Praise for the works of Amanda Kabak

Playing with Fire

…*Playing With Fire* is an emotional rollercoaster that masterfully captures a journey of healing and self-discovery. This story is a testament to the author's ability to craft a story that tugs at the heartstrings, making readers reflect on the power of resilience, love, and the human spirit.

-Shimere A., *NetGalley*

…Beautifully written…I really enjoyed this!

-Kerrie V., *NetGalley*

Training for Love

I'm a big fan of authors who take the time to really develop their characters and both Charlie and Elizabeth were really well written. I do like slow burns and this definitely fell into that category.

-D Booker, *NetGalley*

If you're looking for a book with characters you can't help but like with conflicts that are "real," then this is the book for you. If you want a well-paced book that is also well-written, do not pass on this book.

-Abbott F., *NetGalley*

Paying Her Way

Other Bella Books by Amanda Kabak

Training for Love
Playing with Fire
Changing Her Tune

About the Author

Amanda Kabak is the author of multiple novels, both romance and general fiction. Her writing focuses on the deep ties that make us human: love, friendship, and family. She is also the author of award-winning short fiction that has been published in outlets like *The Massachusetts Review*, *The Tahoma Review*, *Sequestrum*, and other print and online journals. Despite a long career in technology, human interactions interest her much more than code, though she can't resist making some of her characters engineers and scientists. She's lived in Boston, Chicago, and the wilds of Florida, but home is wherever her wife, Anna, is.

Paying Her Way

Amanda Kabak

BELLA BOOKS

Bella Books, Inc.
P.O. Box 10543
Tallahassee, FL 32302

First Edition - 2026

Editor: Medora MacDougall
Cover Designer: SJ Hardy

ISBN: 978-1-64247-695-8

PUBLISHER'S NOTE

Acknowledgment

I've got to hand this one to Boston, where I arrived as a child and left, over fifteen years later, as an adult. I found myself in its streets, its parks, its subway, and its river. I wished away broken hearts and made other people cry in the Public Gardens, ran and biked along the Charles, walked through torrential rainstorms and winter Nor'easters, once to hit a stationary store for ink so I wouldn't run out. I spent time in Symphony Hall, both as an audience member and a performer. Forsythia and magnolia and dogwood. The colors and smells of spring never fade in my memory though I moved away almost twenty years ago. Fall is an equal and opposite electricity in gold, orange, and red. History is alive and well, but the city is also always changing as any good town does.

In the midst of all this, I learned and loved (and met my now-wife), sweated through workouts and stress, and claimed so much of the city as my own. It was a pleasure setting these characters within its confines, walking and riding and staring at the trees I adore. Boston, you will always have a part of my heart.

I, of course, need to thank the whole crew at Bella Books, including Jessica and Tracie, who shepherded my manuscript with care along all its many steps to publication. To Nancy, my esteemed editor. It was so good to work with you again in developing the story and keeping my sentences straight. Any remaining errors in the book are my own.

To Anna, again, our lives started in Boston and have gone where I had only dreamed. Thank you always for being my first reader, my greatest champion, and my number-one fan. Without you, I'd be lost.

Dedication

For Anna, as always

CHAPTER ONE

Erin McCallister liked the heavy velvet draperies at Dialogue, the restaurant she went to at least once every week. They were a deep green, swallowed up sound from the tables around her, and were soft to the touch when she couldn't resist putting her hands on the luxurious fabric. Everything at Dialogue, including the Italian-inspired food, was dialed in for maximum comfort without being ostentatious. No wonder she couldn't stay away. Well, that and the fact that she couldn't cook her way out of a paper bag and was still too immature to try to learn how. Why bother when the brined half chicken, herb-roasted potatoes, and sauteed shaved brussels sprouts were so delicious and enough food for two meals?

She went out to eat a lot, but Dialogue was her favorite and in that sweet spot where entrees went for between thirty and fifty dollars. Not that money mattered to her. But at more expensive places, she didn't feel comfortable sitting alone and reading—a magazine, the latest business bestseller, or the occasional novel. Dining alone didn't put her off, but unstated rules were often more stringent than ones posted for everyone to see. Besides, the dress code here suited her: dark jeans and a blazer made her blend right into the scenery.

Dialogue changed its menu regularly, and she made a point of tasting everything on offer while she could get it. Tonight it was trout in a mustard cream sauce she wanted to lick off the plate. Between bites and paragraphs in the latest issue of *The Harvard Business Review*, she glanced around the medium-sized dining room. It was creeping toward nine, and the second seating was proving to be smaller than the first. She liked to play witness to the ebb and flow of the tables around her, the waitstaff weaving their way around obstacles with big trays loaded with divine-looking, earthenware plates in deep jewel tones. She'd been served multiple times by everyone working tonight—everyone except a small, striking woman with dark hair in a braid as thick as Erin's arm. She must be new, but she looked like she knew what she was doing, making the diners at her tables nod and laugh along with her.

Erin bet she got big tips, though probably not as large as the ones Erin made a habit of leaving. Fifty percent was typical for her, and it went up from there. Why not? Since Nuvio had acquired her company almost three years ago, she felt uncomfortably made of money. Twenty-one million dollars and change the last time she looked at her accounts. The least she could do was spread it around to people working hard for a living.

She ran her fork across the plate to catch some stray sauce and woke from her food daze long enough to see that she wasn't going to be toting home any leftovers tonight. It was getting to be too late to hit a market on the way home, so she'd have to go scavenging tomorrow. Within a minute of her setting her silverware on her plate to signal that she was finished, her server, Greg, was there to clear it and replace it with a dessert menu. Dessert was a different story from the savory dishes; if she ordered it every time she went out for dinner, she wouldn't be able to make it through the door of her house. She glanced at the small sheet of thick, cream paper and wistfully pushed it away, replacing it with her magazine.

Despite the hour, she wasn't ready to go home, and Greg took the hint, staying away except to top off her water glass. She'd sit here undisturbed until she finished this article on bias in blind hiring practices. Then she would settle up and walk the mile back to her place, taking it slow to delay the inevitable. She didn't mind living alone, but thinking back to the tiny apartment she used to share with Catherine Wu, her best friend and former business partner, her memories were often tinged with the honeyed glow of irresistible, revisionist history. They'd hated that place while they'd lived there. They'd made do with what little they had while bootstrapping a new company just out of university. Boxed mac and cheese was a splurge back then.

While she wouldn't want to go back to eating ramen several times a week, she missed the closeness she'd had with Catherine then: in it together, dreamily pragmatic. And it had worked. Four years after they'd started out with nothing, TriBar was acquired for a sum remarkably close to the number Catherine had written on a sticky note hanging off her laptop the whole time. The money had been more Catherine's aspiration than Erin's, who had taken a detour from law school for the tantalizing prospect of making something of her own. Though her father had done that for himself with his construction business, he'd never understood what Erin had been doing at TriBar. Now here she and Catherine were, rich and validated and strangely separated from each other. After the two years they had contracted to Nuvio as part of the acquisition, Erin had left and Catherine had stayed.

It wasn't that Erin didn't want to work. She just hadn't wanted to work there anymore, where she felt alternatingly useless and stymied by the powers that be. During their partnership, roles had been clearly split, with Catherine taking the technical work and Erin accountable for everything else. Their product was a piece of middleware missing from the legal space, a ligament knitting together bones of data critical to law firms. Erin, with her prelaw degree and multiple internships at local firms, had played the domain expert while Catherine actually built the thing, eventually hiring a small technical team to assist her. Erin's job was figuring out how to keep the lights on, at least until she'd landed a five-million-dollar investment that had left them breathing easily until their acquisition.

Nuvio didn't need funds, Erin's team had come over with their hard-earned successful culture, and the product was already defined. All of which left her feeling like tits on a bull, as her father would say, even though he'd never been near a bull in his life. So she'd left.

Running a company at such a tender age had been nauseatingly thrilling, full of bruising lessons and occasional wild victories. After that, where was there to go but down? In comparison to those early years, she was tiptoeing toward being a useless relic before she was even thirty. She told herself she had time to turn things around before she officially hit middle age. The problem was she didn't know where to apply herself.

Erin finished her article, closed the magazine, and glanced at Greg, who came over and delivered her bill before she could even blink. Knowing he wouldn't grow impatient if she sat around even longer gave her a warm—but fleeting—feeling. Being a regular had its benefits beyond them always finding a table for her, no matter how busy it might be.

When Greg came back with her change from her cash payment, she said, "The trout was unbelievable tonight. Give Suzanne my compliments if you can."

"It was the sauce, wasn't it?"

Erin smiled. "If you sold it in quart bottles, I'd buy it."

"I'll let Chef know about the idea."

"Tell her I'm sure she could be very successful with it." She picked up her magazine and stood. "Thanks for taking care of me tonight."

He gave a slight bow. "My pleasure. Have a good rest of your evening."

She nodded and made her way out of the restaurant to the sidewalk, where she stood for a minute, soaking in Boston's early-summer night. The soft air caressed her skin while she rolled up her magazine and pointed herself home. Dialogue was in the South End, which made for a twenty-minute walk to her place in Beacon Hill. The path she took went past blocks of brownstones and a couple of hotels and design stores before dumping her out on the road that separated Boston Commons from the Public Gardens, both of which were quietly lit this late in the evening.

Erin dipped into the Gardens to prolong the walk and to give her regards to her favorite tree, a sprawling weeping beech with branches that turned abruptly downward after reaching their peak, leaving exposed knobs of tree above the cascading, dark-green oval leaves. Under the skirt of branches and leaves was a clearing down to the dirt, no grass able to grow within the permanent shadow the tree cast.

Some people thought the tree was sad looking or vaguely menacing, but it was majestic to Erin. It left everything on the table and was true to its nature. Stepping under its canopy, one was treated to leaves that turned a lighter green when kissed by the sun, and the rest of the world faded away to insignificance. It was where she went when she was chewing on a problem too big to solve or when she didn't know quite what she felt about something. She would look at the old carved graffiti on the smooth-barked trunk and think and not think at the same time.

Tonight, she gave it a little nod before caving to her desires and pulling out her phone to call her best friend.

Catherine answered with, "Are you walking home from dinner?"

"I didn't want to wait until I got home because you might be asleep."

She laughed but said, "You're probably right. Nathan and I were meandering in that general direction."

Catherine had been with Nathan since the second year of their startup, and they shared not only a very nice house about five miles away in Brookline but also a devotion to "Early to bed, early to rise." Not like her. She and Catherine used to joke that they pretty much operated the company twenty-four seven, with Erin going to sleep about the time Catherine was waking up.

"Fish tonight, in case you were wondering. At Dialogue. It would have been heart healthy if not for the luxurious sauce it was served with."

"I wasn't wondering, but I'm all for a luxurious sauce. What's up?"

"Nothing." Literally. "Just wanted to say hi. Even though it's been months, it's still weird not to talk to you every day."

"I doubt you miss me nagging you to find a girlfriend."

Erin sighed. She for sure hadn't missed that. She stood at the light to cross Beacon Street and waited for the walk signal. Charles Street shone bright with streetlights and a healthy number of people leaving restaurants or popping into ice cream shops for dessert.

"You don't get it. You met Nathan well before the acquisition so you started on an equal footing. Now I've got this money, and you know very well how that changes things."

"I get it, I do. But you can't stay alone just because of what Hayley did. Not everyone's like her."

"Anyway, how's work?" She got the light and crossed. From here she could see the side street she'd turn on to walk uphill to her place near the top.

Catherine's pause was as rich as that sauce had been at dinner. "Can we not do this?"

"I'm asking how things are going for you, not whatever you think is happening."

"Things are okay. No fires, at least no big ones, and that's all I'm going to say."

"Fine," Erin said, frustrated. "Will you at least tell me when you're available to get together? I know this great restaurant in the South End."

"Let me check." Catherine put her phone on speaker while flipping through her digital calendar. Erin didn't have to look at hers, because she was generally free. They made plans, she let Catherine go to Nathan and their bed, and she made her way uphill past old redbrick houses and condos, the street sometimes claustrophobically narrow.

That conversation had *not* been what she'd been looking for, though she couldn't put her finger on exactly what she'd wanted from Catherine. How had such a short conversation been laden with so many landmines? She didn't know which of them not to think about first.

Definitely not the one that was Hayley, her ex, who had turned out to be more interested in her money than her. Catherine's parry to her simple question about work came in a close second. Catherine thought Erin wanted to know all the dirt about the product road map and marketing efforts, and, well, she was right. Just because Erin had left didn't mean she'd stopped caring about what they'd built together—the technology and their people, both. And last, but not least, there was the fact that her schedule was wide open, which riddled her with shame.

The light by her front door offered a warm greeting, haloed with the faint humidity in the air. The three-story building she'd bought after the acquisition sat on a corner a few minutes' walk from the State House. Because it had already been subdivided into a first-floor apartment and a unit that spanned the second and third floors (and a roof deck), she continued to rent out the apartment, using a property management company so the tenant didn't know he was living downstairs from the owner. He and Erin passed in the night—or the front hall—every so often, but otherwise it was like he wasn't even there.

Her key rasped into the lock, and she opened the door into soft quiet. She took the stairs, clad in a red runner, without making a sound, like she was sneaking up on the emptiness of her apartment. If you could call 2,500 square feet in the prime of this neighborhood a mere apartment. She could have gotten a house like Catherine, but if she thought this solitude was tough to take, she couldn't imagine having a whole house of it.

She let herself into her space, dropped her keys on the entryway table, and started her circuit around the main floor, turning on every light and starting some low music to keep herself company. Distressed wood floors and paneling that ran up one of the walls in her living room warmed the whole space. She had worked with a designer to make the place hers, transforming it into a harmonious whole that reflected tastes Erin hadn't even known she'd had.

It felt both hers and not hers. She was most comfortable watching TV from the sectional in front of the wood wall and making calls and putting together presentations at her desk in the spacious office nearby. The rest was top of the line but not quite…right. When hunger forced her to, she pulled something ready-made out of the fridge, often eating it while standing at the counter instead of at the nearby dining table.

She perched now on a stool at the breakfast bar, her head resting on her hands, one finger stroking back and forth across her lips, and stared into the gleaming space she rarely used. Whatever was wrong with her home was entirely her fault, but she hadn't found her way to fixing it yet. What a waste. The whole place was a waste. *She* was a waste.

And this was why she was supposed to keep herself busy.

Officially, she was a consultant—at least that's what her business incorporation papers said. It wasn't completely a lie: she'd had a few short gigs since she'd hung out her shingle. Drawn by her name and track record, some people were interested in paying her good money to tell them what a healthy corporate culture looked like and how to achieve it. She'd quickly found that consulting mainly consisted of telling people what to do and just hoping that they would actually do it after you walked out the door. Engagements that were longer, where she could help them with follow-through, would maybe be more rewarding, but she'd have to actually try to find those.

She shook her head. She could build a company out of a few packages of ramen, but she couldn't seem to put her mind to this. She told herself she didn't have to work, ever, but that didn't sit well, not just with her stolid middle-class upbringing but also with her sometimes overactive brain. It didn't cope well with stillness, but since leaving Nuvio—or, to be honest, throughout her last year there—she hadn't been able to choose what to charge off into. Her engine was revving in neutral, but she had crippling ennui and no partner to brainstorm exciting ideas with.

To say it was a bad combination was like saying Moby Dick was a guppy.

She'd cut all ties to the group she and Catherine had built, relinquished responsibility for its road map and marketing, and left Nuvio to "do something important." That's what she'd said to Catherine, and here she was, months later, having done nothing but find a favorite restaurant and make more embarrassing money on her few consulting engagements. She used to have a ton of reasons to respect herself, but they'd evaporated with each week that peeled off the calendar. Honestly, she had a hard time looking at herself in the mirror.

Tonight, unlike Catherine, she still had hours before she'd be able to sleep, so she hauled herself over to her couch, shrugged off her blazer, stretched out, and turned on the TV. She'd find something mindless to watch, a series that would lead her from one episode to the next without conscious volition, all without shutting off the music that was playing through speakers throughout her downstairs. The more she put between herself and echoing solitude the better.

CHAPTER TWO

Mugar Library at Boston University spanned seven floors, though to be honest, Iris Patterson only ever used two. Libraries were about the best thing ever—with librarians running a close second to the books shelved all around her. As a graduate student in history, she made use of the research librarians on the first floor and ranged up and down the shelves on the fourth, even though at this point the source material for her PhD research practically had to be begged, borrowed, and stolen from other locations.

A lot of things needed to be begged, borrowed, or stolen these days, especially time. Oh, and money. Even with a partial scholarship, she had racked up a harrowing amount of debt during her undergraduate career. So far she'd been able to cover tuition in graduate school through a combination of grants, other academic awards, and multiple jobs, but when she finally finished in a few years, she would have to get a good job and fast to avoid staring down the barrel of bankruptcy.

Mostly, she tried not to think about that. If choices were anything, they were consequences. Wasn't that what her mother had taught her by example? Good or bad, decisions lead to a shift in the world, sometimes in a direction you hadn't bargained for.

Not that any of that mattered, because Iris had things under control, especially with her first week as a server at Dialogue under her belt. It was the perfect restaurant if you couldn't break into the Michelin-starred tier. The prices ensured good tips, and the turnover meant at least two seatings at every table. It didn't hurt that the food was delicious and she got to eat dinner there gratis a couple of times a week. At any rate, she could pay all her living expenses with what she earned there, and she'd landed a big grant that, if she could renew it, would float her through the three years she planned on for her PhD.

It was officially summer, but graduate school knew no seasons. She wasn't in a position to dawdle with her research and writing, so hitting the nearly empty library in the middle of June wasn't just smart; it was a necessity. She was immersed in reading a political history of the Congo (including how the United States had messed around with the idea of Congolese sovereignty in the 1960s and beyond). This was critical background to her thesis topic, which concerned the interplay between how missionaries in the region had affected the rural population and how that, in turn, had rippled up to the different political movements in the countries in that area.

She was interrupted when her phone buzzed a soundless ring. Usually she'd let it go to voice mail when she was in these quiet confines, but a glance at the screen showed that it was her mom. She glanced around to make sure she was alone and answered.

"Hi, Mom. What's up?"

"Just wanted to see how you're doing."

The tone of her soft, high voice belied the casualness of that statement. Iris pulled her phone away from her face long enough to check the time. "Are you on break?"

"Just resting my feet before the dinner crowd. Let me guess— you're in the library."

"You know me so well." She really did, but Iris knew her mother equally well, so she spared her the burden of asking by saying, "I'll get my first paycheck in a week, but it'll only be a week's worth of wages, not two. But with that and tips, I should have a decent amount out to you soon. Are you okay for now?"

"I don't know what you're talking about. I'm always okay."

Iris couldn't stop a small head shake, knowing her mother suffered when Iris couldn't send anything home for a while.

"Tell me about what you're reading."

"A political history of the Congo that covers some of the time Grandma lived there. It's color commentary for what I'm actually going to write about. I just wish she were still around so I could interview her."

She could hear her mom's sigh. "We both could have used her around much longer."

"Have you heard from Grandfather?" Iris couldn't remember the last time she'd asked about him.

Naomi laughed. "You know how busy he is with his spiritual work." Even with no video, Iris could see her mom's finger quotes. Iris's grandfather had been a foreign missionary before he brought his Congolese wife back to America with him and had Iris's mom. He'd stayed in the States until his wife died, through Iris's mom having Iris much too young, putting a baby-sized dent in their never-close relationship.

"We'd hear if something went wrong, so I guess no news is good news."

"Agreed."

They sat with that for a while, long enough for someone to stumble on Iris's little hideaway and cast a disapproving glance at the phone in her hand. "Hey, Mom. I need to get going, but are you sure you're all right for the next few weeks? I have some savings now, and I can—"

"I'm fine. You worry too much. Go finish your reading. Call me soon, okay?"

"I will, Mom. Love you."

"Love you more."

Iris disconnected the call and put her phone face down next to her open book. No matter what her mom said, everything wasn't fine. Everything hadn't been fine since her grandma had died and her grandfather had taken that opportunity to pick up where he'd left off, spreading the news of Christ in all the jungles of the world. He was somewhere in the Amazon this time, a whole different continent from where he'd saved Iris's grandma so hard she'd ascended straight from the small, Angolan village she'd fled to from the Congo all the way to Bethlehem, Pennsylvania. Iris's grandfather wasn't completely the fire-and-brimstone kind, but he had strong opinions on what was right and proper and what wasn't. Needless to say, Iris being born out of wedlock to his twenty-year-old daughter hadn't given him the warm and fuzzies.

It had been push and pull since then, with Iris's grandma helping to raise Iris until she died when Iris was nine. Iris's grandfather oscillated between pretending nothing was amiss to being appalled by the state of his family, and Naomi worked two or three jobs, since there was no free ride in that house. Now, even with Iris out of the apartment, Naomi had a hard time making ends meet, there being no good opportunities for a Black woman with only a high school diploma. Then there was the pressure of her own student loans from her two years in college. She'd negotiated a thirty-year term to reduce her monthly payments, but she'd been under them her entire adult life and could never get ahead.

Sometimes Iris felt guilty for her very existence. If her mom had given her up for adoption, she would've been able to move on, go back to college, and have a completely different life. But she'd made the choice to keep Iris and had managed to give her a childhood rich in love even though it was poor in other respects. If nothing else, Iris had been taught an iron work ethic and the value of a dollar.

Speaking of which… She moved her focus back onto the book in front of her, wanting to get as much done as she could before her shift at Dialogue.

* * *

Iris had studied Dialogue's menu with as much attention as she spent on her research materials. Nothing killed the urge to tip more than a server who didn't know what they were talking about.

At Dialogue, this included recommending wine pairings as well as having enough knowledge about their whole wine list to be able to describe each offering in a few succinct words. Fruit notes, tannin, oak, smoke, light, tart, and so on. She had to be helpful but not pushy, friendly but not presumptuous, efficient but not rushed. Good thing she'd been doing this kind of work for the last eight years, a chip off the old block. Iris knew her working as a server dismayed her mom, but she could make good money at it, and it was temporary.

In the lull between seatings, Iris talked to Greg, one of Dialogue's veterans.

"The duck is going like hotcakes tonight." She pushed some hairs that had strayed from her braid out of her face and behind her ear. It had a texture similar to her mom's but a curl more lazy than kinked. "Isn't it funny how that happens, everyone getting an itch for the same thing all at once?"

"Too bad we're supposed to be highlighting the trout."

"I've tried in a low-key way, but it's been much more turf than surf so far. Maybe we'll have better luck with the later seating." She peeked out at her tables, trying to gauge if anyone needed anything and noticed that one of her empties was now occupied by a lone woman. "Hey, didn't I see her last week? She was reading a magazine."

Greg smiled without even looking to where Iris was indicating. "That's Erin. She's our most regular regular. Don't pressure or rush her. She only needs the specials menu, and even if you screw something up, she tips like you only dream of. She deserves excellent service for the tips she gives out. You'll learn what she likes. We all have."

"Thanks for the tips, no pun intended."

"Yeah. I've never heard that one before." The orders came up for one of Greg's tables, and he said, "Duty calls," before loading warm dishes on a large tray and hefting it to his shoulder, grabbing a stand with his free hand.

His instructions about her new customer made her nervous for no good reason. Now she wanted to do perfectly—and not just for the tip. She bypassed the menus in favor of the water carafe, took a deep breath, and headed in the woman's direction. She was younger than Iris had thought, no more than a handful of years older than Iris was. What Iris had thought was brown hair sparkled an obvious red in the small lights strung across the ceiling, and she blended into the rest of the diners with a starched shirt and dark slacks—more classy than casual. Then Iris was at the table, and it was too late to catalog the woman's traits except to note that her head was bent toward a book she held open on the table with one hand.

Iris hovered to the side of the table, waiting for Erin to clock her, but when that didn't seem likely to happen, she said, in a near-whisper, "Would you like some water?"

Erin's head snapped up, revealing light-blue eyes.

"Sorry. I didn't mean to startle you."

She waved Iris off with her free hand. "Don't worry about it. I just got absorbed."

"I can come back in a bit if you'd rather."

"No, really. Now's fine."

Iris filled her water goblet. "Are you interested in the specials, or would you like more time to settle in?"

Erin smiled and tilted her head a little bit. "You're new."

"Yes. I'm Iris, and I have the pleasure of being your server this evening."

Her laugh was short but genuine. "I doubt it's as pleasurable for you as it will be for me. Where's my menu?"

Iris's heart gave a panicked thump. Was this some kind of hazing ritual? Setting her up for embarrassment? "My apologies. I'd been led to believe—Let me grab one for you right away."

"Iris, right? I'm sorry. I was giving you a hard time. Greg must've told you that I come here often enough that I don't need a menu except when it changes. How about we start over? I'm Erin." She held out her hand for Iris to shake, which Iris did after juggling the water carafe.

"Good to meet you. Are we at the point in the evening where you want to hear the specials or am I doing something else wrong?"

"Hey, there's very little you can do wrong. Seriously. And I'd love to hear the specials, assuming they're different from last week, which they usually are." Erin sat back and gave Iris the same attention she'd been giving her book earlier.

Iris felt both warmed and intimidated but made it through the specials recitation without any blunders. She gazed at Erin when she was done, her long, straight nose and light eyes. A smattering of freckles crossed her cheeks and nose like the footprints of tiny elves. Okay, that was a bridge too far. She got control of herself. "Let me give you some time to decide—and read another chapter. No rush."

Without waiting for an answer, she did a circuit of her remaining tables, facilitating payments, topping up coffee, or greeting new folks with menus, water, and introductions. When moving from here to there, she felt Erin watching her. Iris made her way back to Erin's table a little later than she had planned. She refilled Erin's half-drunk water, cradled the carafe against her abdomen, and said, "Anything strike your fancy?"

"Now that I've had it once, I'm tempted to have the trout again, but the duck special sounds outstanding. Who can resist sour cherries?"

"You can't go wrong with either, as I'm sure you know. But Chef could make a fortune bottling the sauce she serves with the trout. I guess it depends if you're in the mood for fish or fowl."

"I asked Greg to tell Suzanne the exact same thing about the sauce. All right. I'll have the trout. I almost never have the same dish twice in a row, but you made a very persuasive case."

"Well, you won't be disappointed."

Erin's smile was wide. "Why do you think I keep coming back for more?"

"So just the trout, then?"

"Why? Are you recommending something to start?"

"No. Not unless you want something. I'm just making sure you want the trout as is. No substitutions."

"Absolutely not." She frowned. "Do a lot of people request substitutions?"

"Not necessarily here, where they're discouraged, but you'd be shocked at what people have asked for at some places I've worked."

"As you said, I'll have my trout as is with my compliments to the chef. Nothing to start, but I never turn down an amuse-bouche if one's on offer."

"I'll see if we have anything in the back for you. Something to drink?"

"What do you recommend?"

Iris cast her gaze up and to the left to bring the wine list into mental focus. It would have to be by the glass and white. Something bright and easy but not too sweet. Normally that would disqualify Rieslings, but the one they had by the glass was mildly citrusy, which would cut through the sauce on the fish without clashing with it. She blinked back into the here and now.

"I'd say the Australian Riesling. The Perry Vineyard one? Or I could get you anything you want from the bar. Or just water, of course. Needless to say, it's up to you."

Erin answered that with a quiet golf clap. "Well done on just your second week. Top of the class. I only drink every once in a while, but you sold me on the Riesling. A glass would be great."

"Coming right up. Anything else I can help you with?"

She raised her book a few inches off the table. "I'm all set, thank you."

"I'll leave you to it then."

Iris made her way out of the dining room, collecting a couple of requests from her diners on the way. When she was out of sight, she leaned her back against the closest wall and laughed at herself. She hadn't been that thrown off guard since her first table back when she worked at the same diner as her mom. Greg had psyched her out (really, how much was this fabled tip, anyway?), and Erin unwittingly playing along had doubled down on her discomfort. Though it had turned out all right in the end, there were plenty of things she still could do to screw things up, including dropping a plate of food right in Erin's lap as, yes, she had done once, though not recently. Serving was threading the needle between being helpful and becoming a pest. It required attention to detail to usher a party through their meal seamlessly with it feeling completely natural to the diners. Knowing Erin didn't like to be rushed had gotten Iris all tangled up, but all it meant was that Erin was in charge of the pacing and giving Iris all the right signals to follow. Easy, right?

Iris serviced all her tables and kept an eye out on Erin, who seemed to delight in the amuse-bouche the kitchen had come up with for her before taking her time eating her fish, engrossed in her book again. Could she even taste things properly with that level of concentration? When the plate was clean, Iris cleared it as quickly as she could, offered more wine, and when she was turned down, refilled her water glass and cleared the table of crumbs.

Then, a slow, inexorable game of chicken commenced. How long would Iris keep her nerve and not run the check over to Erin before she'd made some sort of definite signal that she was finished? A long time, it turned out. Most of her other tables had left, and the restaurant went from a din muted by curtains and upholstery to a lush quiet that transmitted each clink of silverware against plate clearly. It was her favorite part of a shift: the rush behind her, a few tables to serve at her leisure, everything getting fuzzed and soft as dusk lingered outside the hushed lighting of the restaurant in this end to a long summer evening.

Finally, Erin closed her book and looked for Iris in a way that made it clear she was ready. Iris brought the check over, leaving the folio to the side of Erin's book, which was about "transformative management"—something that seemed way too dry to command Erin's attention the way it had, though Iris supposed some of her sources would rival that text.

Iris said, "Thanks for coming in. I hope you enjoyed your meal."

"I always do. Oh, except for Suzanne's sea bream experiment." Erin shuddered and smiled. "I hope it doesn't sound patronizing, but you did great. Everything was perfect, down to the wine."

"I'm glad to hear it. I aim to please. Have an excellent night and get home safely."

Erin slid the check toward herself. "Thank you for taking care of me tonight."

Iris left to tend to someone flailing wildly for their check as if she were in the next county over and not fifteen feet away. After dealing with a couple of her tables, she looked back at Erin's to see that she'd slipped out. Even though she had something else to do, she couldn't help herself from taking the check folio into the back to peek at this fabled tip.

Erin had paid in cash and, after doing some quick math, Iris's eyes practically fell out of their sockets at the size of the tip. Two hundred percent, including the alcohol, which way more than made up for the fact that she hadn't gotten a starter or dessert. It was easily four tables' worth of tip. Even after it got divided with the back of house staff, Iris would be pocketing a nice sum of money that she (and her mom) needed sorely.

Greg walked by while she was still absorbing the tip. He laughed. "You're not seeing things. What was it, a hundred percent?"

"More like two." Almost exactly like two.

His eyebrows raised. "You did something right, though as far as I know she never tips less than fifty percent—and that's if you've done something wrong. Needless to say, we like her, even though she almost never orders all three courses and more than one drink."

"What's her deal? Was she a server in a former life?"

He shrugged. "I don't know, and I don't care. I love having her in my section, though Justin tries to switch her up among all the servers. I've got to get this check out so we can start closing soon."

Iris had a table lingering as well and was ready to get home and off her feet, but she looked at Erin's check one more time to caress the tip with her gaze. She'd already liked Erin, but now she liked her even more.

* * *

When Iris got home, her roommates, Candice and Trish, were watching TV, which they must've been doing for a while because crusty dinner dishes were still on the trunk they used as a coffee table. She didn't even want to know what the kitchen looked like. Their apartment was a study in entropy she tried her best to keep in check.

She let her bag drop to the floor. "You guys will not believe the tip I got tonight."

Candice, hair in a perfectly formed Afro, leaned forward to grab the remote and mute the TV. Iris had known her since they'd been freshmen, and they'd shared this apartment for the last two years with Trish coming into the rotation only six months ago. "Good or bad?"

"Very, very good."

Trish, her skin as pale as Erin's, said, "Was it a pervy old man? I only get really good tips from pervy old men trying to look down my shirt. Sometimes I think about undoing another button to see how much more I might rake in."

"No pervy old man."

"Amazing. How much?"

"Two hundred percent. An even hundred on a fifty-dollar bill."

Iris reveled in their expressions of surprise. Candice asked, "What did you do to earn that?"

"Nothing. It's this regular who's known to be a big tipper, but another server seemed to be surprised at the amount."

"Sounds like he's got a crush."

"Actually, it was a woman."

Two sets of raised eyebrows greeted that. Trish said, "An old pervy woman?"

Iris laughed. "No. She was pretty young, actually. And perfectly nice. I think she was gay. I got the vibe."

"Ooh. A potential sugar momma. Did you give her vibes back? Because nothing about you screams gay."

It was true that Iris usually flew below the gaydar, for better or worse. Sometimes she wished everything about her was more obvious: her Blackness, her gayness. "I don't need a sugar momma." Though that could be up for debate. That she would never accept one was closer to the mark.

Candice said, "We all need a sugar somebody. Was she cute? You've been single too long. All work and no play makes Iris a dull girl."

Iris walked to the couch. "Scoot over." Candice made room, and Iris got off her tired feet. She pictured Erin. The low lighting made her hair a deep red, and it was cut chin length in a no-fuss style. Her features were well proportioned, and her smile was warm and wide. Truthfully, that smile had hooked something in Iris. "She was good-looking."

Trish said, "But she was with her girlfriend? Wandering eye?"

"Nope. She ate alone. Or with a book. I guess she pretty much always comes in by herself."

Candice and Trish looked at each other.

"What?" Iris said. "I see what you're doing there."

Candice said, "It's like something in a movie. You need to get her to make the first move."

"No one's making a move on anyone. She was a customer. I did my job well. She always tips a lot. End of story."

"You're no fun."

It wasn't the first time Iris had heard that—not even the first time Candice had said it to her. She couldn't stop herself from stiffening against it. "I don't have time for fun." She let her head fall back to the couch, suddenly exhausted.

"Hey," Candice said, serious now. "We're kidding around with you. We just don't want you to burn out. We practically never see you, and you're not even TA'ing this summer. Besides, it's fun to fantasize."

Iris had been so blinded by the amount of the tip that she hadn't even gotten far enough to wonder if Erin were fantasy-worthy. She reviewed their interactions, the way Erin looked when she was concentrating on her book, the frequent smiles she'd bestowed. Her smile really was swoon-worthy in its clear genuineness.

She said, "Would you guys really want a sugar daddy?"

Candice said, "No," while Trish said, "Yeah."

Iris and Candice looked at her.

"What?" she said. "I can admit that I wouldn't mind being taken out to a nice dinner every once in a while instead of just serving them up. I'm not saying I want to be a kept woman or anything."

Iris said, "Money always comes with strings."

"Seeing as your mystery benefactor is the closest any of us are going to get to a sugar anybody, I think it's safe to fantasize."

They talked for a while about nothing until Iris started to yawn and excused herself to the orderly haven of her room. In bed, waiting for sleep to overtake her, she thought of Erin again. She admitted that with any other person on any other day, she would have been at least a little put off by the exorbitant tip, no matter how much it benefited her. Someone throwing their money around like that was distasteful, but something about Erin felt different. Genuine.

Iris closed her eyes and felt the warmth of Erin's gaze again. Okay, maybe she was fantasy-worthy. Some other time, when she wasn't so tired.

CHAPTER THREE

Just because Erin wasn't doing much consulting didn't mean she wasn't doing any. She might not know exactly where her life was heading right now, but occasionally being able to play "culture doctor" to a few companies at least gave her temporary satisfaction. Today's client was having a huge retention problem across multiple departments, and she'd spent weeks interviewing people both in management and in the trenches. To put it in medical terms, she had taken the patient's vital signs and health history and was now in the diagnostic and treatment phases.

If she was known for anything, it was leading a high-performing team, though that wasn't the only thing she'd done at TriBar. Had she done everything well? Not necessarily. There'd been a couple of notable disasters over the four years she'd run things, but she guessed it all turned out well in the end—and left her with at least moderately bankable credentials. If only she could feel the same deep certainty that she'd felt when starting out with Catherine, maybe her life would make sense again. Back then, coming up for the idea of the software gave her the opportunity to have something of her own, which had caught her by the throat. Both her older brother and sister were involved in the family contracting business, leaving Erin adrift on her own path. She'd thought it would be law school, but building something from scratch was so much better.

Her current client was mired in a world of hurt and was at least paying lip service to making changes in the guise of improvement. Her approach and techniques were based on the latest research, but she'd always worked to make it (and herself) as approachable as possible. Really, it boiled down to just a few fundamentals: empathy, respect, honesty, and communication. Easy, right? Yet so many of the companies she'd seen over the years weren't even near the road to corporate nirvana, let alone making any headway down that long, winding path. She just wished she was as excited when educating these companies about what to do as she'd been actually doing it with Catherine.

Regardless, she had to deliver a diagnosis and treatment plan this afternoon, which always brought on a case of the nerves despite being confident in her findings and recommendations. She was new to consulting, and it was pleasant—though in the same way she imagined those Nordic saunas were where you were beaten with tree branches.

She sat in the back of an Uber on the ride out to the company's suburban office. During the interview process, she'd dressed in well-worn jeans and knit tops a step above T-shirts when meeting with individual contributors and in one of her three suits, tailored and coordinated and with slick, cool, satiny linings in bright colors when meeting with executives. Today, she'd landed somewhere in the vast middle, wearing dark jeans with a navy blazer over a deep-green blouse that reminded her of Dialogue. Chunky black wingtips rounded out the ensemble.

She smiled at the thought. Dialogue really was her home away from home, even more comfortable than eating at her kitchen bar. That new server had been delightful, competent, and nervous all at once, at least in the beginning. Iris had rich, tawny-beige skin and a broad, striking face. Her smile was an easy benediction, pulling her large, shapely lips wide. It wasn't hard to like her, even with the beginning awkwardness.

What was the staff saying about Erin outside the dining room? Yes, she was a little particular but only in the pacing of the meal—and her tips—but that was a good thing or should be, at least. Iris had checked on her partway through the meal the way the other servers had stopped doing, and Erin had been charmed instead of annoyed at the interruption. Was she so starved for human interaction that the briefest of chats with a server meant so much? With a grimace, Erin guessed the answer was in the question.

Before the acquisition, work and her social life had been inextricably entwined, partly because of the hours they'd kept and partly because she'd genuinely liked the people that they'd hired. Working and playing with them was easy despite the difficulty of what they were doing. In ways, it felt like an extension of college, only with bigger stakes. Then came the acquisition and the colder, impersonal conglomeration they were suddenly part of, and Erin, the one who supposedly knew how to talk and make connections, felt uncomfortably alone.

The Uber swooped around the curved exit ramp toward the suburban office park that was her destination, and Erin shook off those thoughts. She had to get her head in the game and be prepared to nail her boardroom presentation.

* * *

Erin had made a handful of slides for this meeting, but for the most part she just stood at the front of a large, full conference room and talked. She was speaking primarily to managers and an executive or two, and she was telling them things they ought to know and probably wanted to deny.

"The results of the anonymous employee surveys I sent out are pretty clear. Eighty-six percent of those who responded feel out of the loop, sixty-two percent don't trust upper management, and forty-five percent are under the impression that nothing they do is good enough. If I surveyed the folks who left the company in the last year, I don't doubt that these would be the most common reasons why people moved on. Salary matters, but it's not a cure. Same with vacation and benefits. Feeling valued is what leads to loyalty, and people don't feel valued here."

She continued in this vein for a while, doling out the tough love as well as suggesting a potential light at the end of this tunnel with a step-by-step road map for how they could turn things around without just firing everyone and starting over, something which had actually been suggested by an executive she was glad wasn't attending this session.

Wrapping up, she said, "I know this is a lot to take in, and you'll need time to digest and decide on the best course forward for you." Now was when she should sell them on retaining her to help facilitate the changes they needed to make, but her brain stumbled on the words, keeping them from getting to her mouth. She ended her presentation with a weak, "You know how to find me when you're ready to take the next step. I'm happy to assist in whatever way would be helpful." Lame. So lame. But she stopped projecting the slide that had her contact info on it and shut her laptop softly. She slid it into a padded compartment in the backpack she'd had ever since she and Catherine had started out, the one that was festooned with national park patches—not patches of the ones she'd been to, which were very few, but the ones she had fantasized about walking around in. She hoisted the pack on one shoulder, shook hands, and made short conversation on her way out the door.

During the Uber ride back to her house, she alternated between giving herself a stern talking to and trying to understand why she hadn't pushed for more work. Was she already so used to a life of relative leisure that she found honest work beneath her? Was it this company, specifically, which had a cesspool in the place where competent middle managers should be? Did she think they were a lost cause? Were they? She definitely wouldn't want to work further with them in that case, leaching money from them while they either did nothing or did the opposite of what she would recommend.

She actually didn't think they were a lost cause. It was pretty hard for a company to truly be hopeless. That would take executives actively conspiring to create a culture that was downright rotten, treating people like they were as disposable as tissues. She knew a couple of places like that, but most companies were somewhere in the muddied middle, a resounding blah shot through with veins of both terribleness and bliss. Those were countless and could keep her in business for the rest of her life, could eventually even require her to have a staff of her own, leaving her free to be an idea person again. That sounded exactly like what she should want, but she'd choked in that meeting before offering the next step down that path. She'd become such a mystery to herself. The money from the acquisition was the big difference, of course, but, honestly, most of the time she felt like it didn't exist. In the beginning, she'd let herself go on a small spending and giving spree: buying her house, paying off her parents' mortgage and a loan on the contracting business, buying a couple of new work trucks for her dad and brother, setting up generous college funds for her young niece and nephew, and initiating a small endowment at Tufts for women pursuing management studies or headed for their MBA. Not to mention creating a trust that would confer a legacy of generosity to friends, family, and charities when she ascended to the great beyond.

Would she rather give it back? Obviously not, as her brokerage statements showed. But the pathetic end to today's meeting was another clear indication that she hadn't figured out what to do with herself when she didn't need to make a living anymore. Nor had she beaten back her fear that she might be a one-hit wonder. Though she was a devoted night owl, this definitely helped keep her up at night. The hours between ten at night and one or two in the morning had always been her most productive ones, but they felt haunted now.

Having someone else around the place wouldn't hurt, but she was as lackadaisical about trying to find a girlfriend as she was about landing longer contracts with the clients that had already engaged her. At least she'd have some company this afternoon. Her mentee/assistant was meeting her at her house, and she was looking forward to spending a useful hour in conversation and tutelage with her. She'd also delegate a couple of small tasks to her so Shannon would feel like she was doing something useful for the money Erin was paying her.

Erin had conjured this summer position out of thin air and filled it with help from a former professor of hers at Tufts—her alma mater. The work was largely on Erin, given the large mentorship aspect, but she had to fabricate five or so hours of things to do for Shannon every week as well. Catherine joked that Erin had grown so accustomed to leading people (including Catherine herself sometimes) that she didn't know what to do without minions. But it wasn't just minions she enjoyed. It was the work that brought them together.

Shannon was sitting on the steps to Erin's building when the grumpy Uber driver pulled over to let Erin out. She tipped him fifty percent and slung her backpack over her shoulder while Shannon got to her feet. The woman was a business major between her junior and senior years at Tufts, and they were a month into this relationship.

Just inside the building's entryway, she asked, "How did the meeting go?"

Erin was halfway up the stairs to her space before she answered. "They didn't throw things at me, so it's not all bad."

"Were they just not interested or actually negative?"

Erin turned around so Shannon could see her, giving a wide smile. "Yes." She unlocked the door and waved her inside. "I'm being dramatic. I could tell some people were interested or at least agreed with the tenor of my findings, but I don't think there's institutional support for actual change."

"I swear you said that exact thing about the last place you did an initial assessment for."

They reached Erin's office, and Shannon flopped down in her spot on the love seat, her curly light-brown hair bouncing with the movement. Erin took the chair opposite, both of them ignoring the actual workspace in the corner across the room.

Erin said, "Change is hard, especially systemic change. I mean, look at me." She slipped her laptop free of her bag and settled it on her thighs. "I know I should learn to cook instead of buying all my meals out. I've been telling myself that for years—without any success. And I'm not trying to change a company, just one person."

"How do you convince companies to change?"

She placed her hands flat on her laptop. "You don't. You can give them information, but they need to convince themselves, which usually only happens when they experience enough pain. Pain is the best motivator there is. Given that, one approach you can take is to reveal their pain to them."

Shannon opened her own laptop. "How do they generally take that? Is it like an intervention?"

"Kind of. In an intervention, at least a properly facilitated one, change happens immediately if the subject agrees that they need help—because they go right from the intervention to rehab. But the subject can also disagree that they have a problem, and there's no change. It's rarely that black and white with corporations. They may agree that they have a problem but face uphill battles to do anything to rectify it."

"And that's where you arm them with information."

"And strategies. That's where Cialoni's book *Influence* comes in. Are you finished with it yet?"

Shannon made a face like she'd tasted something questionable. "Not quite. I was slammed with a new schedule at work and that one summer school class I'm taking. I'll finish it soon, I swear, but…Didn't you feel kind of sneaky in a bad way about reading it?"

Erin laughed. "How so?" She stretched her legs out and knocked her shoes together.

"It just feels like one hundred and one ways to manipulate someone, you know?"

"I get it, and you're mostly right. At its root, influence is the endeavor to sway someone's thoughts or output, which could be considered manipulation. Or an attempt at manipulation. Of course you want to use your powers of influence for good—"

"With great power comes great responsibility?"

"Sure. You need to be driven by your own moral code, which can be harder than you'd think it would be."

"My mom used to talk about peer pressure like it was a deadly disease."

"And yet you don't want to miss out on being positively influenced. You need to be the one in charge of what parts of what you hear or read go into your head."

They talked a while longer about influence, Shannon almost losing control of her laptop in her animation. Erin liked her, though undergrads had started to seem impossibly young lately. They spent some time on a draft proposal for continued consulting for the company Erin had just been at. Some parts of it might make it into a real thing, but it was mostly practice for Shannon in how to write clearly and persuasively. Erin gave her a short list of contacts to cold call for consulting services, and they worked on the script she would use on them.

All in all, it was a pleasant hour, and Erin paid her for the small amount of administrative work she had done that month. But when Erin was alone again, she crawled with dissatisfaction. The mentoring was one thing—she was good at it and enjoyed it—but the make-work left her with a sour taste in her mouth. It felt suspiciously like paying for someone's company, especially since she was halfhearted about pursuing her consulting work. As she'd said to Shannon, there was only so much impact she could make at most places, no matter now nefarious her attempts at influence could become.

She just felt useless—maybe not to Shannon but in a broader respect. She was supposed to be doing something important by this point, making a positive impact whether she was earning money at it or not. She'd set the bar so high with the startup and its sale that everything now felt tepid in comparison. Inspiration eluded her. She was also supposed to have someone to go through her days with her, someone who would truly see her and even be her champion. Not Catherine, obviously, but someone like her, someone she fit with, someone special.

That thought came with a pang of despair, which was about the best excuse ever for having dinner at Dialogue again. At least her desperation would be drowned out there by the low murmur of conversation, silverware, and the occasional blurt of laughter. Not to mention delicious food.

She went upstairs to busy herself with mounds of laundry before heading out on foot past her favorite tree to the friendly confines of the restaurant, which was packed. Good thing she'd called ahead to make sure they could fit her in. They'd managed to do so every time she'd called or just shown up, except for when they'd been closed for a private party. Tonight they seated her closer to the kitchen than usual, but she didn't mind the background noise of plates against metal and the hiss of the espresso machine's steam wand. Sometimes some good and steady background noise was the best thing to dial her concentration in on what she was doing, even if it was just reading *To Kill a Mockingbird* for the fifth or sixth time. To Erin, Maycomb, Alabama, was as friendly a place to spend time in as Dialogue.

Kaylee was her server tonight. It wasn't lost on Erin that they tried to seat her in a different section each visit, presumably because of her tips. The redistribution of wealth, she supposed, and she was all for equity. She really needed to figure out the best way to do more with what she had. That endowment was a start and the mentorship, but it was ultimately insufficient. Maybe she should give it away after all. It wasn't the worst thing to have to work for a living, but based on her experience at Nuvio, she wasn't cut out to work for someone else.

She shook herself out of her stupor of self-doubt, dragged herself from her book, and glanced around the room while working her way through a bite of the kale salad she'd gotten to start. The usual crew was there, and Erin grinned at the smile Iris was giving to one of her tables. She had a great smile, white teeth set in her mouth a little haphazardly, like they were a bit tipsy, and a squint to her eyes, which made it seem all the more genuine. She was good-looking overall, petite with intensely dark hair Erin could only describe as full-figured even though it was tucked away in a thick braid.

Iris nodded at her diners and walked directly toward her table, which made sense because Erin was so close to the kitchen, but she so rarely looked around while dining that she was taken aback when Iris smiled right at her. She smiled back before it got weird, and Iris detoured from the dark, swinging doors with their face-height porthole windows and came to a stop across the table from her.

Iris said, "I like your shoes." Erin reflexively pulled her feet back under her chair. "How are you enjoying your dinner?"

"So far so good. I'm looking forward to the squash tart."

"Getting your vegetables in tonight."

"I'm told it's good for me." Erin half picked up her book to end the conversation before wondering why she wanted to do that. Wasn't she here to have some kind of socialization?

Iris glanced at the movement. "I love that book. Even though it perpetuates the white savior myth."

Now Erin looked at the book as if it had grown horns in her hand. "I, uh, never really thought of it like that. Man, now I have to rethink everything."

"Mostly everyone has to rethink everything, but I'm interrupting, and I only meant to say hello and thank you for your tip."

She waved Iris off with the hand not occupied by the newly troublesome book. "Don't mention it."

"It was beyond generous."

"Really, don't mention it." The words were flat.

Iris's smile faltered. "Okay, I'll leave you to your meal. Enjoy."

Erin opened her book but didn't resume reading. What had just happened? More to the point, what had she just done? Killed an entirely pleasant conversation, that's what. Granted, Iris had put a huge kink in her enjoyment of one of her favorite books, but that didn't call for Erin to shoot her down like that. What was wrong with her? Had she been spending so much time alone that she didn't remember how to have a simple conversation when it wasn't about business?

It had been Iris's mention of her tip that had gotten to her, a topic of conversation she had tried to slap down, but instead she'd slapped Iris.

The tips were supposed to go gracefully unnoticed and unremarked upon, and they had since a month after she'd started coming here a year ago. But was that so important that she would go as far as behaving badly about it? They *were* generous, but they were nothing in the face of what she could give.

Was that it? Some kind of existential guilt? She hadn't come into this money without effort on her part, through an inheritance or winning the lottery. She'd worked hard for it, even though the amount she had been rewarded was vaguely embarrassing. She didn't want it acknowledged, not like that. That wasn't what Iris had been doing, though. It had been a simple thank you, and Erin had flubbed her response.

Her concentration shot, she made her way through the rest of her salad, reading the same paragraph three times before giving up and waiting for more distraction in the guise of food—the summer squash and mushroom tart, to be specific. She wished for something more complicated, like crab, where she had to hunt for food already right there on her plate. While she waited, she was forced to glance around the restaurant, at all those two- and four-tops of people enjoying the food and each other, some serious, some happy, some clearly a little bit drunk. She imagined herself among one of those parties, participating in conversation she was ready for, that included topics more in her wheelhouse than her own money.

After their ramen phase, she used to go out with Catherine all the time. She and Hayley had even double-dated with her and Nathan before their relationship had gone to shit. She'd had work dinners and dinners with people from work, which were entirely different things. She was an asset to the kind of conversation that flowed over good food and wine, having wide-ranging interests and at least some knowledge of a bunch of different things. People generally liked to be around her. So why did she sit here so many nights monumentally alone?

Just like those companies that wouldn't change, this must be because this was how she wanted it, which was as depressing a thought as there being serious problems with *To Kill a Mockingbird*. Now, because of Iris's comment, she'd be spending the rest of tonight's long evening hours researching modern interpretations of this classic. Granted, she loved it for much more than its story: intrepid and insistently curious Scout, Atticus's formal and loving parenting style, and the language itself, which was chewy with idiom and bits of stunning vocabulary.

Despite being a lesbian and those years eating ramen, Erin knew her privilege was now both broad and deep. Even if she were to start over from scratch, she had so much on her side it was laughable: education, experience, white skin…the list went on and on. The only thing she could hope for was to use her privilege for good, but she wasn't sure how to go about it. She guessed that's what her tips were about, but now she wondered what problems lurked beneath them. There was only so much that giving money away could mitigate. Iris had thanked her, though, and it had seemed genuine—at least until Erin had screwed it up.

Kaylee brought her tart out along with questions of how else she could be of service, and Erin almost asked her to send Iris over so she could apologize. That seemed problematic on multiple levels, so she busied herself with vegetables and pastry and a cream drizzle so perfectly savory she would have marveled at it any other night. The whole time, she sensed Iris moving through the room, imagined her smiling at other diners and participating in easy chitchat about food or wine or the weather. Erin kept her attention on her dinner, her book open next to her like a prop, though if anyone was paying attention, they'd notice she wasn't turning pages.

When Kaylee took her plate and offered dessert, Erin uncharacteristically ordered some to give her more time to figure things out. She looked around the dining room and saw Iris walking by, carrying main course dishes for diners who had ordered just before the kitchen was shutting down. The staff was going to have to stay late to usher these diners to their departure before going about shift-ending tasks. Erin ate late but usually not that late.

She looked down when Iris turned back toward the kitchen after delivering the food, and she cursed herself. For so long everything had been easy in its difficulty. Problems were challenges to rise to instead of insurmountable obstacles. Even when she didn't know what to do, she was pretty sure she would eventually figure it out—or find someone who could help. Now, everything was amorphous, with whole areas of her life having no solution other than abject avoidance.

Surely her misstep with Iris wasn't at that level. It could be walked back with the right words, and Erin spent the time until her panna cotta arrived trying to figure out what those were. She was halfway through the dessert—the smooth creaminess and sharp raspberry of the firm custard under curls of dark chocolate providing a pleasurable counterpoint to her tied-in-knots head—when she made a decision. She raised her eyes to find Iris, who was delivering a check to a couple clearly having a successful date in a table by the window.

When Iris turned in her direction, Erin made a "check please" gesture that was so spastic it was mortifying. Iris made a little stutter step and frowned before clearly deciding to ignore it and dig up Kaylee to deal with whatever it was Erin wanted.

"Iris," Erin said, just loud enough for her to hear. "Do you have a second? It'll be quick, I promise."

Iris glanced around as if looking for guidance but ultimately made her way toward Erin. "How can I help you?"

"What I meant to say earlier was you're welcome." When Iris made no indication that she'd even heard Erin, she tried again. "About the tip. You thanked me, and I didn't handle that well?" It wasn't a question, but it sure came out like one. "I mean, I'm glad you appreciated it, and it was my pleasure."

"Okay."

"Okay?"

"Yeah, okay. It's fine."

But it still didn't feel fine. "Don't you want to pierce my ignorance about another classic piece of literature?"

One corner of Iris's mouth quirked up, but Erin realized she was working for a full smile. Iris said, "I don't want to blow your mind all at once. Going out too hot can cauterize receptiveness."

Erin smiled first. "Cauterize is a great word. I need to put it into the rotation."

"It's surprisingly versatile."

"Yeah, like the kitchen cauterizing the top of the crème brûlée that's sometimes on the menu."

Bingo. There came a smile. Maybe not fully unrestrained but pretty good for an apology conversation. "Points for style. I noticed you got all three courses tonight."

Only in order to have this conversation. "Yes, and I'm stuffed. But happy I got to clear things up with you. I apologize for having absolutely no points for style earlier, and I do hope you forgive me."

"You're only saying that because you don't want me to spit in your food next time you're in my section."

Her head shifted unconsciously away from Iris. "Does that really happen?"

"What goes on behind those doors stays behind those doors. Let's just say that I've been tempted before but have never let loose. The diner where my mom works is a different story, though. I swear they do it just for the hell of it."

There was a lot to untangle in those last sentences and no time to do it in, especially when Erin saw Iris glancing around at her tables. "I've kept you too long, and I'm not even one of your tables. To recap—I'm sorry and you're welcome and please don't spit on my food."

This time the smile was wide and bright, and Erin felt it tug at her. Iris said, "I make no promises." Then she was gone.

Erin pushed her half-eaten dessert away from her, her own signal for a check. She paid quickly with a customary tip and gathered her book up. At the door to the outside, she glanced back, finding Iris taking away some dishes and looking right at her. She smiled, nodded, and left. The air outside was muggy, which usually would be a reason to head directly home, but she turned in the opposite direction, not ready to be deflated by discovering the truth about *To Kill a Mockingbird*. Not ready to be deflated at all. That conversation with Iris had been the highlight of her week, and Erin wanted to savor it, not examine what it meant about her life.

CHAPTER FOUR

Iris's advisor's office was on the third floor of a brownstone at the end of Bay State Road, a quiet, tree-lined street that paralleled busy Commonwealth Avenue, where the T rumbled through crosswalks with its two green-painted carriages. This side street was shoulder-to-shoulder brownstone dormitories, each fronted by a set of concrete stairs and a small, desolate plot of earth host to nothing but weeds. Despite the dire lack of landscaping, Iris took the opportunity to walk along here whenever it was remotely on her way.

The faculty offices were sequestered from the congestion, housed in buildings bigger and reposing behind grass instead of bare dirt. Iris climbed the stairs to a front door with its leaded glass inset and made her way up two creaky flights inside and down a hall to Professor Rawling's office. Iris had been working with him in various capacities since she'd made the transition from undergraduate to grad school, which, given that she hadn't changed universities, had been seamless. The professor's door was half open, and she stuck her head inside while she knocked. He was a balding Black man with a graying beard and the perfect sized potbelly. If he wasn't such a taskmaster, Iris could imagine him as her grandfather, albeit someone much more loving than the man she and her mom had been stuck with.

He said, "Come on in, please, and close the door."

A window air conditioner hummed out a cool breeze that made her shiver when she seated herself in one of the chairs across his large desk from him. Before he could even ask, she started bringing him up to date about her research. "I'm waiting for the books I have on order to come in, so I'm going back to some of the firsthand accounts of Congo before independence through to Mobutu getting installed as president. I'm pretty sure I can get another one from my grandfather's church since they had missionaries out there before independence."

His nod became a headshake, and Iris sat back. "I have some bad news about your grant."

Her heart thumped and squeezed. "What is it?"

The deep breath he took made her own lungs seize. "The Foundation for Modern Historical Studies split the aid it's providing into four different grants. You've been grandfathered into one of them, but that's all they offered, and there's no possibility for renewal."

"But I was awarded the full grant months ago. I've been counting on it."

"I know you were. They acted in bad faith even though they appear to have been trying to do a good thing."

Iris laughed. "Bad faith?" She put a hand over her mouth and inhaled sharply to beat back nascent tears. "Is that what you call it? What good thing were they trying to do? Less for more?"

"I understand, and I know this grant meant a lot to you."

"It means *everything* to me. It's what made this even possible."

Professor Rawlings placed his hands on his desk and interlaced his dark fingers. He was lighter than her coal-black grandmother had been but not by much. "What about loans?"

Iris couldn't have this conversation, not with this calamity sitting like an undigested piece of gristle in her esophagus. At the same time, she was welded to the chair, able to move only enough to keep breathing. She hadn't even blinked since getting the news.

"I'm already swimming in debt from the part of undergrad that my scholarship didn't cover and most of my graduate work so far. Any more and I won't have any hope of repaying it when I graduate and get a job. I mean, I know how it is. I'm sure you're not even paid as much as an entry-level software engineer in Silicon Valley." She stopped talking well after she should have. At least she didn't mention her mom and how much money Iris sent to her every month. That would evaporate with more loans once she graduated.

"This doesn't mean you'd be without funding for the three or four years you have left. There are always new grants, and you can apply for some of the smaller grants that are still available for this coming year."

If she took a year off and found a more upscale restaurant to work at, she might be able to save up enough to be able to continue with the small grants he had mentioned—assuming she'd be readmitted into the program. That would delay everything, though, and still leave her with frankly terrifying debt at the end.

"I need to look at my finances and think about it." That was a lie. Her finances were depressingly clear in her mind at any given time.

"I understand. I'm having Irene"—the ancient department admin—"pull applications for all the grants we can find that still have submission windows open. She'll email all of them to you by the end of the week. Your record is stellar, and I'm sure you'd have a good chance at a couple of them, which would offset part of the loans you'd have to take out." He clamped his lips into a thin line and pushed a small stack of papers away from him. "I'll be honest with you. I'm appalled at the behavior of this organization and blame their recent change in leadership for their shift away from African history. They've behaved dishonorably, and you of all people don't deserve it. I would hate to lose you as a student."

Though she appreciated the sentiment, she huffed out a short breath. In her mom's words, "deserve" was a concept for those already lucky enough not to be poor. "I appreciate that, but I have to think about my future. Right now I could stop and be a teacher at a private high school almost anywhere. Betting on anything else might be a terrible idea." She got up. "I have to go to work."

That was a lie—she wasn't due there for hours. "Thanks for your help with those applications. I'll let you know what I decide."

With as much poise as she could muster, she let herself out and hustled down the stairs to the cloudy, humid day outside. She stood in momentary indecision until cutting across a small expanse of well-maintained lawn and making her way to Marsh Chapel.

Any real religious feeling had been driven out of her at a young age, a result of the way her grandfather had treated her mom, but churches were still places where you could share misery with high rafters and intricate stained glass. Marsh Chapel was Methodist with stained glass nods to nondenominational welcome, a stone edifice with heavy wood doors that she wrenched open before stepping across the threshold from summer into quiet somberness. She slid into a cushioned pew a few rows in and let her head fall back, closing her eyes after a long look at the wood rafters far above her. This was why she'd come here: to let the quietness and tranquility help suppress the scream that had been fighting to burst from her throat since Professor Rawlings had spit out the news. Her pent-up dismay beat against her eardrums in muted waves. Or maybe that was the sound of her own blood racing through her arteries and veins.

She squeezed her eyes shut. She'd worked too hard to have this happen—though Iris knew well from watching her mom her whole life that hard work often didn't translate into any rewards. She'd think unfairness ran in her family, but she knew it was more endemic than that. Being furious about it made perfect sense but solved nothing. Naomi had shielded Iris from any of these types of reactions she might have had to their circumstances, putting her head down and getting on with it even though their situations had been more dire than Iris's now. Naomi had dropped out of college at the end of her sophomore year when she came down with her pregnancy like a virulent flu. Neither her boyfriend or an abortion being viable options, she worked and sweated through a Pennsylvanian summer with Iris growing heavy inside her. As if that weren't bad enough, Naomi had had the added complication of dealing with her father, a Baptist preacher and missionary.

Noah Patterson had spent years in Africa, largely in rural villages in Angola, not far from the impenetrable border of what was, at the time, Zaire. Whites were not welcome in Zaire during Mobutu's dictatorship. Not that they were exactly welcome elsewhere in Africa at the time, not even when they were spreading the good word. Now, if they brought medical supplies and other necessities, that was another story. Noah visited the closest missionary hospital regularly, ministering to those suffering from one of the innumerable diseases that flourished in the African forest. It was at the hospital that he met Naomi's mother, Kiala Domingos.

Iris had known her grandmother as a whip-thin woman who spoke English with a French accent and suffered from recurrent malarial fevers and dreams that persisted even after she was out of Africa. There wasn't enough of the right drug to rid Kiala of the poison her blood had sopped up from mosquitoes while she was growing up a hundred kilometers from the mission hospital. Iris still wasn't certain exactly why she'd been at the hospital, whether it was due to her own ailment or that of someone in her family, but by the time Noah met her, she'd been there a couple of months, had mastered a surprising amount of English, and was helping around the hospital like she'd been born to it.

Noah showed his affection by making a concerted effort to save her soul. After they married, she followed him back into the bush to the congregation he'd carved out of the jungle. They lived there for a number of years before Kiala fell ill in a way the mission hospital couldn't handle, and they came back to the US and a new congregation in Bethlehem, Pennsylvania. Kiala volunteered at the local hospital, never missed a Sunday sermon, and sang Angolan village songs while she tended to their garden in the backyard. "There's room for everything," she'd told Iris more than once.

For Kiala, there was room for Naomi's baby. For Noah, it was more complicated. Iris was kicking and screaming evidence of a transgression hard to swallow. How was he supposed to face his congregation and preach chastity and purity when his own daughter had flouted his teachings? He was gracious enough to let Naomi and Iris live in his house, but actually acknowledging them (forget about loving them) was a bridge too far.

His hospitality had ended when Kiala passed away, too young, when Iris was nine. Shortly thereafter, he sold the house out from under them and went back to his mission work, though in South America this time, leaving Naomi and Iris to fend for themselves. They ended up in a run-down one-bedroom apartment, only moving to something marginally larger when Iris was old enough to start working and pitching in.

Iris had had plenty of time over the years to think about her grandfather's many bullheaded contradictions. He wasn't a bad man, as hard as Iris had tried to see him as such over the years. His offenses were no more pronounced than those of most people, but so many of them, appalling ones, had been done in the name of the good word of God and Jesus himself. Noah was genuinely trying to make a difference in whatever jungle he had set up camp in, but in his ardent desire to save all the souls around him, he had forsaken those closest to him.

Iris opened her eyes and straightened up to look at the large, round, stained glass window nestled inside the tall pipes of the chapel's organ. Inside the circle was Jesus floating with a nimbus in one hand. While she didn't have her own close, personal relationship with the son of God, she considered his teachings to be pretty good ways to live in general: loving your neighbor and enemies, forgiving others, serving others, and having faith—without substituting belief for hard work. Those lessons could be easy to forget or ignore, as her anger at the grant administrators showed. It was going to take a lot of time for her to forgive their callousness and not let her anger calcify in her arteries and strike her dead like her grandmother's heart had done to her.

She was too worked up to think productively about it now. She'd been planning on going to the library to while away the couple of hours before she had to show up at the restaurant, but that would be useless. Words would just slip past her eyes like rain sliding down the outside of a window, an endless progression of letters, spaces, and punctuation that would mean nothing.

Her apartment was a half hour away by train plus a ten-minute walk, so by the time she got there, she would practically have to turn right around and leave. Not that her apartment would provide any kind of balm.

She'd lived for three years in what was dubbed "transient housing," during which she'd had seven different roommates. Her room was nice enough. The biggest of the three bedrooms, it was decorated with African masks and landscape watercolors. Her desk, perpetually covered with papers, books, and journals, sat under an east-facing window which lent a cheery brightness to the mornings.

The rest of the place, though, was only one step above a dorm. The living room was furnished with castoffs accumulated over the years: a futon couch, a precarious rocking chair, a beat-up trunk that served as a coffee table, and a TV that had a corner that showed everything in magenta. The walls were white and bare of any decoration. The kitchen existed in various states of disarray, all depending on how much Iris cared about the place being clean. Keeping it tidy was entirely on her; Candice and Trish would let the dishes pile up until they were eating everything off of paper towels.

Realizing now that she might actually be transient again soon, depending on how things panned out, she got to her feet and moved out of the chapel and up Commonwealth Avenue toward downtown and the restaurant. If she lingered in the Public Gardens first, she wouldn't be too early for her shift.

After passing through Kenmore Square with its iconic Citgo sign and the glimpsed silhouette of Fenway Park, Iris took Newbury Street all the way to the Gardens, allowing herself to get distracted by the stores and foot traffic. She passed the bistro she used to work at, seemingly countless clothing stores, and a couple of salons. An overcast sky gave everything a slightly ominous look, though maybe that was due to Iris's mood. Her quick stride ate up each long block, ticking down the alphabetical cross streets from Gloucester all the way to Arlington.

She squinted at the darkening sky. Was she going to get caught in the rain without a jacket or umbrella? That would be the burnt dessert on the rotten main course of this day. But then she was in the Gardens, entering in the middle of one side of the rectangular park on a paved path lined with a riot of flowers. The whole place was aggressively verdant, and Iris let her gaze stop where it wanted: tulips, various beds of flowers and green plants, the stone footbridge in front of her, a swan boat on the pond. The bridge was too crowded for her taste, so she made her way to the path that circumnavigated the pond and strolled her way down and around the south side before turning back north. In this part of the park, the main features were a heavy handful of wonderfully mature trees. Iris couldn't identify any beyond a weeping willow and maybe an elm? Or was it an oak? Whatever they were, they were beautiful and calming in a way her walk over here had failed to be, melting away the top layer of her consternation.

She took a deep breath. While she wasn't anything like a tree, she could probably take a lesson from one about perseverance. Tomorrow was going to come and the next day and the next, and she was going to live through it one way or another, just like her mother.

The problem was that she didn't want just to live. She wanted to get herself into a position that was the polar opposite of her mom's subsistence work. What she'd said in Professor Rawling's office had been true. She had options. With just her master's degree, she could make a good life for herself and still help her mom. The problem was that she'd let herself want more, envision more, count on more. Now anything less than that "more" felt like failure—or punishment.

She ended up by a large tree that looked like a partially opened umbrella. Maybe she could take shelter under it if the heavens opened—as they now seemed poised to do. The downturned branches were heavy with deep-green leaves, and the ground below them was bare of grass. It reflected her mood, and she walked toward it.

As she got close, she noticed a woman on a bench nearby, her deep, red hair vibrant against the steel-gray sky. It took a few seconds and some blinking to place her. Erin from Dialogue. Her hair was brighter outside the restaurant's warm, intimate lighting. She was leaned back on the bench, one foot over the other knee, eyes fixed on this somewhat improbable tree. No doubt, her ever-present reading material was on the bench out of sight beyond her legs.

Iris stopped where she was, considering backtracking before she was potentially spotted, though Erin's focus on the tree appeared absolute. She was torn between wanting and not wanting to talk to Erin, especially given her current state. Their interactions last time had been dizzying, ranging from inexplicably curt to actually pretty nice. She had turned out to be charming in a low-key way. "Please don't spit on my food." Iris felt the smallest hint of a smile form on her face, which was a miracle considering this day.

Riding on that and their shared interest in this tree, Iris approached the redhead. As she got closer, she cataloged everything she could see about Erin: medium-wash jeans, a dark-gray V-neck T-shirt, bright yellow Chuck Taylors, and…an aggressively neutral expression. It was more like an antiexpression: masklike and freakishly steady. Iris stopped again and watched, waiting for her to blink. When it came, the blink seemed to loose something in her. She tilted her head back to look at the sky and felt around on the bench—looking for her umbrella, Iris realized.

Then Erin glanced in Iris's direction and sat up a little straighter. Iris gave a small, tentative, misguided wave. Though she wasn't in the mood for small talk, she covered the rest of the distance between them, pulled there by Erin's incongruous seriousness.

"Take a load off," Erin said, motioning to the empty spot next to her.

Iris sat, twisting to face Erin, one leg bent and resting on the bench while the other jiggled on the paved path in front of them. "This tree…" She indicated it with a tilt of her head.

"I know. It's my favorite. Not necessarily this particular one, since there are some magnificent ones in Forest Hills Cemetery, but weeping beeches in general."

"Weeping? But it doesn't seem exactly sad to me."

"I don't think it's sad, either, but weeping describes how the branches grow downward from their peaks. I love that if you look closely through the leaves, you can see the tops of the branches before the downturn. In winter, the whole skeleton is exposed, of course, which is interesting on its own." Erin had illustrated her points with sharp gestures, slicing her hand through the air to mimic the shape of the tree's branches. She pointed behind them at a large tree that oversaw part of the pond. "Weeping willows do the same thing, but it looks different because their branches are so thin and flexible."

"You really like trees, huh?"

"Not like in a horticulture way, but they're both salve and inspiration to me. My family used to camp growing up, so I ended up with an appreciation of nature. And this one, come on…" She smiled and threw her hands apart to encompass the tree in front of them. "It's special."

"I know I like white birches, and that's pretty much it."

"Well, sure, who wouldn't like them? They're wonderful whether they have leaves or not. The poplars along Memorial Drive out by Harvard are pretty magnificent, too. But," she said with a wry smile, "I think I've talked about trees too much at this point."

"No, that's okay. I like the idea of salve and inspiration."

"Yeah, it's almost as good as cauterizing everything in sight."

They sat for a long moment in quiet, both of them contemplating the tree again, though Iris sneaked peeks at Erin from the side of her eye. Like her hair, her freckles were more pronounced out here, a steady smattering across her cheeks and nose as well as on the backs of her hands and arms. She was pale otherwise, a prime candidate for some sunblock and a hat. Iris, on the other hand, had a built-in tan, though it was light enough that sometimes she felt the need to prove her Blackness by trotting out her literally checkered genealogy. She'd been mistaken as Hispanic, Indian, Spanish, Brazilian, though never Asian. She existed in that uncomfortable place of being too light to be Black and too dark to be white. She embraced her Black identity but was too often in the position of having to justify it to other people, a conundrum her mother never had to face, given how much darker she was than Iris—even though she'd gotten "good" hair from Noah. What a load of crap that was, assigning qualitative judgment to the texture and curl of someone's hair. The ways Blacks were devalued were legion.

Finally, Erin said, "What brings you to the Gardens this afternoon?"

"I'm early to work, so I thought I'd stop by." Some part of the truth was better than an outright lie. Iris didn't intend on going into why she was early. Thinking about it made her chest tight. She chased the discomfort away by asking, "Are you going to be dining with us today?"

Erin shook her head. "I have a grocery-store salad waiting in my refrigerator for me."

"Ah, so you're avoiding it by sitting here."

She huffed out a laugh. "You got me. It's far less inspiring than Dialogue, but I have a feeling when I get older I'll have to move on from eating whatever I want, whenever I want it. I'd better start practicing now."

"Or maybe take advantage of the time you have left. What do you do when you're not working at the restaurant?"

"I'm a graduate student at BU." Her breath failed her for a moment. She paused, not knowing how long it would last.

"What do you study?"

"History." The jiggling of her foot increased exponentially at this shift in the conversation.

"What part of history?"

"Don't worry. You don't have to ask to be nice or anything." She shifted on the bench so both her feet were on the ground and she had to turn her head to see Erin.

"I'm interested in all sorts of things, so it's not like you'd bore me. But if you don't want to talk about it, that's fine."

Iris wanted to refute that while still not talking about it, which seemed impossible. While she was trying to think of what to say next, a raindrop splatted on her nose.

Erin said, "Was that…?" Then, within the span of one second to the next, that opening salvo transformed into a heavy, cold rain. Before Iris knew what was happening, Erin had her large umbrella open and was shielding most of them both, though each had an arm outside the cone of safety. "Now that was impressive."

"The rain or your quick draw with your umbrella?" Despite herself, Iris scooted a little closer to try to get her shoulder under cover.

"Oh, Mother Nature, definitely." Her voice was raised to carry over the drumming of the rain on the fabric above them. "I'm guessing this downpour is going to last for a while. Do you have an umbrella in your bag or can I walk you somewhere? Over to Dialogue?"

"You really don't have to do that. I've tested it, and I don't melt in the rain."

"But you'll be wet all through your shift. Come on. It won't be much more than ten minutes if we walk like city people."

"Don't you have something better to do?"

She tilted her head, seeming to consider the question. "No, I don't." She got up, leaning into Iris's personal space to keep them both under the umbrella. "Are you going to walk with me, or am I going to Dialogue by myself?"

So Iris got up. Under the umbrella, she smelled rain against concrete and asphalt and a sharp, woodsy scent that felt like it had peeled off of that tree and followed them back through the Gardens and down Arlington Street into the South End. It was Erin, of course, and after their conversation, Iris could see how well the scent suited her. Erin and the rain were perfect distractions from the disaster of her financial situation. As they shuffled toward Dialogue, she tried to knit together everything she knew about Erin into a consistent whole: dining alone, reader, exorbitant tipper, tree aficionado, free to sit and contemplate a weeping beech in the late afternoon on a workday.

"What do you do?" she asked as they hurried across an intersection, trying to avoid the instant puddles at each curb. "For a living, I mean. Unless tree staring is your actual vocation."

"If only. I would ace that, though I doubt it would pay much. I'm a consultant."

"What do you consult on?" The irony of the possibly prying question didn't pass her by, given how firmly she'd stopped the conversation about her history studies at this exact point.

"This and that." Iris was pretty sure that was all she was going to get, but Erin went on after they'd walked past a few brownstones. "I try to teach companies how to build and maintain high-performing, happy work teams. The corporate world is generally a disaster in that respect, so I have my work cut out for me."

"How did you get into that?"

Erin glanced at her, which was disorienting this close together. Her eyes were the blue of worn denim. "I guess I built a high-performing team, and word got around. Consulting is challenging, but I like that I don't have a typical nine-to-five job. Those are soul killers."

Iris's affection cooled a few degrees at that incredibly privileged statement. Before she could stop herself, she said, "Unlike, say, knitting together multiple minimum-wage jobs to barely survive?"

That shut Erin up, and they walked the last block to the restaurant in an uncomfortable quiet. But after jogging with Iris around the side of Dialogue to the staff entrance, Erin stopped them. "I know how lucky I am. I try to deal with that luck in multiple different ways, though it's never enough. I've had my struggles along the way, but someone has always struggled harder, and I don't know what to do about my privilege—like in a systemic way, not just giving people good tips to help make up for their ludicrously small salaries." She opened the black, rust-flecked door and leaned over with the umbrella so Iris could make it inside without getting any more wet than she already was. "Have a good shift. I'm sure I'll see you sometime in the next few days." Then she was gone.

Iris let the door close on the rain but didn't move further inside the restaurant. Her shoes were soaked, just like her pants, which were wet nearly to her knees. The cuff of her right sleeve dripped water on the floor, and whatever hair wasn't in her braid was kinked with moisture.

She catalogued these things because she didn't want to think about how they'd just left that conversation. She usually didn't feel bad about reminding people of their privilege, but Erin's contriteness had taken the wind right out of her self-righteous sails. Erin had clearly been aware of it already and struggled over it. Iris didn't know her well enough to know if her privilege came from the luck of her birth, being white, hard work, or, most likely, a combination of all three, but a lot of it was probably out of her control or had been cemented long before now.

What did Iris expect her to do about it? Be a crusader of one? Renounce her position and join Iris as a server at Dialogue instead of just being a very good patron? That was ridiculous. And yet wasn't that how Iris had just acted? The fact was that she didn't know Erin but had gone ahead and judged her regardless. Whatever Christian values had sifted down to her through the generations and past her pretty formidable shields made it clear that this was a casting-stones situation and that she had her own work to do.

As much as Erin's privileged situation had triggered a deep jealousy in Iris, she wanted to apologize to her—and to do it exactly the way Erin had done it: from the heart and admitting culpability. Unfortunately, Erin had a salad waiting for her at home tonight so the apology would have to wait.

Iris headed to the staff room to dry off, put on the serving uniform she had in her bag, and think more about what had just happened. She had learned a lot about Erin in a short period of time, she realized, but she still knew next to nothing. What was surprising was how acutely she wanted to learn more. As a rule, she didn't google people, but since she didn't even know Erin's last name, she wasn't tempted. Besides, she didn't want to find things out through the Internet. She'd rather hear it from Erin herself.

CHAPTER FIVE

Catherine was already in line at Sweetgreen when Erin got there, and Erin apologized her way past people to her side. They gave each other a one-armed hug and talked while surveying the menu board.

"Isn't it weird that there's always only one vegetarian special? This is a salad place. You'd think the vegetable would be celebrated a little more," Catherine said without looking at Erin. One of her ears was pierced stem to stern with silver hoops, and her black hair was shaved tight to her head under a cascade of long, thick hair. Her Chinese immigrant parents had tried mightily to mold her into something more acceptable looking to them, but she had repelled their attempts like she was water and they were oil.

"You can just have them leave the meat off if you want to fully celebrate."

"Then I'd feel like I'm missing out on something." This time she glanced at Erin and gave her a wide grin.

"Just don't start crusading on behalf of vegans everywhere."

"I could never give up cheese."

"Or meat? You make these declarations all the time. In fact, I seem to recall you also saying you could never live in a bougie neighborhood."

"Brookline isn't bougie. Its great schools attract a certain demographic."

Erin refrained from reminding Catherine that she wasn't in any hurry to increase the size of her family. Nor was she becoming a vegetarian. Instead, they ordered, paid, and went outside and across the street to sit on the steps of the Boston Public Library. They chewed in companionable quiet until Erin couldn't stop herself and asked, "What do you do with your privilege?"

"Enjoy it."

"I'm serious."

Catherine held a bite suspended between her bowl and her mouth. "Are you insane?"

"Maybe?" Erin's appetite began to flag at this exchange. She wished she could take back her question and just have a nice time with her best friend, but who else might understand?

Catherine dropped her fork into her bowl. "Why are you so intent on feeling bad about what we accomplished and how much we got paid for it?"

"It's not feeling bad so much as…conflicted."

"Erin, you are so newly privileged that the shine hasn't even gone from the finish. You were drowning in student loans until our payout, and you're a woman—not only a woman but a lesbian."

"My parents gave me every opportunity growing up."

"That's a good thing."

"I'm just saying that I'm much more fortunate than so many people, and I don't know what to do about it." Erin hadn't been able to shake Iris's damning statement from her mind. She'd been stewing on it for days now and hoped Catherine would untangle the knots she'd put herself in just like she could slice and dice her way through programming code.

"If you have such a problem with the money, give it away and really start working again. Of course, then you'd probably be privileged with a generous salary. How much are you charging for your consulting?"

Erin ignored the question and stared out at Copley Square and Trinity Church across the street from them. The church's ornate symmetry invited contemplation, just not now. It turned out to be harder than one would think to gift that much money in a thoughtful, impactful way. If she put her mind to it, she could make it happen, but she kept avoiding putting her mind to it.

"I'm working. I have a deliverable half done at home I need to finish in the next week."

"You're playing at being a consultant, which is fine if that's what you want, but you have to admit you're not serious about it."

Erin set her salad down next to her. "Is it too early to have a midlife crisis?"

"Not unless you only intend to live to be sixty." Catherine punctuated that with a large bite.

"Why are you being such a hard-ass?"

She spoke around the food in her mouth. "Because you love that about me."

It was true and illustrated another thing she appreciated about Catherine and that had made them such spectacular business partners: she told it like it was. "I do. And we can stop talking about this now."

"No, not yet. What's got you thinking about privilege specifically?" Catherine tucked hair behind her pierced ear. The sun glinted off one of the hoops.

Erin considered evading the question but thought better of it. Keeping it to herself would only continue to torment her. "I ran into a server I've had some short conversations with at Dialogue, and after a perfectly nice time talking in the Gardens and walking under my umbrella to the restaurant, she pointed out how privileged I was. It stuck with me."

Catherine hummed. "Was it mean-spirited?"

"No, just devastatingly factual. Pretty much how you'd deliver it."

"Why do you care what your server says?"

That was a good question. They each ate a few bites as Erin considered it. This was another thing she loved about her friendship with Catherine: they were both okay with giving conversational space to deep and extended thought.

Finally, Erin said, "I like her, and she still wanted to talk to me after I was stupid and put my foot in my mouth the last time I was there."

Catherine nudged Erin with her shoulder. "Like her or *like* her?"

"I don't know. I hadn't gotten that far before she so neatly took me down a notch. Or several, to be honest."

That wasn't exactly true. When sitting in the Gardens, Erin had noticed Iris's bronzed skin, her full lips, and her light-brown eyes. Her braid had been disheveled, leaving many tendrils loose around her face. Outside of the restaurant, in the muted light of the overcast day, Erin could see her well enough to decide she was quite attractive. The question of whether Erin was attracted to her was a little fuzzier, especially given how they ended things.

"Well, you like difficult women, so you should buckle in for a rocky pursuit."

"Difficult has the wrong connotation."

"Fine, what would you call Jane, Denise, Hayley, and now… what's this woman's name?"

"Iris. If they were anything, which I'm not admitting, I'd call them challenging. Why would I want to be with someone who doesn't push me?"

"I wouldn't call emotional manipulation pushing, but you say tomato, and I say what's for dinner?" Catherine put her hand on Erin's forearm. "I'm just saying a relationship shouldn't punish you for who you are—it should celebrate it. You have too much Catholic guilt."

Erin laughed. "You know I went to church all of ten times before leaving home. I doubt that was enough opportunity for me to soak up anything about Catholicism besides the Holy Trinity, and I never really got the Holy Ghost."

"Fine." Catherine squeezed her arm before relinquishing it. "I'm just saying that you deserve to be happy, so maybe you should dedicate some brain power to getting out of your own way."

With that, they changed the subject, talking about their families, the broad strokes of Catherine's work, the Pops' schedule at the Hatch Shell along the river, and so on. The daily ease of it was soothing, and after they'd sat and talked for an hour, Erin was still sorry to say goodbye, even though it was paired with promises to have dinner at Catherine's place one night soon. She sorely needed that. When she'd left Nuvio after her contract was up, she hadn't just left the job but also separated herself from most of her friends. Now they were all on different trajectories, and she felt adrift.

It had been well over a year, too, since her relationship with Hayley had blown up in her face. Or since a rogue part of herself had blown it up by setting the explosives without the rest of her knowing. The two of them had started dating six months before the deal closed with Nuvio, though that was already in slow, hazy motion. Erin had clawed some semblance of a normal life out of her previously all-encompassing work schedule and was having fun. They'd go to dinner or a bar and back to one of their apartments, dodging roommates and communal pets, having quiet or raucous sex, depending on who was around.

The lead-up to Nuvio's acquisition of TriBar had been shrouded in a thick cloud of nondisclosure agreements, so neither Catherine nor Erin was legally able to tell anyone anything, not the least of which was the eight-figure payout that Nuvio was dangling in front of them like a big, fat carrot. Every last thing had to be negotiated, and the lawyer fees were ridiculous. They joked that the deal had better go through or they'd be up to their eyeballs in debt to their attorney.

But it did go through, all the previously secret particulars became public knowledge, and things started to change. Hayley seemed to take endless glee in looking at the growing balance in Erin's brokerage account and became full of ideas about how to spend it: trips abroad, the Beacon Hill apartment, a second house in the Berkshires and a car to get them there, Michelin-starred restaurants, and, finally, jewelry.

Erin had explained the terms of the buyout to her, but Hayley didn't understand why Erin was still working. She wanted to launch into retirement together right away. When Erin stopped spending after paying off debt, setting up a small endowment, and buying the building she lived in, Hayley had doubled down on envisioning their future together and hinting, in a very heavy-handed way, that there was something wrong with Erin for not jumping onboard with her ideas, in which they were married world travelers, rubbing elbows with other millionaires—or, hell, billionaires.

One evening, Erin had sat on her couch, her head tilted back, her gaze on the smoke detector mounted to the ceiling right above her, and explained once again. "I have to work at Nuvio for at least another year or the penalties will wipe me out. Besides, it's my company. I want to see it be successful for years and years."

Hayley sat cross-legged one cushion over. "Why did you bother selling it, then?"

Erin rotated her head to glance at Hayley, who had practically moved in with her. She still had some clothes in her apartment, but Erin couldn't remember the last time she'd been over there. Hayley's hair was freshly cut and colored to the tune of five hundred dollars. Giving her a card on one of Erin's accounts—one with a generous limit—had seemed like a good idea at the time, a time when Hayley herself had seemed like more of a good idea than she was seeming at the moment.

"Catherine and I wanted to give it the best chance possible, and Nuvio had resources we couldn't match on our own, not for years, at least. They gave us the best terms out of a few other companies that were interested."

"The best terms meaning the most money?"

Erin sat up. "No, meaning things like dedicated resources and autonomy and a fleshed-out road map with some real research behind it."

"So they weren't offering more money than the other companies?"

"No. They were in the middle. The top offer was ludicrous, but they weren't going to be a good environment for our employees."

It took a moment for Erin to recognize the expression on Hayley's face: disgust. "You didn't owe them anything. You said you paid them fairly as soon as you could, and they wouldn't be fired or anything."

"Yes, they could get fired. That's what big companies do. They cut fat, and some of my people had been with us since practically the beginning, living paycheck to paycheck in the hope that something like this would happen and they'd be rewarded."

Hayley laughed. "Don't tell me. You rewarded them out of your own pocket after not even getting the most money you could for your company."

Erin got up, barking her shin on the coffee table as she rounded it to open space between them. "Of course. Catherine and I agreed. We never got around to setting up options, but we wouldn't have gotten here without our employees." She rubbed her leg. "They deserved every penny we gave to them. Why not? We could afford it, and it was the right thing to do."

"Listen, I'm not saying that you didn't have help in getting to this point, but it was your idea, your company, and your payoff. If you're not careful, you're going to give it all away before you know what you're doing. Don't you want to travel with me? To do everything you ever dreamed of? You need to be smart about what you have now since you did something stupid like not taking the best offer you got."

Anger bubbled up in Erin like acid reflux. "That's exactly what I was telling you, but you don't want to hear it." Her voice was too loud. "We went over those offers to every last detail, talked to as many people as we could, researched how other acquisitions went, and Catherine and I agreed that this was the best offer overall. It's beyond me that you can think twenty-five million dollars isn't enough."

"You just wait and see how quickly it goes."

"If it's going to go quickly it's because you want to spend it on everything."

"It's the cost of getting set up the way you should be."

Erin crossed her arms. "Why do you think you know everything about me?"

"We've been together for a year and half, and we've already covered richer or poorer. I don't know why you're being so stubborn about this."

"Maybe because you've been way more interested in my money than you've been in me since the acquisition."

"Because you've been totally uninterested in your money. I'm thinking of our future."

Erin scrubbed her hands over her face. "I don't want the future you want."

"Do you even know what you want?"

"Not that." She sighed. "And not you."

Their breakup hadn't been finished that night. Even without obtaining the official sanction of marriage Hayley had done such an excellent job of entwining herself in Erin's life that excising her from it had prolonged Erin's pain over the next month or more. It had been both financially and emotionally costly. Catherine may never have liked her, but Erin had let herself fall in love and was mortified that it had taken such an embarrassingly long time for her to wake up from the dream that had existed only in her own mind. It was hardest to free herself from some of the things Hayley had said. They'd gotten lodged under Erin's ribs and had a habit of stabbing her when she least expected it.

Doubts were a hard thing to shake. At least Hayley had been sure what she wanted in life—and she'd seemingly wanted it with Erin. Erin had been less certain. One thing she was sure of, though, was that she and Catherine had taken the right offer and done the right thing by compensating their team. That said, she still didn't know what future *she* wanted. She was treading water. How long could she do that before she got tired and drowned?

* * *

Erin had been avoiding Dialogue, and it had to stop already. At this point, the only person she was hurting by staying away was herself, especially since she'd woken up this morning craving Suzanne's bruschetta, which was the perfect combination of bright acidity, herbaceous basil, and sweet and creamy mascarpone cheese. They were a staple on the seasonal menu, and Erin helped herself to them every second or third time she was at the restaurant.

She didn't want to see Iris until she had a better answer—or at least a plan—for how to use her privilege as a force for good instead of unconsciously wielding it like a weapon, but she might dry up and evaporate into the summer sky if she had to eat one more grocery store meal. Yes, there were other restaurants, but none that felt like an extension of her living room. Or that had food that she loved as much.

So on Wednesday night, she put on some jeans and a deep-purple shirt that she left unbuttoned one extra button from when she wore it to client meetings, checked the weather forecast and her reflection in the mirror, and walked out of her house without an umbrella.

She skipped the usual detour into the Gardens to say an up-close-and-personal hello to her favorite tree and instead powered along Charles Street, which divided the Gardens from the Commons. Every block she went, she remained unsure of what to say to Iris. The newness of her privilege seemed like a pale excuse, but it was the only one she had—though not one she could give Iris. "I'm trying to figure it out," she muttered to herself as she retraced the route the two of them had taken in that rainstorm. "I want to do the right thing," she reminded herself, whispering at the sidewalk. "I've been unbearably lucky. I've also worked hard." Figuring it out wasn't easy, but if it were, she wouldn't be driving herself crazy about it.

At Dialogue, she was seated in the middle of the dining room. She had no idea whose section she was in until Greg came by with the water carafe to recite the day's specials. She was disappointed that it wasn't Iris. Finally, she saw her come out from the back, carrying two desserts with a bunch of sharing spoons held tightly in three curled fingers. She didn't see Erin, or at least didn't let on that she'd seen her. Erin couldn't tell if that was a good or a bad thing.

After ordering her food, her head bent over an article in the *CIO* magazine she'd brought with her, she surreptitiously kept an eye on Iris, enjoying again the way she interacted with the diners in her section. She was so quick with a smile, used ready hand gestures to indicate the sizes of things, and tilted her head toward whoever was speaking to give them her full attention. Okay, Erin clearly *liked* her liked her, but where could it go after their last conversation? Iris had no idea the full scope of Erin's privilege—

and Erin wouldn't disclose it so soon after meeting someone. Perhaps in time.

Erin was done with her main course and deep into her magazine when she heard a throat clearing next to her. She jerked up, her heart giving a jump of surprise.

Iris said, "I kept waiting for you to wave me over like you were flagging down a taxi."

"Have you ever even done that? Or only seen it in the movies? Rideshares have been around longer than I can remember."

"Well, I think that wave you gave me the last time you were here would have definitely gotten someone to at least slow down for you." Three pens resided cozily together, clipped to a pocket in her black apron.

"Thanks for saving me the embarrassment tonight. Since you're here, though, I need to say something."

Iris got serious, which was a look Erin liked on her as much as her smile. "No, it's my turn to apologize. I put my shit on you in a way you really didn't deserve."

"You were right, though. About my privilege. Which was what I wanted to say. Maybe more than that, but that as a start."

"There's being right or maybe just having a well-informed opinion on something, and there's weaponizing it. I was having a terrible day, if that's any excuse. I assumed a lot about you and your situation, and we all know what happens when you assume."

Meaning it made an ass out of you and me. Unfortunately in this case, Erin was sure Iris's assumptions were way short of the full truth—at least in some areas. Erin twirled her water glass, spreading out the ring of condensation at its base. "Should I ask?"

"No. Not that I would have time to go into it."

An electric energy took hold of her, and before Erin knew what she was doing and despite her fears of Iris's justified judgments, she said, "What about somewhere else some other time? If you're interested, of course."

Iris gazed across the dining room. Erin held her breath, steeling herself for rejection, but Iris said, "I'd like that." She pulled out her order pad and scribbled something on it before handing the top sheet to Erin. "That's my number. You can text me, and we'll coordinate something. I've got to get back to work now, but I guess I'll see you later?"

"I'm looking forward to it."

When Iris was safely out of the dining room, she gave Greg her customary nod and took advantage of the pause while he got her check ready to take a picture of Iris's number and text it to Catherine with the caption, *I have a date (maybe?)*

Catherine's response was immediate. *You go, tiger.*

Erin shook her head, paid her check, and left, her step a little lighter at the thought of sitting near Iris soon. She still needed to solve the problem of how to deal with her privilege, but now she had even more motivation to do that than before. Iris may have apologized for her delivery, but she was right about the advantages Erin shared that many didn't. Including Iris. Erin knew almost nothing about her, but her statement about minimum wage jobs had sounded personal.

Iris didn't know much about her either. She was the first person in her family who had gone beyond community college and had worked her way through school in an attempt to minimize the ballooning debt she'd been racking up. She'd washed dishes at the student union cafeteria, made sandwiches until she could no longer stand the smell of salami, worked in the library, and, finally, landed a cushy position as a research assistant to one of her professors. She'd paid a few dues. It would be ridiculous, though, to trot out that history to prove she understood the plight of the working poor, especially in the face of where she was now, dealing with an existential crisis about work and worth brought about by all the money she had in the bank.

That money would not be making an appearance when she got together with Iris, which was a relief. Still, it felt disingenuous to go into something new and withhold such a whopper, especially since she already wanted to know everything about Iris. She made Erin want to be truthful, however problematic her truth was, but she'd learned her lesson with Hayley. She wished her worry could be merely about whether Iris saw this as a date or not.

CHAPTER SIX

Iris and Erin had coordinated to meet over the weekend at The Thinking Cup, a café and coffee shop in a basement space on Newberry Street, not too far from where they'd run into each other in the Gardens. It was public and sometimes loud and a splurge that Iris rarely indulged in, especially if she bought one of their pastries. The weather was so glorious she wished she'd had them meet at the weeping beech instead.

She had complicated feelings about this get-together. She liked Erin despite the two of them clearly existing in different worlds and despite there being a whiff of an unequal power dynamic, given their customer-server relationship. But Erin's invitation had seemed so genuine and in the moment that Iris couldn't resist.

The truth was she didn't want to resist. Despite Erin clearly being well off—having a fancy job and no doubt impressive billing rates—Iris liked her. She liked Erin's focus and her wide-ranging interests. She liked her attempt to spread some of her wealth around in the form of excessive (but appreciated) tips. If she were honest with herself, she also liked how Erin looked: the snap of her short-but-still-long red hair with strands that sparked fire in the slow burn of the rest of it, the playfulness of her freckles, her ease in clothes that ranged from college-student casual to boss business lady, the dark eyeliner that accentuated her light eyes, and the three chunky silver rings she wore on long fingers with short nails.

Iris really hoped she wasn't reading something into this invitation that wasn't there, but she'd seen Erin looking at her, and straight women never looked at her that way—unless they were trying to puzzle out her genealogy. She wondered what Erin thought about her. Despite her fairly strict but reasonable rules about her dining experience, she seemed pretty easygoing, taking things as they were, though not in a way that precluded thoughtfulness.

As Iris approached the coffee shop, she realized she'd gotten way ahead of herself for the lead up to a first date, a realization cemented when she saw Erin resting a hip against a low, wrought iron fence, her head tilted to the sky and eyes closed. She wore slim, dark jeans and a baby-blue T-shirt with a deep V-neck, and Iris envied her ease, her ability to make any space her own.

Iris got close but not too close. "Hi," she said, trying to make the word gentle enough not to startle Erin out of her reverie.

Erin opened her eyes and treated Iris to a slow smile. "Hi. I checked it out inside, and there were plenty of tables, so I thought I'd get some fresh air."

"No interesting trees around?"

"Sadly, no. How are you? No, wait, we should probably get settled before the questions start. One more, though—Are you going to let me treat you?"

An offer to pay was a clear indication of a date, but maybe Erin just thought she needed the help, given their disparate positions. "No," Iris said. "But thanks. I'll just use part of your last tip to cover it."

Erin frowned, the expression pulling together eyebrows several shades darker than her hair. "Are those somehow condescending? It's not how I mean them."

Iris reached out and touched her arm below the short sleeve of the shirt that matched her eyes. "No. They're generous. Everyone at Dialogue thinks of them as a treat."

"Well, that's a relief. I'm rethinking a lot of things lately, and that was one of them. Shall we go inside?"

They ordered and sat at a table in the back near the bathrooms, usually a strategic error, but it gave them a little space from the other patrons.

Erin wrapped her hands around her mug of tea like it was chilly in there. "I have to admit, I'm out of practice with this, but I'm pretty sure we start with the basics and work from there. So… where are you from? Or if that's way too boring, what are your deepest hopes and dreams?"

"I'm from Bethlehem, Pennsylvania, but the rest of my childhood is so complicated that it's at least fifth-date territory." Even in the dim lighting, Iris could see a flush crowd out the freckles on Erin's cheeks—maybe at the mention of future dates so early in this one. "But we can start with yours if that's okay with you."

"Oh, sure. Mine's so milquetoast that it's suitable for strangers on a bus. Two parents, one older brother, one older sister, suburban childhood north of here. We're literally the most boring family. I went to Tufts, just far enough away from home that I could figure out who I was—at least partly."

Iris laughed. "Somehow I doubt it was that simple."

"Oh, sure. The bottom line is that I like my family well enough, but I don't really fit in, and we don't manage to hang out very much for some reason, which says something about priorities, actions speaking louder than words, and all that."

"That's the way I think about your tipping. Action."

"This isn't weird, right? Some kind of power dynamic given how we met?"

Iris laughed. "I was wondering the same thing on the way over here."

"What did you decide?"

"That sometimes I should stop trying to examine everything and go with it."

"Oh, no. You, too?" But she said it with a smile. "Sometimes it's a wonder I can get out the door. Some days I've been paralyzed by inner turmoil about what socks to wear. I'm not joking."

"What socks are you wearing today?"

She hiked up her jeans and moved her leg into Iris's sight line. They were a deep purple with multicolored fireworks exploding up from the part hidden under her shoe. "They seemed appropriate for the occasion, and it only took me about five minutes to choose them before heading over here."

"I'm guessing your sock collection dwarfs mine."

"No doubt. It's a whole thing. Anyway." She took a sip of her tea. "What was bad about your day, the rainy one?"

Iris hesitated, searching Erin's face for interest or nascent judgment, wondering how that topic remotely followed the sock conversation, and trying to conjure up some precognition about Erin's reaction to aspects of Iris's financial situation.

"Or if it's complicated, I can ask again in a couple of dates. Believe me, I've got some twenty-seventh-date skeletons in my closet myself."

The joke lightened things inside Iris enough for her to say, "I found out that day that I'd lost my funding for my PhD studies this coming school year."

"Ouch," Erin said, which matched her furrowed brow. Her hand drifted across the midpoint of the table but didn't quite make it all the way to Iris. "What are you going to do?"

"Decide which of all my bad options I'm going to choose— more loans, taking a year off to save money, or dropping out and trying to find a high school teaching position."

"Wow, okay. That really is bad news. When do you need to make up your mind?"

"Yesterday?"

Erin sat forward, her gaze firmly on Iris, who found that she liked to be the focus of Erin's considerable attention. "Will you tell me now what kind of history you're studying?"

Surprisingly, Iris did, and the telling made the sting of her dilemma both sharper and mellow. She left out the part of her very particular inspiration for the topic. Twenty-seventh-date territory indeed. Erin was an active participant in the telling, asking questions and raising interesting points.

"Does history dig into correlation versus causation? Or is it mostly concerned with the what of it all—at least that's what I remember of it when I was forced to take it in high school. No offense."

"Oh, God. Don't judge historians on junior-year world history. I'm fascinated with correlation versus causation. Sometimes digging out causation is the whole point. We know what happened, but why it happened can be incredibly complex and fascinating— or infuriating a lot of the times. Knowing who has the power at any given time is critical."

"Why infuriating?" Erin slid her mug to the side and intertwined her fingers on the table top, leaning toward Iris, telegraphing her engagement.

"Practically everything's about how people in power want nothing more than to stay in power."

"Do you think those with means are always corrupted by the power they get from those means?"

Iris took a swallow of cooling coffee. "I think history has had its say about that over and over again."

"Yeah, that's what I thought." Erin sat back with a downturned expression. "Sometimes I think I might secretly be a communist, but that never turns out well, does it?"

"I think that depends on who's writing the history. It's easy to ignore starving people and stagnation of innovation when you've got plenty yourself."

They moved even farther from the personal by talking about different social, economic, and political structures for a while. Finally, Erin laughed. "My best friend, Catherine, would be horrified at our conversation. I think we skipped right to the eighth date. Next time I see you, we'll be talking about genocide."

"If I didn't already tell you that it's dangerous to get me started about history, consider yourself warned now. Why don't you tell me about Catherine?"

That made Erin smile. "Her first talent is being a tech wizard. Her second is giving me a hard time."

"I like friends like that. You can't get anywhere in life if you're afraid of the truth."

"Sure, but there's the truth and there's how Catherine swings the truth around like a sharpened sword. She's first-generation American, so she's all-in on the immigrant work ethic. We were a lot alike that way."

"But not anymore?"

"I've slowed down, for better or worse. But we had some crazy times at Tufts and after. She's so good at convincing me to be a prankster. Practical jokes, long cons, and whoopie cushions."

Before Iris could ask about "for better or worse," Erin went on to share a number of anecdotes about her younger self and Catherine. Letting that question go was probably a good thing because Iris was enjoying herself too much.

At the same time, there was clearly a lot they weren't telling each other, and Iris couldn't forget that Erin was definitely someone of means. She didn't know what that meant, but holding her most dear cards close to her chest seemed wise. What had Erin said? Twenty-seventh-date stuff? It had been a while since she'd made it that far with someone.

After Iris had chimed in with some choice tales from her own undergrad years and her current roommates, Erin glanced around the café. It had grown crowded while they'd sat there, their conversation tucked into the general din of other patrons and the espresso machine.

Erin said, "I don't want to, but I feel the need to look at my phone and see if I'm taking up too much of your time."

"You're not. I blocked out two hours on the off chance that things went well."

She laughed. "I think I'm offended."

"Considering how our last extended conversation ended, there was a not-insignificant chance we'd talk ourselves into another problem."

"I don't mind hitting a problem, not as long as we can find a solution."

"Ah," Iris said before she could stop herself.

After a beat, Erin said, "Ah?"

"Of course, you're an optimist." It was obvious, but it still felt like a surprise, one that she didn't know if it was good or bad, though she was rooting for good.

"You say that like it's a bad thing."

"It's not. It's just that a lot of people aren't in a position where they can maintain the same sunny disposition."

"Privilege again." Erin's face closed off, her gaze drifting to the table between them.

Damn it! Why did she feel compelled to share every truth that waltzed through her mind? Things had been going so well.

"I don't deny it," Erin continued. "But I also think you get back what you put out into the world—or you have a better chance of getting something good if you don't spend all your time being shitty about your situation." Erin put a freckled hand over her mouth and dragged it down across her chin. "And that just makes me sound more privileged. I told you before that I'm working on it."

Erin wasn't entirely wrong, but Iris had brought the carnage of their previous problem out of its tentative truce. She felt bad enough about it that she reached for Erin's hand and squeezed it. "I'm sorry. If it makes you feel any better, I'm working on it, too. But when you exist under a pile of minority identities—Black, woman, lesbian—it's hard not to have a hair trigger."

Erin squeezed back. "It's okay. I hope we have another date coming up where we can work on making it through that topic without it going off the rails."

"Definitely. Let's see what rules we can break on our second date."

"Just three more until I get to hear about your complicated family."

Iris laughed. "Wait, did I say fifth date for that? I meant twenty-seventh."

Erin's thumb brushed the back of Iris's hand, sending energy up her arm. "I'm not the most patient person, but I think I can manage that for you."

Because there was nothing to say to that, yes, optimistic but touching statement, Iris just smiled. Then they were upstairs at the sidewalk, in the awkward part of the date where you have to say goodbye gracefully.

"I'm that way," Erin said, pointing down Newberry to the Gardens.

"I'm that way," Iris said, pointing over some brownstones toward Boylston Street and the T.

"In case I haven't been clear. I'd like to see you again if you're interested." Erin's gaze was intense.

"I'd like that, too."

"I want to schedule it now, but I'll be cool and say that I'll text you."

"Okay." Then, because she didn't care about coolness, Iris took a step closer, tilted her head up, and kissed Erin. It landed somewhere between chaste and deep, and when she disengaged, Erin's cheeks were flushed. Iris was quickly growing fond of provoking that reaction.

"Okay," Erin said. She gave an adorable little wave and walked off.

Iris watched her go, smiling until she blended in with other pedestrians and effectively disappeared from sight. Then she called her mom, who didn't answer. Iris waited where she was, leaning against that wrought iron fence, and her mom called back seven minutes later.

Iris asked, "Is it busy?" She could picture Main Street Diner, where Naomi had worked for most of Iris's memory.

"Everyone can wait. How are you?"

Just the question made her smile. "I had a profoundly good first date."

"Profoundly, hm?"

"We skipped all the first-date stuff and talked about ideas. Causation versus correlation, the corrupting influence of means and power. She's thoughtful even when I get a little aggressive."

"You? I can't imagine you getting assertive and judgmental."

"Hey, I didn't say judgmental."

"Potato, po-tah-to. What's her name?"

"Erin McCallister." They'd finally exchanged full names.

"Ah, so not Black, then."

Iris had dated both Blacks and whites, but Erin might be the whitest one yet. "No. Pretty clearly Irish, complete with the red hair and freckles."

"'Profoundly good.'" Iris could see Naomi's wink.

"I like her." It came out like an admission of guilt. "I met her at work. She's a regular customer and tips like she means business."

Naomi went so quiet Iris could hear the bustle of the diner in the background.

"It's fine," Iris said.

"I know how expensive that restaurant is."

"It's fine."

"If you say so."

"I say so. Don't rain on my parade. She's thoughtful about herself and me and our positions, which is more than I can say about most people." Going into the conversations they'd had about money and privilege would only worry her mom more, so she said, "It was just a first date. It's not like I'm super attached."

"'Profoundly good.'" This time there was a small edge to Naomi's voice that Iris decided to ignore.

She laughed. "Okay. Man. Don't you have customers that need something?"

"Nothing takes precedence over my daughter, and I'm pretty sure you were the one who called me. All I'm saying about Erin is that we both know there's a difference between what you want and what you get. Or even what you deserve and what you get."

"You sound like me."

"Oh, the horror. Just be careful."

"I'm trying to just let things unfold."

"Really? I know how you get."

Meaning that Iris tended to overthink things, a tendency her mom claimed had skipped a generation, from her father to her daughter. Iris didn't like to have anything in common with her grandfather. Sharing a quarter of his genes was plenty.

Naomi had to get back to work, and for once, Iris was happy enough to let her go. They were close as far as parents and children went, their slim age difference facilitating both chumminess and strife, at least during Iris's early teens. It had been maddening to be sure that Naomi didn't understand something only to have her prove that having that exact experience was still within her recent memory. They weren't exactly friends, but they were deeply there for each other.

Still, the end of that conversation threatened to erase her elation at the ninety minutes she'd just spent with Erin. She wished for a moment that she was back at their table inside, Erin in a gently defensive position about what she had that others didn't—not trying to justify it but seriously conflicted in a way Iris admired. It hadn't hurt how her eyes sparkled in the dim lighting or how her thin but shapely lips pulled wide into frequent smiles. Or how her breasts rose and fell with her breaths while she listened to Iris, always letting her take her thoughts to completion before interjecting with her own.

Yes, "profoundly good." She already couldn't wait until their second date and what that might unlock between them. But first, work.

* * *

Iris unlocked the deadbolt to her apartment and muscled open the sticky door. On the couch, Trish was scrolling on her phone, not watching the TV that was playing too loud across the room from her. "Is Candice here?"

Trish shook her head without ungluing her gaze from her device. "She's at the latest boyfriend's."

"Do you mind if I turn this down?"

"No, wait. It's getting to the good part. I've been waiting forever for it."

"You know that you can fast forward on Netflix."

Finally, Trish's eyes flicked up away from her small screen. "It's not the same. You need the lead up for it to make visual sense."

Iris stopped herself from pointing out that Trish wasn't even looking at the TV and made her way into the messy-but-not-yet-disastrous kitchen for a glass of water before securing herself in her room. She'd had way worse roommates than Trish, and the three of them hung out on a fairly regular basis, but sometimes she wished hard that she had her own place. Though she knew she should do a pro/con list for her school options, she put her water on the upturned wooden crate that served as her nightstand and flopped back on her bed. She should at least change, because her clothes smelled like the restaurant, but she felt a lovely kind of lassitude. Warmth from her date had persisted through the evening even though she had been stupidly disappointed that Erin hadn't shown up. Would that have been weird? Would it have been weirder if she'd been seated in Iris's section or someone else's?

As if Iris's thoughts had conjured communication out of thin air, her phone buzzed where it was still nestled in her back pocket. She lifted her hip and slid it out, unlocking it as she brought it up in front of her face.

It was Erin. *How was your shift?*

Iris considered saying it had been boring without Erin but thought better of it. *Thankfully over. There was a run on the quail, and we all had to start hinting that something was wrong with it.*

As if.

I know. I'm beat now.

Iris watched the bouncy dots that indicated that Erin was typing…and typing…and typing. She put the phone down and shucked off her shirt and bra, pulling her pajama T-shirt over her head before she heard the chime of a new message.

Friday's supposed to be beautiful. Would you like to walk a few miles along the Charles with me? We can start and end at the Harvard Bridge if that's convenient. I just like long walks and getting caught in the rain.

She smiled harder than those personal ad clichés really warranted. *And staying up late?*

I'm just getting started. Please don't propose we meet for an early breakfast.

A Friday walk sounds great.

They coordinated time and place, and Iris grinned her way through putting on the rest of her pajamas, brushing her teeth, and washing her face. That exchange had pepped her up enough that sleep wouldn't come easily. The image of Erin awake in her apartment somewhere in the city accompanied Iris as she sat at her desk and slid a notepad in front of herself, flipping it open to a blank sheet and resolving to focus, finally, on a much less pleasant situation.

A good pro/con list could clarify, but it was a subjective affair, which made it easy to put your thumb on the scale in the column you secretly (or not so secretly) wanted. Judging the results could be problematic as well, since it wasn't just about the number of items in one column or the other but also the *weight* of each—and their downstream effects. Writing something as simple as "increased student loans" was an a priori negative, but the real problem was that it meant she would start out far behind her peers. It would take her longer to get a down payment on a house, money meant for retirement savings potentially would go to servicing the loan for decades, she'd remain constantly on a budget, and other negatives she couldn't accurately imagine right now.

What was all that compared to being able to continue on the plan she'd been imagining since before she'd learned how to drive? To becoming a professor and teaching at the college level as soon as she was able? To earning unequivocal respect? Because wasn't that part of it? Being able to put herself in a position in direct opposition to her mom's?

That thought put a damper on the exercise, and Iris pushed the notepad away from her, only half finished with one of the options. Not that she would ever ask her, but she sensed Erin might be good at this kind of thing…or good at helping Iris do it. She seemed appropriately analytical and thorough. It seemed like she'd managed to achieve something professionally noteworthy and then spin that into a career, which sounded a lot like success to Iris.

They were in such different places even though they'd felt so in tune with each other this afternoon. But her mom was right: Dialogue was an expensive restaurant, and someone who made such a habit of going there had to be very well off. That said, Erin didn't talk down to Iris or treat her as lesser for being a server, so did her salary really matter? Their next date said it didn't: all Erin wanted to do was take a walk, which was free no matter who you were. But there she went again, tilting the scale of the pro/con list of her romantic life. All she had to do—besides go to sleep, based on her gritty eyelids—was to remain unattached like she'd assured her mom.

She broke even that simple rule by texting Erin after getting into bed.

Don't stay up too late.

It only took a few seconds for the response to come through.

Good night, Iris.

CHAPTER SEVEN

Spending time with Iris made Erin anxious to develop an actual purpose in her life.

In the absence of one, she decided to work on developing her consulting business. If she shook her network hard enough, surely it would lead to more business. She also contracted with a lead generation firm that would do initial outreach for her based on the marketing materials she'd paid a pretty penny for when she was just starting out.

Sales was something she hadn't relished even when TriBar had relied on her to do it. Back then, though, the wins had been so tangible, building and building until the startup was out of the red and into the black and then making enough to hire more people and then enough to capture the attention of investors and acquiring companies. Everything had been steeped in purpose, thrilling and tinged with the real possibility of failure.

What would professional failure mean to her now? A small, private embarrassment? No one was counting on her to be successful in any of this, not even her. She could give up before she even really started, and nothing would change.

Okay, maybe she'd find it even harder to face herself in the mirror every morning, but she wouldn't call that substantive.

At the very least, the sales calls she was making, pitching her services and reminding people of her track record, took up some of her day. Seeing Iris did the same and in a much more pleasurable way. They'd danced around each other at Dialogue a couple of days after their first date. Erin's walk to the restaurant had fizzed with anticipation even though Iris surely wouldn't have time to talk with her. And she hadn't, except for when she'd intercepted Erin in the hallway to the bathroom when they didn't get much past "hi" around the thirsty gazes they gave each other.

Now, Erin waited on the river path underneath Mass Ave, hands in her pockets, swaying back and forth a little. Her attention was zeroed in on the ramp down from the road to where she stood, getting passed by runners and cyclists and a few other walkers. This date was more calculated than she hoped it seemed to Iris. After her aggressive insistence at paying for herself at The Thinking Cup, Erin had brainstormed activities that were free or close to it, removing money from the equation as much as possible. It was a good thing this city was full of no-cost entertainment. They would be set for things to do for months.

Walking along the river was genuinely enticing to her, even aside from the fact that Iris was going to be with her. Their first date had exceeded her expectations, which she'd tried to hold at modest but had failed. It had reminded her a bit of spending time with Catherine and their tendency to skip to the good stuff. Iris's passion about history in general and the topic she'd chosen for her dissertation specifically was an aphrodisiac of the highest order. Her light eyes, sensuous lips, and exuberant hair came in a close second. Making her smile felt like more of an accomplishment than most of the work she'd done since the acquisition. Iris was a woman you had to earn your place next to, and Erin relished the challenge of doing so.

Her naturally impatient side wanted to know everything about Iris right now, but the rest of her knew that the slow unveiling would make the knowledge gained even sweeter. Still, just knowing what Iris was keeping close to her chest told her a lot, most notably her family situation but also the challenges she'd had getting to where she was and where she was going—if she could work out her money situation. Already, the struggles she was having around her funding made Erin want to swoop in to help, but she knew that not only would Iris hate that, but that it was a spectacularly bad idea in general.

Derailing her from this dangerous train of thought, Iris came striding down the concrete ramp, moving over for a cyclist making his weaving way up toward her. She wore a flowing skirt and baby T and looked stunning. Erin couldn't glance away, cataloging her shapely arms, strappy sandals, the mass of hair that flowed unrestrained past her shoulders, strands blowing across her face and getting swiped away brusquely.

Erin raised her hand when Iris was halfway down the ramp and said, "Hi," as if Iris might miss her standing there like a doofus. She tucked her hand back in her pocket and took a few steps to meet Iris, who gave her a too-short hug and a kiss on the cheek that Erin reciprocated.

Erin said, "Do you have a preference which direction we go in?"

"I thought you were the one driving this date."

"West it is. Toward downtown is always more congested, though arguably more interesting." She offered her hand, which Iris took, and started them walking at a leisurely pace. "Depending on how you got here, this may take you back the way you came, but at least you'll have company this time."

"I've been at BU for the last six years, so I would have to be hiding under a rock not to have walked this countless times."

"Oh yeah? Is this where you went for your most important dates?"

Iris glanced at her with a smile. "It didn't even break into the top-ten date destinations."

"What are those? Dorm room hookup, coffee shop, which we've already covered, pizza place, movie theater, a club, a home football game...? I can't think of anything else."

"A concert, study session, a drive if someone had a car, shopping."

Erin groaned. "A walk ranks below a study session?"

"In its defense, there usually wasn't much studying happening."

"True. I remember those."

"How old are you?"

"Old enough to know what I'm doing, but still young enough to get it done."

Iris laughed. "I feel like that's from a commercial."

"That's because it is. Just for Men, which is not just for men—or at least the tag line isn't."

"Are you going to make me guess?"

"I wasn't going to, but now I'm getting ideas."

Iris squeezed her hand. "I'm historically bad at this, but I'll say thirty-four."

"Ouch."

"Okay. So too high."

"I'm twenty-eight going on anciently boring, apparently."

"I'm just giving you a hard time. I think this is a lovely date. I'm twenty-five, in case you were wondering. I took a gap year to earn some money."

They strolled under an overpass and made their way into the part of the path that paralleled BU's campus, trees blocking the shoreline on one side and the backs of brownstones on the other. Erin always liked conversations in motion, walking or driving, each focused at least partly on where they were going, words coming easily outside of a direct gaze, the rolling out of scenery as the perfect accompaniment to revelations. It had a certain quiet intimacy, and she worried about getting caught up in it and saying something she didn't mean to.

Iris said, "Tell me more about your consulting. You mentioned high-performing teams, but what are you helping people do?"

"Mostly to remember that we're all human beings."

"As opposed to what?"

"Cogs. Automatons. Obviously there's more to it than that, but that's a big part of it."

"What are the other parts?"

"It has to do with culture. It's about norms, what's accepted behavior, what social contracts are in place, what forms of punishment are used and for what." Erin went on, describing signs of a sick culture and what she thought were essential aspects of performant ones. All throughout, Iris kept asking questions, urging Erin to get deeper into the subject, which she was happy to do. The more she talked, the more she remembered that she loved this topic and how much she'd grown to know about it, first at Tribar, then at Nuvio. It gave her renewed inspiration to pursue her consulting even as she knew it still wasn't tripping her passion switch.

They were well past BU and into a narrow part of the path that was completely treelined. No one else was around, and the seclusion felt achingly intimate. They lapsed into quiet, looking around themselves, their fingers still entwined loosely between them.

Erin said, "You're easy to be around."

"You, too." Iris looked at her. "No, easy's not the right word."

"Right. It's more like the perfect kind of challenging. Like you don't give me any place to hide, but I'm not interested in hiding."

"Am I really that bad?"

Erin pulled them to a stop. "No, that's not what I mean."

"I know. Or I think I know. You're *interested*. In everything, which makes your interest in me genuine."

"Exactly. Not to be crass, but do you know what else I'm genuinely interested in?"

"Do I get multiple guesses?"

Erin leaned close and waited until Iris looked at her mouth before she erased the distance between them. Her hands landed at Iris's waist while one of Iris's drifted up to the back of Erin's head and the soft, fine hair there. She had remembered exactly right: Iris's lips were that soft. They were pillowy and undemanding and opened eagerly to Erin's tongue. Erin's fingers tightened against Iris's flesh, and Iris pulled them closer together.

Their kiss was sweet and savory like the best dish at Dialogue, slow and sensual like they had all the time in the world, like they'd always been kissing and would always be kissing. Erin, whose job had been so much about pushing—the status quo, the glass ceiling, the capabilities of her team, the valuation of their company—

relaxed into the irresistible here and now with Iris. They kissed the way they'd talked, an easy give-and-take, a desire for a deeper understanding, a meeting of the minds.

A cyclist buzzed Erin, and they pulled apart and laughed. She said, "That was almost a tragic end to a terrific kiss."

"Oh, good, so it wasn't just me."

"No, that was definitely us both. Though I'd like to stand here kissing you for hours, I think we've covered a lot of ground and should probably make our way back." They turned around and started walking. "Since you got me monologuing most of the way out here, maybe a bit of turnabout would be fair play?"

"You say that like it's hard to get me talking."

"All I know is that you've got all these rules about what you can say on which date, none of which was the second one. Or… this could be our third. If you count the rainstorm."

"Let's not. I wasn't on my best behavior that day."

Skipping to what she wanted to know, Erin said, "Will you tell me more about your grant situation? What exactly happened?" She glanced over to Iris and watched her smile falter. "Or if not, that's okay. I don't want to bring things down, but I want to know."

Iris shrugged, which tugged at Erin's hand. "There's not much to say. The grant administrators changed their mind about what they wanted to support, and they pulled my funding."

"Can they do that?"

"It's unusual but not unheard of. They're the ones with the money, so they have all the power, and they did it before we had a signed contract."

"What foundation was it through? I'm good at strongly worded letters."

"I'll bet you are. It's the Foundation for Modern Historical Studies. I was supposed to get the Margaret B. Johnson Grant, renewable over three years, but that's vaporized. I've applied for a few smaller grants that would help offset some of my tuition, but I still haven't decided what I'm going to do. There are a lot of factors in play."

"I imagine there are. And you're already working, what, four days a week at Dialogue?"

"Yeah. It helps, but it's not remotely enough. My mom—"

Erin waited for the end of that sentence, looking at the path ahead of them to remove even the pressure of her gaze, but it didn't work.

Iris continued but not from where she'd left off. "It's a question about debt, really, and that becomes such a huge game of conjecture that pro and con lists are useless. I have to make a decision soon, though. I've basically been pretending that this isn't happening, which is far from what's needed in a situation like this. Reality is king, isn't it? It's like what you said about culture: everyone needs to honor reality and work within it."

"That doesn't mean you can't curse it out."

"Believe me, cursing has been covered, but it didn't make me feel much better."

"I wish there were something I could do."

Iris squeezed Erin's hand tightly. "I know you do, but this is up to me. Can we drop it now?"

Erin made a twisting motion with two of her fingers in front of her mouth. "My lips are sealed on the matter."

"Thanks for letting it lie. I really can't stand when people have a savior complex."

"You mean like Atticus in *To Kill a Mockingbird*?"

"Don't get me started."

"But I want to hear about it."

"Are you sure, after that kiss?"

"After that kiss I'm only sure that I want more kisses."

Iris smiled so widely her cheeks bunched with it. "I think that can be arranged."

And they did arrange it, though it was truncated because they ended their walk where they'd started and more people were around. Even without adequate kisses, their parting took several minutes of one-last-things and what-are-you-doing-nexts. But then Iris squeezed Erin's hand before letting it go and disappeared up the ramp she'd come down over an hour before, and Erin walked toward downtown, watching crews rowing on the river and a flock of small sailboats out for a group lesson. MIT stretched out on the other side of the Charles, and small groups of people sunned on square floating docks that toed out into the water.

While she walked, she replayed her time with Iris, searing all its glorious little details into her memory: Iris pointing out an improbably large leaf with what felt like little-girl glee, the warmth of Iris's fingers on the back of her neck, the anger about her grant that radiated from her, the feel of her tongue against Erin's.

When her thoughts felt like a broken record, she called Catherine. "Busy?" she asked when her friend answered with a distracted snap to her voice.

"Just got out of a meeting. I'm only just now understanding how many of those you got me out of by running interference. Somedays I have no time to get anything real done."

"Now there's your problem. Going to meetings *is* doing something, whether you like it or not or if it feels like it or not. I would have been useless to the company if I hadn't sat through all those meetings you hate."

"I think useless is stretching it, but I get it."

"Practice acceptance, and if that doesn't work, change things. You're the boss there." Erin sat down on a bench facing the water and kicked her legs out in front of her.

"I miss you around here."

"Come on. I was window dressing at the end, redundant in almost every way."

"You weren't redundant to me." She paused. "One sec. Let me get into my office and close the door." Erin could hear general office buzz and two different people asking Catherine questions before quiet reigned again. "What's going on?"

"Nothing. I just finished a date with Iris that went really well. Date two and a half, and I like her more every time."

"Have you told her yet?"

"What? No, of course not. It's way too soon for that. I'm already plotting how to keep us away from my apartment for as long as I can."

"What does she think you do?"

"Consulting. Which is the truth."

"Hey, I'm not judging you. I'm just trying to understand. Neither of us has had to navigate this before."

Erin tucked her feet back under her knees and leaned forward, propping herself up on a forearm draped across her thighs. A pair of ducks paddled their way past her. "I'm afraid it'll change everything—the same as when I show up at Dialogue sometime and they seat me in her section. I don't want it to get weird."

"Erin, you have millions of dollars. It's going to get weird no matter what."

"Well, see, that's what I was calling about, actually. If you give an anonymous donation for a personal reason, does it still count as anonymous?"

"I think most places don't care why you give as long as you're giving. What do you mean by 'count'?"

"Nothing, never mind. It's a stupid idea. It's just that some targeted donations are basically like putting the cash directly in the recipient's pocket. I mean, you might as well bypass the middle man."

"Unless you actually want to remain anonymous. Who do you want to give money to?"

"Nothing, no one. Forget it. It's a dumb idea."

"Is it Iris?"

"I said forget it. I'd never be that stupid."

"I never said you were stupid. I just want to make sure you're being careful, just like you've been for the last few years."

"I hate that I'm lying to her."

Catherine's breath was a gale-force wind in Erin's ear. "You're not lying to her. You're protecting yourself. You're trying to figure out who she is without that massive complication between you."

"That's a lot of fancy words that mean I'm lying."

"Why did you call me if you didn't want to know what I thought?"

Erin took a beat and brushed her sandaled foot across the stubby grass in front of her. "I just really like her. A frightening amount for so early on. Integrity oozes from her, and she's not going to understand."

"What isn't she going to understand?"

"Everything."

"Erin, really? If she's the quality person you think she is, there might be an initial shock, but she'll come around when you explain things. Don't forget that you earned every dollar. Until then, though, you need to be careful about more than your money."

They talked for a few more minutes even though both of them had had their say. The conversation had done an excellent job at deflating the high of that date. She thought again about donating all of her money except for what would be a decent start on a retirement account. But in the same breath, she imagined diving into the startup waters again and trying to reproduce the success she'd had with Catherine, though another substantial payout might be her undoing. Through it all, she felt like a terrible person for having any problems whatsoever with her wealth. She was so far beyond fortunate that it existed as a tiny speck in her rearview mirror. If Iris saw her now, she'd be disgusted—and for good reason.

She had to start doing better to earn the hours she hoped to spend with Iris, the kisses and touches they were on the path to having. She wanted to be good in an uncomplicated sense but found all she could do was think about the Foundation for Modern Historical Studies and its now apparently defunct Margaret B. Johnson Grant. Fixing that would take so little for Erin, and it would do so much good for Iris. Iris would never have to know; in fact, she could never find out.

She knew what a burden debt could be. When their payoff had come, Erin had been swimming in student loans too, paying them off as quickly as she could with the little money she had coming in. They hadn't paid themselves all that much even when they'd started having success in the market, and she'd had plenty of months where it was a squeaker from one payday to the next.

All that went away when they'd been acquired and she'd paid the loans off, but it was still fresh in her memory, not that anyone else saw it that way. They looked at her wealth now as if it had wiped clean everything that had come before it. As much as she liked Iris, she had no doubt that would be exactly how Iris would see things too.

If she knew Erin had money, would Iris ask for help with her student loans? Would she push to move in with Erin? Would she start wanting to do more expensive things, assuming Erin would pay? Erin didn't want to think of Iris like that, but that had been exactly how things had gone with Hayley. Money did things to people.

Erin just wanted to be sure. Had to be sure. But that didn't mean she couldn't do anything to help in the meantime. She hadn't actually wanted Catherine's opinion when she'd called her. She'd already known what she was going to do and just needed some way to justify it to herself. She was supposed to be doing good with her money, and the Margaret B. Johnson Grant was a prime opportunity for that.

She got up and walked to her apartment with crackling purpose, passing the Hatch Shell and the community boathouse before leaving the path. Blocks of Charles Street disappeared under her stride, and she powered up the hill to her house. She sat at her desk, squared her laptop in front of her, and started googling. Then she started calling, tailoring her vocabulary to be the most effective for what level of person she was talking to, until she'd made herself sufficiently clear about donating a sufficiently large amount of money that she got to someone who made decisions.

Even then, her directed donation was decidedly specific—the same grant, the same awardees. They didn't want to go along with it. They wanted to put her donation into their general fund and decide how to use it themselves, but she opened her checkbook a little wider, made a concession or two, and it was done. She was left with assurances that her "anonymous" wishes would be carried out and gave her wiring instructions to hold up her end of the deal. A quick call to her financial guy (actually one in a small team of financial guys, one of whom was a woman), and it was done.

She prowled through her rooms, unable to settle down, split down the middle with the certainty that she'd done the right thing and the certainty that she'd just made a terrible mistake. Under it all was the churning knowledge that it was past the point of taking back, so she'd have to live with the consequences either way.

CHAPTER EIGHT

Iris exited the train at the Arlington stop, thinking about when she'd come this way for her first date with Erin. She didn't know what she'd expected, but it was definitely not what had happened. They just *matched* despite their differences. It didn't even bother her that Erin undoubtedly made a good salary as a consultant and probably wasn't saddled with a mortgage-sized debt unless it was an actual mortgage. They met on a middle ground where all that mattered were questions and answers, looks and easy touches, and too brief kisses. It was all about now and not about then, which is exactly where Iris wanted to live, because the past was too difficult and the future too uncertain. Erin was passionate and funny, an acute observer of the world if not quite conversant on the questions of class, race, and privilege that Iris lived under all the time. But Erin actually tried to be better, which was such a relief. Iris was counting the days until they would see each other next.

Erin somehow made her current problems seem solvable, which was a foolish idea but persisted nonetheless. She made it seem like everything was possible and problems were transitory. These red flags, her idealistic optimism, were now soothing and inspiring. They had even helped her make a decision about school. She was going to take a year off and work as much as she could to both help her mom and put herself in a better financial situation—and to allow her to apply for more substantive grants. This option came with its share of risks beyond maybe having to start over somewhere else or else giving up, dropping out for good, and becoming a high school teacher where she'd have no time to do research of her own.

The other problem was that if she left school, even with the intention of starting again in a year, the required payments on her loans would start, and she wasn't ready for that. She wouldn't want to take a real job with a decent salary, because she'd hopefully just be quitting it a year later and that seemed like the height of disingenuousness. The money at the restaurant was good, but it wasn't nearly enough, especially with her mom in the picture. She'd have to get a second job. So, taking a year off was not a great option even outside of the simple disappointment she felt at delaying her work. But there was a small pleasure at least in having determined a solution for now and giving herself more time to figure out how to get through her program without dooming herself to even bigger loan payments she wouldn't be able to afford.

She was halfway to Dialogue, thinking that taking a year off wouldn't necessarily keep her from continuing her research, when her phone rang. Erin, she thought and smiled, but it was Professor Rawlings, probably checking up to see when she would make a decision.

He said, "I've heard something unofficial from the Foundation for Modern Historical Studies."

"What, that they're screwing more people out of their funding?"

"No. That they are reinstituting your original grant. In full and renewable for all three years."

Iris stopped walking, making someone behind her stumble, curse, and dance around her. She moved to the edge of the sidewalk. "Say that again."

"It's unofficial, but I know a couple of people in the foundation, and they say that a large anonymous donation just came in, and they're using some of it for the Margaret B. Johnson Grant—and saying that you'll be a recipient, of course. They'll tell you directly when all the financials are squared away. I'll say this—whoever made the donation caused quite a stir at the foundation. It sounds like they don't know what to do with themselves."

Iris's breath had a hard time making it to her tight chest. She put out a hand to a low fence to keep herself steady. "You know what I think about unofficial things."

"I know, and I wouldn't have told you at all, but everything sounds legit and like it's coming out in your favor."

"How long before it becomes official?"

"They said a matter of days."

Before she could stop it, a sob roared up from her clenched gut, through her battered lungs, and to the space in her head behind her eyes and nose, both of which started dripping. Her chest convulsed, and she wished she could sit down—or, barring that, not make a scene. But that burp of tears and snot turned into full-fledged crying. The relief was unbearable. She managed to tell Professor Rawlings that she had to go, put her phone in her pocket, and covered her face with her hands. Public crying was about the last thing she wanted to do, but she had no say in the matter.

Though she was indescribably happy, that feeling existed alongside a buildup of struggles and bad breaks and a lifetime of being the underdog in just about every situation, overcoming the stigma of free lunches and secondhand clothes, food stamps and after-school programs for the poor. The news about the grant had loosened up everything inside her, and her body was taking the opportunity to expel as much as it could as quickly as it could. It was a good thing she was in a New England city as opposed to her neighborhood in Pennsylvania. People left you alone here—sometimes too aggressively—and she could count on other pedestrians giving her a wide berth while she had this cathartic breakdown, instead of asking how they could help.

Eventually, everything slowed down, and she could breathe again. She tried to do damage control on her eye makeup with a cuff of the black shirt that was part of the restaurant's uniform, then took a deep, shaky breath, then another, and laughed. Man, what a sight she must be. She itched to tell someone the news even though it was unofficial and could still go sideways. Any other time, she would call her mom, but she hadn't gotten around to letting her in on the situation, not wanting her to worry—or to try to influence Iris toward a particular decision.

Erin. She called her without a second thought, even though they usually texted. While it rang, she recalled their last conversation, Iris already in bed and Erin far too energetic for the hour. They'd easily continued from where they'd left things at the river, talking about books this time and the usefulness and dangers of historical criticism, where the work was read through the lens of the history and culture that the author had lived in when they wrote it. It wasn't just dry ideas, though. They'd each peeled back another layer of who they were and how they saw this world around them.

Erin answered in a bright voice that sounded like a smile. "Hey. I was just thinking about you but figured you'd be at work. Aren't you supposed to be at work?"

Those words reminded Iris of the here and now outside her incandescent happiness, and she started walking again. "I'm almost there, but I wanted to tell you something."

"You don't want to do the Freedom Trail and the North End on Saturday?"

"No, I do. What historian would say no to that? It's something else, but, listen, it's unofficial, so I shouldn't even know about it, let alone tell you. It could up and evaporate at any minute, and I believe in money only when I see it in the bank."

"Wow. Now I'm wondering if you should let me in on the secret with all those caveats. Maybe you should wait until it's official."

"My grant is funded again!" It felt ridiculously good to say and, more specifically, to say to Erin.

"That's fantastic! How did that happen?"

"Something about an anonymous donation. I honestly have no idea, and I only partly believe that it'll become official."

Erin said, "Hey. How about I believe it enough for both of us?"

Iris's voice was low when she said, "I'm so relieved. You can't imagine. All I had were bad options. I've got whiplash from it all. I just spent the last ten minutes crying on the sidewalk."

"Crying?" Erin sounded stricken.

"Don't worry about it. It was good, I swear."

"If you say so. I'll bet you're relieved, and I know I can't imagine, not exactly. But I know what it feels like to have a big load of worry taken off your shoulders. The other thing I know is that we should celebrate when it becomes official."

"If it becomes official."

"*When* it becomes official. The universe tends to reflect what you give out."

Erin wasn't totally wrong, but sometimes the universe heaped it on no matter if you had a sunny disposition or not. "Then, fine, you can be positive enough for both of us. I'm at the restaurant, so I have to go. I just wanted to tell you."

"I'm so incredibly happy for you. Maybe I'll change my dinner plans so I can come over there and see you."

"What were your dinner plans?"

"A chef salad from Stop and Shop. I know—the height of luxury."

"Ah, iceberg lettuce. You know I'll be busy here, but it's always good to see you."

"I should probably remain at least a little mysterious so I won't wear out my welcome."

They finally said goodbye. Iris thought it was unlikely that she was going to get sick of Erin anytime soon. Erin was disorientingly optimistic sometimes, which made the distance between them open up almost far enough to swallow Iris whole, but then Erin would say the perfect, balanced, down-to-earth thing, and they would feel almost uncomfortably close again. While the differences between them had made Iris suspicious in the beginning, they felt less daunting the more time they spent together. Maybe Erin was rubbing off on her, because, despite what Iris said, she found herself believing that everything was back on track and impossible choices were a thing of the past.

Erin did show up to Dialogue that night, but not as a customer. She waited out back for Iris to have a couple of minutes and engulfed her in a hug. Iris's nose was in Erin's neck, and she could smell the faint remnants of Erin's perfume, which now reminded her of a rainstorm. The firmness of Erin's arms around her shoulders and waist and the delicious closeness they stood in, not talking, breathing slowly and deeply, burrowed into Iris. Instead of trying to stop it, she urged it on until, when they parted, she stood in a pool of want.

She said, "You give good hugs."

"You're easy to embrace. I wish we had more time."

"Then kiss me now before we waste any more of it."

Their kiss outdid the one along the river, and Iris knew if they were in private somewhere, she wouldn't stop until they had devoured each other. When she finally pulled away, she could see Erin's flush even in the orangey glow of the streetlamps.

"I should tell you good news more often."

"I want only good news for you. I know that's impossible and that it's a privileged kind of wish, but it's true." Erin flexed her fingers, which were buried in Iris's hair between her braid and the back of her neck.

"Erin, I don't want you to be on edge around me about that stuff."

"It's just that you make me want to do better, and the first part of improvement is awareness."

Iris's heart squeezed in a way that her mind said was way too soon, but it was undeniable. "How about we teach each other?"

"I'm not sure what I have to offer."

"Positivity, focus, assertiveness, kindness. The list goes on. I really need to get back to work."

Erin's hand was gone from the back of her head, and the space between them was an affront. "I'll see you on Saturday?"

"Definitely."

"Congratulations again."

"Thanks for coming over here just to say that. It means a lot."

Iris waited until Erin was out of sight before going back into the restaurant, donning her apron, and checking the state of all her tables. Even then, her lips remembered Erin's, and her scalp tingled with her touch.

* * *

Candice walked into the apartment while Iris was on the couch, texting with Erin. When Iris looked up to say hi, Candice stopped short. "Wow. What's that smile all about? Still high about your grant?"

"Yeah, and…nothing," Iris said, but she was unsuccessful at wiping the grin from her face.

Candice hummed. "Huh. Maybe I should say, 'who's that smile all about'?"

Iris's phone buzzed with a text, but she kept herself from looking at it. Barely. "It's an ordinary smile." But she was still doing it.

"You met someone."

"You're like the Gestapo."

Candice crossed her arms over her chest. "I'm just getting started. Spill it."

"Okay. I'm seeing someone. It's new."

"But good?"

There went that smile again.

"Really. That's awesome. Where did you meet her?"

Oh. Right. "The restaurant."

"Another server? Kitchen staff?"

Iris cleared her throat. "Customer."

It took a moment, but Candice's eyes went wide. "No way. The tipper? How did that happen?"

"I don't know. I mean, I do, but I don't. I ran into her outside the restaurant. She was interesting, but we kind of argued."

"About what?" Candice dropped her arms and sat next to Iris on the couch.

"Privilege."

She groaned.

"It wasn't like that. Or it was, but Erin short-circuited it."

"But she has money."

Iris's head moved in a combination nod and shake.

"What does that mean?"

"She's careful about it. She meets me where I am."

"I can't believe you even gave her the time of day."

"What do you mean?"

"I can't imagine you with someone who's not barely scraping by. You have to admit you're on a hair trigger about that stuff."

"Hair trigger is a bit much."

Candice gave her a look.

"All right. I take your point." And it was true that there were parts of Erin's existence (that she still didn't know much about) that made Iris uncomfortable, but everything else about her told Iris to let go of her natural wariness around people with Erin's kind of privilege. "She's different, though. She's acutely aware of how good she's got it and works hard to deal with it in a productive way."

"How rich is she?"

"I never said she was rich."

"What does she do?"

"She's a consultant." One who had plenty of time on her hands, though maybe that was because she was always up late? Iris's phone buzzed again. Speak of the devil.

"I think consultants are rich."

"Cut it out."

"Oh. You really like her."

"She basically pretends like she doesn't have money."

"But she's a regular at an expensive restaurant."

"Okay, fine. But she doesn't spend it around me."

"How long is that going to last?"

"Hey. You keep telling me to have fun, and now you're giving me a hard time about it."

Candice raised her hands in surrender. "Sorry. I'm just surprised. You're pretty militant."

"There are always exceptions to everything."

"Well, good for you for finding one. Is she a good kisser?"

Iris shoved Candice's shoulder. "I'm not talking to you about that."

"Have you googled her yet? If she's really rich, it'll probably give us her net worth."

The idea of even having a net worth made her kind of queasy. "No."

Candice pulled out her phone. "Why not? How are you not cyber stalking her yet? What's her last name?"

"No." Iris put her hand over Candice's phone.

"Hey, I know you have a hang-up about social media, but that doesn't mean you can't take a peek at what other people put out there."

Hang-up wasn't exactly the right word, but the gist was close enough. Iris eschewed an online presence entirely, except for what came with being in academics and a coauthor of a number of papers. How could she participate in a system that had given her so much grief when she'd been younger? Try being a bastard from a religious family, try being obviously poor, try being a lighter-skinned kid with a Black mom, and see how the social media world treated you. There was nothing her mom could do to shield her from the cyberbullying of her peers back then, but now, she controlled things by removing herself from the equation entirely.

Iris said, "No. If I want her to know me based only on real life and what I tell her, I need to give her the same courtesy. Don't you ever just want things to unfold naturally?"

Candice laughed. "Are you kidding? I want all the ammunition I can get before things get too serious."

"I don't think a little mystery is bad."

They talked about other, stupid stuff before Candice got a box of crackers from the kitchen and disappeared into her room. Iris looked down at her dark phone, knowing there were texts from Erin waiting, but she hesitated before unlocking it. She had to admit that she had a small urge to look Erin up, if only to see pictures of her that were surely up there somewhere on the web, but she refrained. Online was a different world, a complicated, fraught world, and Iris wanted things between her and Erin to be real. Still, Candice had done a pretty good job throwing cold water on her simple happiness. Honestly, Iris had mostly stopped thinking about Erin's money—however much of it she actually had. Erin made it easy to do that. But Candice wasn't wrong. Erin might be the exception that proved the rule, but the rule was a thing—and for a good reason.

What if Erin were playing some sort of bait-and-switch game, and it was just a matter of time before her money became a thing between them? The truth was that they were fundamentally different in this way, and privilege wasn't something you could ignore indefinitely. Still, Erin took such care and made Iris feel seen and understood. No matter how much it could feel like it, not everyone and everything was out to get her.

She looked at the last few texts from Erin.

Does that sound good to you?

Silence signals agreement.

Did I lose you? Maybe silence doesn't signal agreement.

I'm here, she typed. *And cannolis sound great. I'll see you Saturday at Haymarket.*

Erin's response was satisfyingly immediate. *And I'll text you sooner.*

* * *

Erin had been a good sport on the Freedom Trail, which was full of sites of historical significance to Revolutionary times and beyond. Iris had assumed Erin had suggested it not only because Iris was a historian but also because of Iris's budget. Iris went all in on it, reading every plaque and stopping at every site, spending an inordinate amount of time in Paul Revere's house and at the Copps Hill Burying Ground, where she nosed around among the worn gravestones, looking for the oldest one that was still remotely legible.

They ended up at Modern Pastry in the late afternoon, sitting at a table with two espressos and two cannoli between them. Erin had asked if she could pay, and instead of making a scene, Iris let her. Iris's hatred of incurring debt (real or assumed) was palpable, but she could forgive ten bucks of imbalance right now. She just wasn't sure what was going to happen when they progressed to dinner out. A problem for another day.

Erin's chocolate shell, chocolate filling dessert exposed a sweet tooth she rarely indulged at Dialogue, and it crunched faintly when she bit into it. Her eyes closed, and she moaned behind a smile. Iris watched her chew for a while and swallow, her throat working behind thin, pale skin. Her mouth went dry at the sight and sound. They'd held hands most of the walk, stealing kisses when no one was looking, but seeing Erin wrapped up in pleasure made Iris's stomach drop. She sipped her espresso to dispel it.

Erin said, "Totally better than Mike's Pastry."

"That's a controversial stance."

"Maybe it's the chocolate shell. I don't know. I'm not an expert, but I could eat about five of these."

"And ride the biggest sugar high."

"It'd be worth it. Are you going to eat yours or is it up for grabs?"

Iris shifted her small plate closer to her and put her arm around it. "I'm just savoring it."

"With your eyes?"

"Part of eating is seeing." The tan pastry had irregular bubbles all over it, and slivered almonds clung to the edge of the ricotta cheese filling.

"Sure, but most of it is actually getting the thing in your mouth."

"Fine." She smiled, picked up the cannoli, and took a big bite, the shell cracking under her teeth and barely holding together when she put the rest back on the plate. Creamy, sweet, and crunchy, both from the shell and the almonds. "Okay," she said after she swallowed. "That was way better than just looking. But the plates at Dialogue are very pretty."

"Agreed. I always try to appreciate it before devouring what's on them."

"You don't devour. You're an incredibly slow eater."

Erin shrugged and shifted in her chair. "It's because I like to linger there before I have to go home."

"Why don't you want to go home?"

Erin's gaze was fixed on her cannoli. "It's lonely." She picked the pastry up and took a definitive bite, clearly wanting to end the conversation. What could Iris say to that? That she understood while also not understanding, given that she lived with two other people? Or maybe she could go totally off the rails and say that she could fix that for Erin, that they could go to her place right now and bring life back into it.

Before she could say anything, though, Erin wiped powdered sugar from her fingers, looked at Iris, and said, "Why history?"

It took a minute for Iris to switch gears and set aside the idea of a lonely Erin.

"Because it answers the why of the what of the current moment. We're living in an accumulation of past moments and decisions. Think of Critical Race Theory, which relies on a deep understanding and accounting of history to come to its conclusions. It's important to understand the past, especially the past of the last century, or else—"

"We're doomed to repeat it?"

"Well, yes, but I was going to say that we're making decisions in a vacuum when we should have wisdom on our side."

"Is it personal for you? What you're studying?"

"Yeah. You need to have some kind of connection to the material you're going to spend years getting intimate with enough to make a novel contribution to the field."

"But for you, why the Congo at that time?"

Iris took another bite of cannoli to insert a little pause in the conversation and allow some quick contemplation. Strangely, she didn't feel her defenses rise in response to that question.

"My grandmother was born there. She met my grandfather in Angola after walking a couple of hundred kilometers through the forest and across the border during the time when Mobutu was the dictator propped up by the US, among others."

"Ah, so really personal. Are your grandparents some of the source material you're using?"

"My grandmother died fifteen years ago."

Erin's face spasmed, and her hand slid across the table to take Iris's. "I'm sorry."

"It's okay. I mean, it was a big deal at the time, but I've now lived more of my life without her than with her." And yet, with Erin's sympathetic expression warm on her, she felt some of the grief of that loss again. Because of that, Iris let herself say, "She was my second mother for a lot of my childhood. Oh." She squeezed Erin's hand before releasing it. "I forgot to tell you that I'm going home next week."

"Bethlehem, Pennsylvania, right? Are you going to see your parents?"

"Yeah. Just a quick trip so I don't miss too much work." She felt words about her mom rise through her into her mouth, but she wasn't ready to let them out. She didn't think Erin would judge Naomi for her circumstances, but fear wasn't rational. This time she was the one who said, "Are you going to eat that?" about the rest of Erin's cannoli.

Erin pushed it toward her. "Do you want a bite? It's hella chocolatey but good."

"I thought you said you could eat five of them."

"I could, but I'd love to share with you. Besides, I can always get more, though that might make me look like a pig."

Iris inched Erin's plate back to her. "You don't seem to care what other people think about you."

"I don't? How so?"

"Most people won't eat out alone. People look at you in the dining room. You get up in front of people all the time and tell them things they don't necessarily want to hear. Isn't that what your consulting is?"

"That's part of it, but doing those things doesn't mean I get away without critical voices in my head. These days, I mostly think I'm a terrible disappointment." Erin swiped a finger through the chocolate filling in her cannoli and deposited the gob of custard in her mouth with an air of nonchalance Iris wasn't buying.

"A disappointment to whom?"

Erin flashed a small smile before growing serious again. "I love that you used whom instead of who there."

"This isn't a conversation about grammar. Who do you think you're disappointing?"

Now she grimaced and glanced around the pastry shop. "Myself, I guess. And Catherine, though she'd never say so. People more driven than I am now. A whole bunch of people both known and unknown." She laughed. "Could I be more full of myself? Or spineless? That's an impressive combination if I do say so myself." She took another bite of her cannoli without meeting Iris's gaze.

"Hey," Iris said softly and repeated it again until Erin would look at her. "You're not disappointing me."

"That's because..." Erin raised her hand from the table but put it back down without saying anything.

"What, that I don't know you well enough? Or that you're busy trying to impress me? Or that I don't understand what you're doing with your life right now?"

She squinted with a pained expression. "Yes?"

Iris's chest squeezed at this part of Erin's truth. She reached across the table and put her hand on Erin's forearm. "I'm pretty good at reading people, and I'm not fooled easily. I like you, a lot, and if any of those people are judging you harshly, they need to open their eyes. And if you're judging yourself harshly, you need to knock it off. We all have things we think we don't do well and mistakes that we regret. Isn't it all about trying to be better, not getting mired in everything you think you should be doing?"

When Erin dipped her head, the lights in the shop picked out individual strands of her hair and lit them up like lightbulb filaments. "That's beyond kind."

"But you don't believe it."

"I want to."

"Try harder." Iris softened her remark with a smile when Erin looked at her.

Erin's answering grin looked genuine enough to unfurl a small ribbon of relief through Iris. "Yes, ma'am. Can we talk about something else now?"

"How about we finish these and try to get lost in the maze of streets up here?"

"Now that's a challenge I'm completely up for."

Iris was almost sad that the tone had lightened up so quickly and definitively. Getting to see through this crack in Erin's shell affected Iris deeply. Knowing Erin had doubts and voices of illogic whispering to her made her seem even more worthy of affection. Iris wanted to know as much about her as possible and to be someone who could soothe her demons. It made her think Erin would be graceful in how she would take the story of Iris's own history. It made her want to tell Erin all of it—just not now when things were still raw between them.

She was content to hold Erin's hand while they wandered narrow streets, catching drips from wheezing window air conditioners and getting turned around before they'd gotten anywhere. That realness had been intoxicating, and Iris had delighted in every new facet of Erin that she discovered, loving the unfurling of mystery over their walks together. It was so much better than dinners out or drinks at a bar. The only problem with it was she couldn't get physically close enough to Erin. They took advantage of labyrinthine sidewalks rife with blind spots to steal steadily deepening kisses, Iris tasting the chocolate of Erin's cannoli in her mouth.

Iris might have invited Erin back to her place, but she was due at Dialogue. She had carried her all-black uniform with them in a backpack on this whole date, intending to change at the restaurant when she got there. Back at the Haymarket T stop where they'd met up earlier, they stood close together and spoke softly of nothing, prolonging the time before they parted.

Iris tugged gently at the front of Erin's button-up shirt. "As much as I'd love to be around to monitor you, you need to try to be kind to yourself."

"I make no promises."

"Seriously, Erin. It's okay to have things about yourself you want to change, but berating yourself about them is counterproductive."

"How'd you get so smart?"

"I guess I've just been lucky enough to witness a whole lot of mistakes, so...learning from negative example?"

"Well, thank you, and I'll try. Call me when you're in Pennsylvania."

"I will. Oh, and when I get back, I want to have you over to my place and cook us dinner. My kitchen's a postage stamp, and my roommates might bother us a little, and it's way out on the B line, and I only know a few dishes well enough for them to be good enough for you to eat—"

Erin interrupted her spiral with a bright smile. "I'd love to. I'm sure whatever you make will compare favorably to whatever prepared thing I'd pick up from the grocery." She kissed Iris again and gave her a tight squeeze. "Thanks for a great afternoon. Don't forget to call me." Then she released Iris, gave a little wave, turned, and walked away toward Government Center.

Iris watched her for a while before heading into the station. Erin's hair bounced a little with each step, catching the sun; a spot of sweat marred the back of her shirt; and her incredibly sexy calves flexed and relaxed. This was getting out of control in the very best way, speeding past infatuation to something deliciously more.

* * *

After a six-hour bus ride to Philadelphia and a change to a second bus to Allentown, Iris took an Uber to the Main Street Diner in Bethlehem. It was a blue-collar town, but her experience growing up, especially after her grandma died and she and Naomi were left to their own devices, scraped the bottom of the barrel. Even before she was old enough to join Naomi waiting tables at the diner, carrying on the dubious family dynasty, she worked under-the-table jobs—anything anyone would pay her for. It had separated her from her peers at school, adding to the other differences already between them, differences they leaned on in all the worst ways. Erin's confession of it being lonely in her house made her remember her own alienation growing up, a loneliness she'd buried under work and the drive to ace school and succeed where her mother hadn't.

When the Uber pulled over, her mom was in the middle of her shift. Through the front windows, she could see her taking an order at one of the booths, her hair straightened into the same bob she'd worn for the last ten years, a new pair of glasses—those had been so expensive—perched on her nose. Even outside, Iris knew the smell of the place, the bubbling fat of the fryer, the meaty aroma of beef hamburgers cooking on the griddle. On fish fry Fridays, the air was so thick with beer-battered fat you could taste it. The walls were papered with old advertisements on artificially yellowed backgrounds. Booths clad in a green vinyl similar to Dialogue's draperies lined the windows, and tables filled in the space between them and the bar with its chromed swivel stools.

She'd spent countless afternoons here, doing her homework in a booth in the corner, making her slow way through one of the large cookies they had in a small case by the register. Peanut butter had been her favorite, and she would eat every crumb on her plate. Between customers, her mom would sit across from her and quiz her about her school work, drilling her on math and geography, spelling and vocabulary. Iris could stay the whole afternoon in that lull between lunch and dinner, assuming it didn't get suddenly busy and they needed the table.

Now, to the familiar sound of the bell above the front door, Iris stepped across the threshold, smelled the grease in the air, and met her mom in the middle of the restaurant in a firm embrace. "Baby," Naomi said.

"Hey, Mom." Iris stepped back and nodded at what she still thought of as her booth. "Let me put my stuff down." She dumped her large backpack on one of the benches and gave her mom another hug.

"How was the trip?"

"Fine. The second bus was mysteriously smelly, but it was the short leg."

They sat across from each other, the bench seat making a sighing noise under Iris's weight.

"I'm taking my break now, but do you want something to eat?"

"I would kill for a burger. I haven't eaten since an early breakfast." The pay might suck, but the food at the diner was surprisingly good. Grade A everything and most things made from scratch, including their steak fries.

Once the food was in front of her and Naomi took another short break, she broke open a steaming hot fry and blew on it before dropping it in her mouth. "I have some news," she said. "I've officially signed the papers for my grant, and the money is on its way to BU for this year's tuition." She'd heard the final word on the funding the day before and wanted to wait until she could tell her mom in person even though she hadn't mentioned its temporary precariousness.

She was rewarded by Naomi's wide eyes and smile. "That's amazing. It took them so long I thought they might have given it to someone else."

Now that the crisis was safely behind her, she was able to tell Naomi what had happened, concluding with "They didn't exactly take it away from me. It was more like it vanished."

"No, they took it away from you and gave it to someone else, and, as your grandma used to say, 'I'll hear no argument about it.' I can't believe that, and I can't believe you didn't tell me."

She couldn't imagine anyone being more on her side than her mom. "I didn't want to worry you. Anyway, they got an anonymous donation large enough to fund the grant again."

Her mom stole one of her fries. "Is this going to happen next year?"

"I asked them the same thing, not that I wanted to look a gift horse in the mouth. They said it's funded for the next decade." She took a bite of her burger and hummed in pleasure. So good. A different kind of good from Dialogue, but it hit the spot. "Anyway, now I have too much work to do and not enough time if I want to get out in three years, but first-world problems, right?"

Naomi nodded, her full lips sucked mostly in between her teeth. "You're amazing."

"Mom."

"I'm serious. You amaze me. The way you decide to do something and just go and do it. I'm not sure where you got that from."

"You always did what had to get done even when it was hard and exhausting. I had everything I needed."

"Just barely." Naomi looked out the window, the afternoon sunlight highlighting her high cheekbones and sepia skin. Her frown showed as a wrinkle between her eyebrows, one that had become permanent through the years. Iris had to admit she looked older than she was.

Iris put the burger down and wiped her fingers on a paper napkin that came apart a little under her fingers. "Who cares if it was barely? It was enough. And I got my determination from you—and from Grandma."

"I know I've disappointed you."

She slid her plate to the side so there was nothing between them. "Where's this coming from?"

Naomi waved one of her hands, indicating either the whole of the diner or the whole of the universe. "Nowhere. Everywhere." She went on, her voice lowered, leaning partly across the table. "I know you've wanted me to get a job in Allentown for years."

Iris matched her hushed tone. "Only because I think it would be better for you, not because I think poorly of you for staying here for so long. I know Allentown isn't swimming in fine dining options, but there are a few, and I think you'd do great at one of those places. And the tips are so much better."

"I don't think my car would make the trip every day."

"It's only twenty minutes away. What's wrong with your car?"

Naomi sat back. "Nothing. I've got it under control. You just got here. Can we talk about something else? What's going on with that profoundly good date?"

In a strange turnabout, the more Iris saw Erin, the less she'd told her mom about her. Iris had been hoarding their conversations, the feel of her hand, the touch of her lips. When Erin had revealed her loneliness and self-doubt over their cannoli last week, something inside Iris had squeezed, in the most pleasurable way. Getting a peek behind that façade of competence and experience had been thrilling. Now, sitting right across from Naomi, Iris didn't want to be evasive.

She said, "More profoundly good dates. They're different. I mean, we started with coffee, which is pretty typical, but then she took me on a walk along the river, and she actually put up with my history obsession all along the Freedom Trail."

The fact that Erin had been proposing free or cheap outings without any conversation on the matter warmed her with Erin's easy thoughtfulness, given how much she could surely afford. "She's ridiculously easy to talk to, and it's not just surface stuff. We seem to be equally interested in each other and the greater world. She—" Iris stopped herself before bringing in Erin's struggles with her privilege, not wanting to open the door to how well-to-do Erin surely was. "She calls me right before I go to bed, and we have these meaningless but wonderful talks until I fall asleep. So, yeah, profoundly good."

Her mom quizzed her on what Erin looked like, how old she was, what she did, what consulting meant, anyway, the whole nine yards, taking up most of the rest of her break in the process. Finally, she asked, "Do you have a picture of this woman?"

Iris unlocked her phone and swiped through some photos until she found the one of Erin standing in front of Paul Revere's house even though it wasn't her favorite. That one was of Erin squatting by an age-worn tombstone, leaning close and squinting to make out the faded lettering. Something about her interest in that stone had tugged at Iris. She reversed the phone and held it out for her mom to see.

Her mom laughed. "Nothing more white than a redhead."

"Mom. What about blondes?"

"I'm not saying anything beyond the fact that you're the third generation in our family to favor white people. Who am I to cast stones?" She kissed Iris's head and went back to work.

* * *

Naomi's boyfriend, Mick, had been living with Naomi for the last three years. Iris was glad she had someone in her life, and she liked him well enough, especially since he contributed to the rent and seemed to help around the house a little bit. He was a manager at a local landscaping store, which meant he wasn't much better off than Naomi. Iris had counselled Naomi until she was blue in the face to keep their finances completely separate, but she wasn't sure how well Naomi had complied.

Iris made dinner for them both on the day Naomi had off from work, and they ate around the well-worn table she'd sat at every night after her grandfather had abandoned them. Even with Mick there, it was strangely comforting. The whole trip was, in fact, unfolding the way they always did: a visit to the salon she'd been going to since she was a preteen to get a trim of her unruly locks that cost a fraction of what it would in Boston, a look at her mom's finances and upcoming expenses, lots of stories about recent problematic or humorous customers, and a quick tour of Allentown restaurants against her mom's will. Otherwise, her mom worked, and Iris either hung out at the diner like she had as a child or surfed the couch, making her way through the book she'd brought with her about the history of Baptist ministry work in central Africa. Talk about a niche tome, one that had almost certainly been this man's dissertation back in the eighties.

When she couldn't read any more—and couldn't resist—she called Erin, who answered on the second ring. "Are you busy?"

"Not too busy for you."

"Now that's laying it on thick." But she smiled regardless. "What are you doing?"

"Reconnaissance for our next date."

"Is that like an engagement with the enemy?"

"More like a close encounter with nature. Did you know they have an entire beech grove at the Arnold Arboretum? I just walked by a few cork trees, which are exactly what they sound like. This place is amazing."

"I was sure you were going to pick the Forest Hills Cemetery next since you've mentioned it."

"I thought two cemeteries back-to-back was a little much so early in our relationship."

Iris smiled at that last word and stretched out on the couch, having grown used to Erin's voice in her ear when she was lying down. "Probably a good rule of thumb." Then, even though she wanted to linger in the idea of being in a relationship with Erin, she said, "If you keep contemplating trees in the middle of the afternoon, when do you get your work done?"

Erin's quiet made Iris uneasy, but when she finally answered, her voice was cheery and light. "First, I'm very efficient."

Iris laughed.

"I'm serious. It has to do with focus. Second, I stay up very late. My creative hours are from about ten until two in the morning. I know I'm lucky to be able to prioritize my quality of life, and being with nature is important to me."

"I have to admit that I don't really understand what you do. I mean, I know what you do, but I don't get how you do it, if that makes any sense."

Erin's breath told Iris she was walking up a hill, and, again, it took a while for her to answer. "It's a lot of talking to people to figure out what's going on, then it's some thinking to figure out the best way to address the problems, then more talking to people to either convince them they should do something or teach them how to do something."

They sat with that between them. In this pause, Iris levered herself back up and replayed what Erin had just said. "That sounds like a lot of jobs. Are you being deliberately vague?"

"I was trying to be charming, but I clearly failed at that."

"Sometimes it's like you refuse to give a straight answer. I'm asking because I really want to know."

"I know you do, and I love that about you. It's just that my work is complicated right now, and I don't like getting into it."

"Complicated how?" Iris wasn't sure why she was pushing this, but that didn't stop her from doing it.

More hill walking. Just when Iris was sure Erin wasn't going to answer, she said, "My work isn't like yours. You're so sure of your path, but I don't know if this consulting is what I'm supposed to be doing."

"Who determines 'supposed to'?"

"I do, but that doesn't make anything easier."

"What would make it easier?"

"Maybe if you stopped this whole Socratic thing you've got going." The words were terse, clipped. "I don't have answers, okay? And I'm well aware that I'm privileged to have this job with this kind of flexibility, and I'm privileged to be able to question if I have a higher purpose or if I'm just—or if I'm just exactly what I see in the mirror every morning."

Iris leaned forward, putting her elbows on her thighs as if that would get her closer to Erin. "Whoa, hey. Questioning your life is for everyone, even if not everyone can fully act on what they decide. You're making this way harder than it needs to be."

"You don't understand how complicated it is."

"Then explain it to me. Isn't that what you're good at doing?"

"Not right now. Not when I'm here in these acres of trees and you're in Bethlehem, Pennsylvania."

"It sucks to hear you being so hard on yourself and not be there to help."

"Talking to you is good for me, even if you have a thing for questions."

By Erin's tone, Iris knew the topic was closed. She didn't push it, asking instead about cork trees and beech groves. When they were finished, she sat on the couch in the quiet of the apartment and replayed their conversation.

"Complicated." It was a cop-out excuse, but at the same time, it had felt real and almost anguished when Erin had said it. Iris had assumed Erin liked what she did, but not everyone had a passion for their chosen work or what they were trying to do. For Iris, making a life in academia might not be the easiest thing, but she was dedicated to that rocky path to what she truly loved. When she'd almost had to compromise (or abandon) her progression, it had felt like the world was crumbling around her.

What kind of higher purpose was Erin seeking, and why did it tie her up in such knots? As for agonizing again about privilege… Erin's continued self-abasement on that subject was almost as bad as its counterpart, being willfully ignorant of your position in the world. Apologizing for your own privilege wasn't what it was all about. Doing something about it was. Changing how you thought, how you behaved toward other people, the assumptions you made, the charitable work you could get involved in, educating your peers on biases and stereotypes. Action was key, as Erin said, to looking yourself in the mirror and being at peace with what you saw.

Now that she thought about it, Iris didn't know what, exactly, Erin felt so guilty about. It didn't sound like she had been born into money or had special opportunities growing up. Solidly middle class was how she had described her upbringing. Public school, a good college but not in the Ivy Leagues or anything, student loans for her education. She must've worked hard to be seen as successful even before becoming a consultant. It couldn't have been easy, especially not with being a gay woman.

Iris wanted to dig into this problem with every question at her disposal, but that clearly wasn't what Erin wanted. The trouble was that she wasn't sure what would help Erin at this point, and she feared falling short. She wanted this relationship to go somewhere, and it was clear that she would have to learn how to balance her need to fix things with Erin's tolerance for her so-called Socratic method.

Mostly, she wanted to be in that beech grove with Erin right now, standing quiet under the canopy of leaves, with Erin's hand in hers, basking in the warmth of her intense contemplation.

CHAPTER NINE

The cake was a problem. Why had Erin volunteered to bring it to her niece's sixth birthday? It had seemed like a perfectly nice, perfectly normal thing to offer—a way to be involved more than by just bringing a gift, which was also kind of a problem. Everything had to be more than enough without being too much. Everyone knew she had money, so if she brought a normal, grocery-store cake or run-of-the-mill doll or outfit, she'd look stingy. But if she spent too much, like getting an illusion cake that looked like a very lifelike ballet pointe shoe (since little Marcie was into dance), people might think she was showing off, throwing her money around.

Family was a tap dance, for sure, and it was disappointing that she couldn't just look forward to seeing everyone without this trepidation. She rode north out of town over the Zakim Bridge in an Uber, the cake, from a very good bakery and decorated with a bouquet of both real and frosting roses, on her lap. The gift, a medium-sized dollhouse she'd cleared with her sister, took up the rest of the back seat. She thought about calling Catherine to keep her company, but Catherine's family wasn't nearly as complicated as Erin's. They had some money of their own so didn't seem inclined to weigh in judgment of how she did or didn't spend hers.

Instead, she thought about Iris, off with her own family in Pennsylvania. She imagined Iris in the seat next to her, everything out in the open, the only nerves in the car the usual ones of introducing a new girlfriend. On paper, her parents should like Iris, though maybe not understand her desire to go "all the way" in her education…and the color of her skin? They were only as bigoted as the next person, but when someone might be joining the family, things changed.

This thinking wasn't helping matters. Despite her objective success, Erin sometimes felt like she couldn't do right in her family's eyes. Or at least her parents' and Stephanie's. Her brother, Rory, was okay, and they actually talked every once in a while. But, first, she was a lesbian, which had taken some time before seriously ruffled feathers had been smoothed down. And then she was going to go to law school, which was too damned fancy for everyone. And then the startup that no one understood, and the money.

And now, they wondered what she was doing with her life. Work, they understood, but this? They'd even asked if she was going to go to law school now, though wouldn't that ultimately make her even richer? It felt like she couldn't win. Sometimes she wondered if all this was in her head, but then she'd get together with them, and there was an awkwardness she couldn't deny. Except for Rory, who, as a middle child, rolled with the punches.

Erin was glad for the chaos when she rolled up to Stephanie's house. She slipped in on the heels of a clot of kids, set the cake on the kitchen counter, and after another trip out front, lugged the doll house over to where the presents were piled. She went out back where everyone was. Her mom was busy organizing some game with Stephanie while her dad and Rory sat on plastic lawn chairs with beers in their hands, wearing matching McCallister Contracting caps.

"Hey," she said. "Cake's in the kitchen."

Rory asked, "What kind?"

"Chocolate with white frosting. Or, pink, really. I assumed Marcie was still in her everything pink all the time phase."

"Is there, like, ganache or something fancy in it?"

"You'll like it. Everyone will like it."

Her dad said, "Well, don't just hover there. Either sit down or help your mother."

So Erin helped even though everything was under control. She facilitated a game of Red Light, Green Light. She set up and put away the ring toss. She cut the cake, which did indeed have ganache between the chocolate layers, and handed out slices. She made herself as useful as possible until she couldn't stand it anymore and went out front for a breather.

Rory was sitting on the steps, smoking.

"Does Mom know you're still with the cancer sticks?"

He laughed out a plume of smoke. "Are you kidding? She would flip her shit. I've cut way back, though. Only, like, five a day."

Erin sat upwind of him. "Dad says business is good."

"Yeah. We're busy. At least we have enough work that we're not always on the same job together. It can sometimes get too cozy, you know?"

She couldn't imagine working with anyone in her family.

"How's 'consulting'?" He put the word in finger quotes, his cigarette dipping with them.

"Hey, it's a real thing."

"I can't believe people actually pay good money for your advice." But he smiled when he said it and knocked her shoulder with his.

"When are you going to get a new girlfriend?"

"I get out there. Unlike you. You're turning into a nun."

She weighed her options for a while before saying, "I actually started seeing someone."

"Hot?"

She grinned. "Beautiful. And smart."

"What does she think about the money?"

"She doesn't know yet. It's too soon."

"What's she going to think about it?"

"I don't know."

"I both envy you and don't. Sometimes it's like you're from another planet."

"I'm the same person I always was."

"Yeah, and it was always kind of like you were from another planet." He stubbed out his cigarette and put the butt in his pocket before folding a piece of gum in his mouth. "Do you think Steph is ever going to get that stick out of her ass?"

Erin laughed even though she knew she shouldn't. "She's always taken being the oldest seriously. Plus, she has the only grandchildren. When are you going to get on that?"

"Ha. When are you?"

At that, an imagined future with Iris flashed behind her eyes, causing a warmth and catch in her chest. Don't get ahead of yourself. First you have to tell her about the money, and despite what she'd said to Rory, she had an inkling how Iris was going to respond, which made her want to kick that can down the road a little more. "Hey, that's one of the benefits of being a lesbian—all expectations are off."

"Lucky you," he said. "We'd better get back in there before Stephanie notices."

She stood and dusted off her hands. "Maybe kids wouldn't be a bad idea. She might judge me a little less."

"It's out of love," he said and laughed.

She laughed along and girded herself for the rest of the afternoon and the long, lonely evening ahead of her.

* * *

Erin walked from the train into Catherine's neighborhood. Brookline was officially suburban, being just outside Boston's city limits, but it didn't have a suburban feel. It was still walkable, existing right in the cradle of three different train lines, the alphabetically adjacent B, C, and D. Catherine rode the train into Nuvio, which had its headquarters in Cambridge, just across the river. Erin had wondered if they'd be on the same train this evening or if Catherine had gotten home earlier.

The sidewalk on this curved street was shaded with mature trees, and the houses were unique from each other, made with different floor plans and building materials, though there was a heavy hint of slate roofs, which Erin enjoyed looking at. Hideously expensive, they lasted at least fifty years and could go as long as two centuries without needing to be replaced. Each house had a meticulously landscaped lawn, and she heard the sound of children playing from the next street over. Catherine hadn't been joking about the appeal of the school district. Erin had heard of a family with a teenaged son who had moved into a one-bedroom apartment at the edge of town just so he could attend the high school.

She shifted the bottle of wine she was carrying from one hand to the other and tried not to let the heat and humidity of this summer day and the frustration of being with her family get her down. She was a walking fool and was never stopped by the weather, but she didn't relish arriving at her destination drenched in sweat. Not that Catherine would mind. They'd seen each other in every state, from hacking up a lung with the flu to dressed to the nines in Nuvio's boardroom.

So why was she a little nervous for this low-key evening? It was just dinner with Catherine and Nathan, which she'd had countless times, but Erin wasn't quite up for a dose of Catherine's telling it like it was. She'd been doing enough of that herself, with Iris out of state and somewhat out of touch.

She'd felt miserable in that last conversation with her. "Complicated." While true, it was an obfuscation, and not telling her what was really going on was starting to chafe. They'd somehow gotten far enough along that divulging the truth now—and all the different facets of it—was daunting. Erin wasn't sure how Iris would respond, but she suspected it wouldn't be entirely positive. She guessed that was better than Iris being bedazzled by Erin's wealth and starting to cook up ways to spend it. Either way, though, letting Iris in on her "complications" could very well lead to an ending she couldn't bear.

Catherine's house, on the corner tucked behind a line of tall hedges, was a Tudor-style with the traditional brown-and-white detailing on the second floor. She turned up the walk and smiled at her favorite detail of the place: a heavy, iron-bracketed, curved-top, wood front door. It looked like something out of the Middle Ages, like there might be any manner of torture going on just inside. The knocker was a large brass eagle's head, and she'd told Catherine that if she changed it, she wouldn't speak to her again.

She used it to signal her arrival and felt a bead of sweat meander down her back to the waistband of her shorts. While waiting, she pondered the label of the Shiraz she'd brought, smiling at the nondescript bird of prey in one corner of the parchment-colored square.

"That's your cousin," she told it, indicating the knocker.

Just then the door opened, and Nathan Sun stood inside, wearing frayed shorts and an MIT T-shirt and brandishing a long pair of tongs, which he clicked open and closed a few times. Nathan had a PhD in chemistry and worked for a green products company. He was a few years older than Catherine and was a bit of a health nut, easily ruining much of what Erin liked to eat by listing out the draconian-sounding chemicals it contained when the bite was just at the threshold of her lips. When he smiled, his black, straight, Fu Manchu beard bunched up at the sides of his mouth. "Just in time. The grill should be warm enough to put the chicken on. It's too hot to cook inside."

Erin followed him into the house. "Don't you have air-conditioning?"

"You know what I mean."

And, of course, she did. At the kitchen island, Catherine was transferring salad greens from a grocery store plastic tub into a large wooden bowl and then chucking on some diced tomatoes.

She said, "Can I trust you with the onion?"

"Hey, just because I don't cook doesn't mean I can't."

Catherine and Nathan looked at each other and laughed. They were hilarious.

"Fine. But I can slice some onions without taking out a finger." Erin set the wine bottle on the marble countertop and took a cutting board from the cabinet where they stood like wood soldiers. She freed a moderately sized knife from the block on the counter behind them and said, "Lay it on me. It's the least I can do."

Catherine plunked a red onion on Erin's board and started chopping up some kalamata olives on her own. "Try to slice it thin."

"Yes, ma'am." Erin approached the onion with all her concentration, not being nearly as cavalier about her competence as she had earlier stated.

Before she even started in, Catherine asked, "Are you interested in a potential client for your consulting?"

"Of course. Why wouldn't I be?" She cheered her first mostly thin slice.

"Last time we talked, you seemed lukewarm on it."

Erin steadied the onion and produced another passable slice. "I like it well enough."

"Now that's a ringing endorsement." Catherine scraped the olives onto the top of the salad. Nathan snagged a platter of raw chicken from the counter and used an elbow to open the sliding door to the patio, then a foot to close it, all without spilling any juice.

"I like it, okay? The interviewing and the problem-solving are interesting, even if I've already seen so many of the same problems everywhere. But half the time, laying out a plan for them is a waste because I already know they're not going to implement any meaningful change."

"Isn't that why you should be selling your skills on the implementation side, too?"

Erin produced a slice that was thick on one end and wafer thin on the other. She set it aside and tried again. "I think I might be lying about it to everyone, myself included. I just told Iris that my work was complicated, and it seemed like the most clichéd and yet true statement ever."

"What does she know about it?"

"About what you do—general consulting. She just doesn't know everything around it."

"Do you think that maybe you're putting things around it that don't have to be there in the first place?"

"I'm playing at it." She put the knife down and flexed her hand after gripping it so tightly. "Is this enough onion?"

"Sure, that's fine. I don't think your clients think you're playing."

"You know what I mean. I'm not making a real business out of it. I'm not even really trying to be successful."

Catherine handed her a block of feta in a blue-and-white wrapper. "Crumble some of this on top while I make the dressing."

"I know I'm whining about it, and I'll stop. It's just that everyone deserves better from me." Erin unwrapped the cheese while Catherine started pouring vinegar and oil in a bowl and squeezing a lemon in with it. She always made salad dressings from scratch and without a recipe, and it confounded Erin.

Catherine rinsed her hands and started in with the herbs and spices. "Who's everyone?"

"You know. Everyone."

"Me? You? Your family? Nathan? Iris?"

"Yes," she said, but it came out sounding like a question.

"Come on, Erin. You know better than that. You're the only one who deserves anything from yourself. Not me, and not Iris, unless you two are way farther along as a couple than you've made me believe."

"Fine, but is it any better if I'm disappointing only myself?"

"No, but won't it make it easier to fix?"

Erin sat with that while she crumbled the cheese and licked the remnants from her fingers. Her tongue curled around the tangy creaminess of the feta. Because what Catherine had said was both true and unhelpful, she didn't directly reply. Instead, she said, "I want things to get more serious with Iris."

"That's good."

"Yeah, but it's also scary."

"You used to like scary things. Our whole business was terrifying for years. When did you become so unsure of yourself?"

But, of course, they both knew the answer to that. Hayley. Erin didn't even say it, and Catherine busied herself with pouring some dressing over the salad and tossing it with a telling vigor.

"Can you get the potato salad out of the fridge and put it on the table?"

Erin did as she was told, shamed, again, at the sight of their orderly and stocked refrigerator. When she came back into the kitchen to get the silverware, she said, "I'm not going to let being scared stop me. Iris is special. She's worth the risk."

"Good, because if she breaks your heart, I'll break her face." Catherine said it with an evil-looking grin.

"How about we limit breaking to the breaking of balls?"

"You used to be fun."

"I used to be a lot of things."

Nathan came in with a steaming plate of chicken, lemon-herb by the smell of it, and they sat down to dinner. Erin waited in the dining room while Catherine took the extra step of transferring the chicken onto a serving platter. When she set it down in the middle of the table, between the two salads, she used tongs to serve everyone, which was a formality she usually skipped.

"Dark, right?" she asked Erin.

"As always." Erin busied herself surrounding the leg and thigh with a mound of greens and a smaller one of potato salad—under Catherine's intense gaze. Was this a new recipe that she was worried about or something? "What's going on? Do you want to say grace or something?"

"Oh, hell no." She cut into her serving in emphasis.

Erin picked up her knife and fork and dove in, ready to separate the drumstick from the thigh, but her utensils practically bounced off the chicken. She tried again, frowning.

Catherine started laughing. "Oh my god. You should see your face."

"Seriously?" Erin picked up the chicken, finally seeing it for what it was: an incredibly realistic rubber version of the real thing that Catherine had made even more lifelike by swabbing with oil and the same mix of herbs that was on the real meat.

"I've been waiting ages to use that on you."

She laughed and shook her head. "Well played. This is impressive."

"Isn't it? I tried it on Nathan first, but he could tell right away, so I had to up my game for you."

"Just remember—payback's a bitch."

"Bring it on."

After Erin traded out the decoy for the real thing, Nathan took the conversation right to politics, which she appreciated for once. He and Catherine were a good match, Nathan being smart enough to handle Catherine's intellectual horsepower but also even-tempered in a way she needed. Erin loved watching him make her smile and chill her out. Being with them tonight made her miss Iris with a startling intensity. She wanted her to be here with them. She wanted her to learn their inside jokes and shorthand phrases. She wanted to watch her question them with the same relentlessness she'd used on Erin more than once.

Mostly, she just wanted Iris to be right here next to her, close enough to touch, solid and irrefutable, in on every secret.

* * *

In a surprise twist ending, Erin and Iris went from the Arnold Arboretum directly to Iris's apartment for Erin's second home-cooked meal in a week. In the Uber on the way, Iris caveated the hell out of her place, citing roommates (who were supposed to be absent), lackluster maintenance in the building, and a kitchen that made a coffin look spacious in comparison. Given that it had only been a couple of years since Erin had lived in a similar place, she could picture it down to the Christmas lights strung up near the ceiling and a cinderblock-and-plywood bookcase somewhere.

On the sidewalk in front of the building, Iris took Erin's hand. "We should probably do this at your place. I'm assuming it's way nicer than mine."

"But if we did it at my place, we'd be subjected to the contents of my refrigerator and to my cooking, and believe me, you don't want that."

Iris pulled Erin's wrist to her mouth and kissed the inside of it softly. They had managed an extended kissing session in the beech grove, and this touch brought it roaring back. Her gut dropped, and she became amenable to almost anything. Iris said, "I'd like to see it, though. I don't even know what neighborhood you live in."

"Beacon Hill," Erin said before she could think of a better response.

Iris became one big pause, still holding Erin's wrist between them.

"I gave up a little space for walkability, and not needing a car is a benefit."

She lowered Erin's arm and let it go. "Invite me over sometime, and remember everything I said about my apartment. Ready?"

"As ever."

The apartment was about like Erin had imagined, though maybe cleaner than she'd expected, knowing the damage a bunch of young women could do to a place. The living room was busy with random, probably salvaged furniture and a futon couch draped in a sheet patterned with dark-blue clock towers. Iris's bedroom was more austere, though here was where the string of lights lived. Her desk was piled high with books and journals, and her bed was tightly made but inviting. Erin thought about trying to convince Iris to skip dinner and settle in here for the evening, but she was hungry and Iris was insistent about cooking when she sat Erin on the couch.

From her perch, Erin could see into the tiny kitchen, and they could continue their meandering conversation. She asked, "What are you making us?"

"Spaghetti carbonara."

"You are a goddess. Suzanne had it as a special a few months before you started. I ate it twice."

Iris glanced at Erin over the half wall between them. "Don't expect mine to be as good as hers. God knows what she put in it. I just make it the very unfancy classic way. I even use ham for pancetta. That's how not fancy I am."

"I'm sure it's going to be delicious. How'd you learn to cook? Was it your mom or your grandma, though you were pretty young when she died, right?"

"Yeah. I was nine." The water ran for a while, followed by the clicking of the stove lighting. "Grandma taught Mom a few things, which she taught to me, but it was the basics, like don't put the flame under a pan too high or you'll end up with something raw in the middle while the outside is burned."

"Is that how it works?" Erin sat back and crossed an ankle over the opposite knee, taking up space and soaking in the atmosphere and Iris.

"Are you really that helpless in a kitchen?"

"I can make pasta with sauce from a jar and a pretty good grilled cheese—unless I burn it. Now that I know the secret, that's going into the regular rotation. Seriously, though, how'd you learn to make this?"

"Partly the Internet and partly a former girlfriend who was into all things Italian."

"Forget I asked."

Iris smiled at her. "I have several exes. Only one that was serious."

"Did you get your heart broken?"

"Yeah. I was unbearable with grief for a few months. Then I got over it."

Erin picked at a thread that had emerged from the base of one of the clock towers. "Same here, though I think I took more than a few months. I remember being thankful that Catherine didn't dump me as a friend by the end of it."

"You two sound so close. I'm kind of jealous. I've never had a friend exactly like that, though I've known my roommate Candice for years. I'm probably closest with my mom, but she's still my mom, so, you know."

Erin tried to imagine having that kind of relationship with her mom and failed. It wasn't that her mom wasn't approachable or had been a drill sergeant or an absent workaholic. She had been busy, working and raising the three of them in a very middle-class way, but she hadn't inspired Erin to confide in her about anything. She wondered what, if anything, Iris had told her mom about them.

The sizzle of something delicious in the skillet made Erin's mouth water. "That already smells amazing."

"You are so very easy to please."

"Better that than the opposite, don't you think?"

"Oh, I'm not knocking it. Sometimes, it's a total relief to have to hurdle only a pretty low bar."

Erin dropped her foot from her knee and sat forward. "It's only a low bar for those things that don't matter very much. I have a much higher bar for everything else, and you're hurdling that with room to spare, even without cooking me dinner."

Their gazes met across the living room and the short wall between them. Iris held hers steady and stood still when she said, "Thank you. You're killing it yourself." They looked at each other for another long moment before Iris turned away and Erin heard the clatter of a pan being shaken against the metal grate of the stove. The smell of cooking garlic followed. "This'll be ready in just a couple of minutes."

"Can I set a table? Is there a table for me to set? Maybe this chest, here?"

"There's a table, but it's being used as an open junk drawer right now, and the chest is too low to be really functional as a table. Are you okay with eating on the couch?"

"Okay? I'm practically an expert at couch eating, and I even have a perfectly functional table at my place. Sometimes I deign to eat at the breakfast bar, but I've spilled a little bit of everything on my couch over the years."

The smells just got better with the addition of the sharpness of grated cheese. Then suddenly they were sitting facing each other, each holding a bowl of spaghetti coated with a creamy yellowish sauce and studded with cubes of crispy ham under a shower of snow-white cheese and a liberal dusting of coal-black pepper. Erin dug in, doing an involuntary comparison to Suzanne's version she'd had months before. She could tell that there'd been more going on in the dish at Dialogue, but this had the same indulgent base.

"This is awesome. If it were on a menu, I'd order it again. You're amazing."

Iris smiled. She hadn't yet taken a bite. "I know you're not a man, so the way to your heart isn't through your stomach, but you clearly like good food, so…" She shrugged.

"You don't know how much I appreciate when other people feed me. It's one of my primary love languages."

"Probably because you'd starve if they didn't."

Erin wound pasta around her fork, spearing a nugget of ham when she was finished for a complete bite. "I'll starve if we don't stop talking and start eating."

They were quiet, then, though their looks were loud with intensity. It got harder and harder for Erin to swallow over the desire that thickened her throat and warmed her whole body. She could feel that her neck and cheeks were flushed, and she couldn't stop watching Iris's mouth and her fingers around her fork. It seemed a travesty that all they'd done so far was kiss with some real fervor. She wanted her hands everywhere on Iris, wanted to see her eyes close with pleasure that Erin gave her.

Erin set her empty bowl on the chest and watched Iris take her last few bites. When she was finished, she, too, put her bowl aside, and then they were kissing, grappling to get closer together. Iris pushed forward, and Erin lay back, in frantic bliss under Iris's weight. Iris's mouth opened wide to Erin's tongue, and Erin stopped breathing with the deepness of the kiss. Her fingers wormed their way between Iris's loosening braid and her scalp while her other hand slipped under the bottom hem of her T-shirt and found the smooth skin at her lower back, warm and velvety.

Iris pulled back, propped up on one straight arm, her hand compressing the couch next to Erin's head. She looked at Erin without saying anything, and Erin submitted willingly to the heat of her gaze. "Yes," she said. Iris groaned and kissed her again.

They progressed further into each other, Erin's body on fire with a vibrating sensitivity, Iris's leg pressed between hers, Erin's mouth on her neck, lightly biting and sucking, her hands busy removing Iris's shirt and examining the contours of her breasts through the lace of her bra. As much as she loved what was happening, the drumbeat of "more" played a loud soundtrack to their press and give and breath.

The front door startled them from the throes. "Shit," Iris said and sat up, casting around for her shirt.

The roommate came into the living room before she could pull it on. She was a big backpack and round Afro. "Oh! Sorry. I see nothing. You must be Erin, though. Hi." Then she was gone behind the closed door of her room.

Iris collapsed back on top of Erin, burying her face in Erin's neck. "I need my own place."

Erin stroked her hair. "It's okay."

"You say that because you're the one with all your clothes on."

"Which I think is a travesty."

She swore she could feel Iris's smile against her sensitive skin. "Did you really mean it? Yes?"

"Absolutely. I want you, Iris. I'm kind of desperate for you, actually. I've wanted you from the very beginning, from when we met in the Gardens. But I'll understand if you want to stop here, given thin walls and an audience."

Iris pushed herself up and off of Erin, and disappointment surged under her arousal. She closed her eyes against the reality of Iris's no. Then Iris said, "Are you coming? Or are you just going to lie there?"

Erin opened one eye to see Iris holding her shirt in one hand with the other extended toward Erin. Erin smiled and took it, letting Iris lead her to her room, leaving their dishes behind. Iris closed the door behind them and stood with her back to the painted wood. "I'm not a fall-into-bed person. I always get nervous when things go this far."

"You seemed pretty relaxed out there on the couch."

"But now we're not on the couch." She ducked her head in a devastatingly adorable way.

Erin stepped closer and captured Iris's hands in hers. "We don't have to do anything you're not ready for."

"The thing is that I want everything."

"Okay." Erin kissed her. "What about if we put you in charge? Everything is your call—what, when, and how."

"You're so good at that."

"What?"

"Saying the right thing. Take off your clothes."

She stifled a surprised laugh. "Yes, ma'am."

She stepped back and unbuttoned her shirt, letting it drop to the floor. Her bra followed it, and when she glanced at Iris, the intensity of her gaze made her a little hesitant—around a bloom of arousal. She unbuttoned and unzipped her shorts, pushing them slowly past her hips until they puddled around her feet. Her heart was hammering in her chest and in regions farther south. She had never felt so exposed or liked it so much. Her thumbs slipped under the waistband of her briefs, and she slid them down past her thighs until they fluttered on top of her shorts. She kicked the bundle of clothes to the side.

She knew her chest was flushed in addition to her neck and cheeks. "What now?" she whispered.

Iris came to her and took her hand. "Come to bed." She pulled the cover and sheets back so Erin could climb in. She scooted over to make room for Iris, who was still wearing most of her clothes. Iris dragged the sheet back over them and ran her hand lightly down Erin's body from her neck, between her breasts, past her belly button, stopping just short of her pubic hair, which matched that on her head. Her hand slid across to Erin's side and made its way back up, stopping at the swell of her breast. That's when her eyes closed and she rested her head on Erin's shoulder, Erin's arm wrapped around her, fingers trailing back and forth across the soft skin of Iris's back.

Erin felt an intense comfort with Iris snugged against her, the warmth of her body seeping into her pores. Iris's fingers found her nipple, and Erin let out a gush of breath, her legs shifting between the sheets as if looking for a grounding for her desire. As Iris pinched and twisted, gently but with clear focus, shoots of pleasure rocketed around Erin's body.

She whispered, "That feels really good."

"You feel really good." Iris lifted her head so they could kiss again.

She climbed half on Erin, her leg pressed against her, making her feel some very interesting things. Her breath grew more rapid, and her hips rose against Iris in a way Erin had very little control over. Then Iris moved her mouth from Erin's down to her breast, and Erin groaned at the warmth and wetness of Iris's tongue against her nipple, which was so hard it almost hurt.

Iris shushed her. "Thin walls, remember?"

"Easy for you to say."

She smiled and went back to her ministrations, her hand meandering across Erin's chest and down her abdomen, drawing circles that dipped closer and closer to where Erin really needed her to be. Her heart was pounding, and she bit her lip to keep herself from some kind of vocal release. She tangled her fingers into Iris's hair and held her close.

Iris's mouth pulled away, leaving cool air against Erin's tight nipple, which was its own kind of pleasure, given her heightened state. Iris said, "Can I touch you?"

"You can do whatever you want to me."

"I doubt that's true."

"It feels true right now."

Without moving her gaze from Erin's eyes, Iris slid her hand down until her fingers found Erin's center. "You're so wet." The words were reverent. She slid her fingers the length of Erin, pausing at her entrance but ending up at Erin's clit, which had grown hard. Her touch was light, almost teasing, and it made Erin want to jump out of her skin with anticipation.

"What do you like?" Iris's face was close to Erin's, her eyes dark in the dimness of the room. A furrow of concentration wrinkled the skin between her eyebrows.

"I love what you're doing. Maybe a little harder." Iris's pressure increased, and Erin pushed her head back against the pillow and closed her eyes. "That, like that. Oh god." Heat surged through her, her muscles tightened, and she knew she wasn't going to last very long. Her fingers gripped Iris's back, and her chin raised, straining her neck. Her breathing was rapid and forceful, probably not as quiet as it should be, but she couldn't help it. It was more and more and even more until it was too much and her orgasm made her clench her teeth so she wouldn't cry out. Iris's fingers kept moving, firm and sure against her, drawing out her climax.

When Erin was spent, her limbs leaden on the mattress, Iris lay her head back on Erin's shoulder, and Erin could feel her rapid breath flutter against her chest, which was tacky with sweat. Erin found the hair tie at the bottom of Iris's braid and pulled it off and gently unraveled her hair from its constraints. It was thick and a little coarse, and it swallowed Erin's hand. She pressed her fingers against Iris's skull, massaging in a way she'd been fantasizing about doing since their first date at The Thinking Cup.

Iris made a sound eerily similar to a purr, and Erin smiled. "I can't wait to find out what you want next."

Iris huffed out a laugh. "I might fall asleep if you keep massaging me like that."

"I can leave if that's what you want."

She tightened her hold of Erin's torso. "That's not what I want."

"You're still calling the shots, so name it, and we'll do it."

"Will you stay the night?"

Erin smiled, not that Iris could see it. "And make me do the walk of shame tomorrow morning?"

"What good are roommates if you can't use them to try to humiliate your girlfriend?"

"I refuse to be shamed."

"I'm sure you do."

"What does that mean?"

Iris raised her head and looked at Erin. "Nothing. It's a good thing." She kissed Erin in a lingering way, then deepened it. Erin's body stirred from its postcoital lassitude. Iris said, "I want you to undress me."

Erin rolled her onto her back and straddled her hips. She slid her hands under Iris, unhooked her bra, and slipped it down her arms, tossing it to the side of the bed. Iris's breasts were small with dark nipples that peaked into tactile cones when Erin touched them. Her skin under the bra was the same warm bronze as the rest of her and hosted a small constellation of moles. She traced widening circles gently with her fingertips from the nipples to the edge of each breast. She did it a few times, watching how Iris's head shifted on the pillow and eyes fluttered closed. Then she bent over and took a nipple in her mouth, savoring the different textures under her tongue. Iris tasted faintly of salt from their walk in the arboretum, and her skin was smooth and pliant.

After Erin had lavished sufficient attention on Iris's breasts, she sat up and raked her nails down Iris's sides, then again. "You're not ticklish."

"No. Is this some patented test of yours?"

"Kinda." Not a test but a certain perverse pleasure.

"What would you do if I were ticklish?"

"I'd want to keep doing it until you were curled up into the tickles, stopping just before it became torture."

"What are you going to do now?"

"Enjoy you as you are." After one more pass down her sides, Erin scooted back until she kneeled across her thighs and unbuttoned her shorts, pulling the zipper down with teasing slowness. When she lifted her gaze to check on Iris, the other woman was looking directly back.

"Okay?" Erin asked.

In response, Iris lifted her hips, and Erin pulled the shorts down, raising up so she could push them past Iris's knees to let her kick them off. Her underwear was next, following the same trajectory as her shorts and letting Erin see all of her.

She took her time looking. "Beautiful," she whispered and covered Iris's body with her own, feeling flesh and heat from her chin down to her toes. She nipped a naked earlobe and sucked gently at Iris's neck. She shifted a leg to fit inside Iris's and felt wetness against her thigh when she pressed it firmly against her. One of Iris's hands cupped her ass and held her close, which was exactly where Erin wanted to be.

Slowly, she rocked forward and back, feeling Iris's chest move against her own and Iris's hand tighten its grip. Erin felt herself unraveling a little with the motion, feeling in control and running on wild instinct in equal measure. She sped up her movement a notch, listening to Iris's breathing become audible and quicken. In a bid to get even closer, Erin pressed her forehead into the side of Iris's neck and breathed humid exhales onto her collarbone.

The world was reduced to rhythm, sensation, and breath. The heat between them ratcheted up, and Iris was moving, too, meeting Erin with a lifting of her hips and a tightening of her grip. She was so responsive, and Erin wondered if she could bring her to climax just like this. She wasn't keen to open any distance between them, but she also wanted to feel Iris with her fingers, explore her in detail, find out what she liked, the contours of her sex, the wet heat of it all.

That desire won out, and she let herself slip to Iris's side, a leg still thrown over one of hers. She slid her hand down Iris's belly, glancing up at her and asking, "Okay?"

In answer, Iris grasped Erin's wrist and moved her where she most wanted to be.

"Inside?"

A further nudge and a press on Erin's fingers was the only answer. Erin took the direction and slid a finger inside Iris, causing them both to groan and then shush each other. Iris was silky smooth, inviting her finger deeper. Erin complied, finding Iris's clit with her thumb and pressing gently. She kept her thumb there while she stroked inside Iris, curling her finger, finding a rhythm that made Iris shift her hips and breathe more deeply.

It continued for a deliriously long time, Iris urging her on but plateauing at a place Erin couldn't seem to nudge her out of. Without breaking stride, she lifted her head and whispered in Iris's ear. "Tell me what to do."

"You're doing it. It's amazing. Don't stop."

So Erin kept going, changing her rhythm from fast to slow, increasing the pressure of her thumb, attuned for any changes in Iris's response that would guide her—breath, movement, quiet vocalizations. Then, suddenly, when Erin moved her thumb in a different way, Iris surged out of a delicious neutral to the fast lane toward climax, and Erin was left trying to keep up. Iris's hand gripped Erin's shoulder, hard.

Then Iris convulsed around Erin's finger, her head lifting up with the contraction of her muscles, her free hand pressed over her mouth behind which faint groans could still be heard. Erin tried to move with her until she was still, when Erin opened up some space between them, kicking off the sheet in the hope of cool air. Sweat slicked them where they still touched, and Erin watched Iris breathe with her eyes closed in the sudden calm that was now upon them.

Iris said, "I can't feel my lips."

"I could try to kiss them awake."

Iris pressed a hand to Erin's chest. "I'm a hot, sweaty mess."

"More like a hot, sweaty goddess."

That got Iris to open her eyes. "If I didn't know you better, I'd think you were bullshitting me."

"Why would I do that?"

"There have been some women who had a problem with how long it takes me to—" She made a circling motion with her hand.

"Really? That seems counterintuitive when pleasuring you is the best pleasure ever."

"I'm glad you think so." She shifted away from Erin and got on her side to face her. "You don't really have to stay here tonight. I know the circumstances aren't ideal."

"I want to be where you are, pretty much all the time."

"Me, too. I love how open you are. I know I guard myself with a kind of righteous indignation, but you put it out there, even the things you aren't sure about. It's amazing, really."

The liquid pleasure that was still coursing through her veins turned solid at Iris's praise. She should tell her. Right now—at least about the money, if not about what she did with the grant. But what they'd just done had been so beautiful, and Iris felt so wonderfully close. The last thing Erin wanted was to let her money insinuate itself in the slim space between them. She reached out and trailed a thumb down the side of Iris's cheek. "Your indignation pushes me, which I love. Seriously. If I get too comfortable it feels like something's wrong. And you can cook."

"Sounds like we're both killing this thing."

"Sounds like it. Now point me at your toothbrush. I can't believe you let me kiss you with this garlic mouth."

Erin pulled on some clothes and wandered down the hallway to the shared bathroom, where she locked herself inside and sat on the closed toilet seat. She didn't want to have any secrets between them. The problem was she could already imagine what Iris's reaction was going to be: the equal and opposite one to Hayley's. Or maybe Iris would surprise Erin and be into her wealth like Hayley had been, which would be a huge disappointment. Either way, the euphoria of the last hour was too new to test with any potential strife. She had a duty to protect what was growing between them. It wouldn't hurt to wait a little longer to tell Iris the truth.

She got up to brush her teeth, the lies she'd just told herself bitter in her mouth.

CHAPTER TEN

Erin made Iris feel dizzy in the best way. She couldn't decide which she was infatuated more about: their talk or their sex. That first night together had been utterly affecting with raw sensuality wrapped in deep caring and communication that had all been effortless. Erin had stayed over a few times since, meeting her at the restaurant after closing (once after being a customer) and coaxing her into taking an Uber instead of the long T ride to Allston. Their sex was quietly spectacular despite Iris's tiredness, but while she fought sleep afterward, it clearly left Erin wired. She would slide out of bed as Iris was falling asleep, and Iris would wake later to see her sitting at the desk in a small pool of light from the goosenecked lamp, reading whatever she'd brought with her. In the small hours of the morning, she would crawl into bed, her skin cool from the fan she had pointed at herself, and mold her body to Iris's. Iris would let her sleep as late as she could before she had to leave for the library. With her bag over one shoulder and Erin's hand in hers, Iris would lead her sleep-mussed girlfriend out the door, down the stairs and to the T, where they rode together until her stop at BU, at which point Erin stayed on the train to continue to Beacon Hill.

The everydayness of their evenings was intoxicating. It was so easy to be with Erin in every way: physically, mentally, and emotionally. Waking up to Erin in her bed was a message from the divine, as her grandma used to say. Erin told her not to change up anything about her routine for her sake, but Iris wished she could speed-read these sources so she could open up hours for Erin before she had to go to work. At the same time, she was inspired to take all this information and make something important out of it, something pointed and meaningful, something that would make people in her field look at her like Erin did.

Iris was typing up notes as she made her way through an article in *The Great Commission Baptist Journal of Missions*, a publication it had taken her ages to track down. There, buried in the second paragraph on the third page, was a reference to a different article in a journal so obscure Iris had never heard of it despite all of her research. She stopped and read it a few times, then searched for a footnote or bibliographic reference that might help her track it down. She came up empty, but just by the title, she could tell it would be hugely influential to her work.

She was about to go down to the reference librarian when her phone buzzed on the table next to her. She smiled, thinking it might be Erin wanting to coordinate about tonight. She could already feel Erin's vicarious excitement about this newly discovered source, but she turned the phone over to see it was Naomi. She checked the time, saw it was the lunch rush, and answered, knowing something had to be wrong.

"Mom. Is everything okay?"

"Well—" Her voice was tight. "It could be better. The car's in the shop."

Naomi's car had been running on duct tape and ardent wishes for the last two years, and Iris had heard this refrain before. Cutting to the chase, she said, "How much?"

"The fuel injector's shot and needs to be replaced. They say $700."

The number made her chest squeeze. "Your whole car's not even worth that. Did you call around for other estimates?"

"Yeah. They're all about the same, and I trust this shop."

"Mom, you can't put that kind of money into that car."

"I can't not have a car. It's at least an hour walk to work, and I haven't forgotten that you want me to get a job in Allentown."

"Hold on a sec, okay? I need to get outside."

Iris pressed her phone against her chest, hustled down the three flights of stairs to the main floor, and pushed out through the bank of doors to the vibrant outside. Before lifting the phone back to her ear, she took a few deep breaths to ground herself. This was so intensely unfair, that this was happening to Naomi— again. And that it was happening to her—again. It was no one's fault, but she desperately wanted to have someone to blame.

When she was a little calmer, she said, "I'm not saying you should go without a car. I'm saying that it's time to get a different one. You can get something reliable for less than twice that repair bill. Is the same place still around where you got this one? I don't think they'll take advantage of you. But maybe bring Mick along just in case."

"I don't have that kind of money. I don't even have what's needed for the repair. And Mick can't take any time off work right now."

Each obstacle she presented to Iris's plan chipped away at the easy, in-control façade she'd assumed. "How much do you have?"

"$500. Maybe $600. I might be able to get an advance at the diner."

Iris pressed the phone hard against her head to keep from throwing it. It was impossible for Naomi to get ahead, and that splashed over onto Iris. It always would, but Iris was trying to get herself into a position where it didn't hurt so much. One of her goals in life was to be in a place where she didn't have to have the current balance of her bank account at the top of her mind. Since she wasn't there yet, she said, "I can send you $900." That would wipe her out, but what was she going to do? Neither of them could go down the road of cash advances on their already burdened credit cards. "You're going to take an Uber to Western Union and then to the used car lot, right?"

"I don't have much choice."

"I'll move as fast as I can, but it could take up to an hour to get the money wired."

"I'll just go there and wait. Iris, you know I don't want to take your money."

"It's going to be fine. You don't need anyone to help you getting a new car. You know how to keep anyone from taking advantage of you. I've seen it. And just think—you'll have a new ride that shouldn't give you trouble for a long time."

"Are you sure you have that kind of money?"

She was going to be terribly squeezed until her next paycheck from Dialogue, but it was nothing she hadn't been through before. "I'm fine. I promise. But I'd better get moving if you're going to be able to get this done today so you can be back at work tomorrow."

Naomi let her off the phone with a few more apologies and declarations of undying gratitude. Iris ran back upstairs to get her things, rushed to the nearest ATM that wouldn't charge her fees, and tucked the wad of cash she'd withdrawn into her pocket. Then, instead of walking, she rode the train two short stops to the Western Union she'd used too many times to feel at all good about. When the wire was complete, she texted her mom that it was ready and left the store to stand outside in the sunshine.

It was a beautiful day, which was infuriating. The whole thing was infuriating. She loved her mom, and they were close enough that she knew how much it bothered Naomi to take money from her. But her mom still repeatedly landed in situations where she needed help. It was no one's fault. Shit happened, and it happened disproportionately to the poor. Her mom was caught in a cycle nearly impossible to escape, and Iris could only help so much without losing her own chance in the process.

Instead of crying, like she wanted to, she called Erin.

"Iris," Erin answered. "Fair warning—I'm going into a meeting in ten minutes."

"That's okay. I mostly just wanted to hear your voice."

"Is everything all right?"

Iris let her head fall back on the storefront's window. "Not really."

"Do you want to talk about it, or do you want distraction from it?"

"I haven't told you everything about my mom."

"I doubt we've had enough time to cover everything about anything."

She took in a slow breath. "She's poor. I mean, we both are. Mine's just temporarily masked by my loan and that grant. She's been working her ass off for my whole life, and she's never going to get ahead, which is partly her and partly the system we all operate under. She can roll with smaller problems, but anything remotely major just ruins her."

"I can't imagine how frustrating that must feel."

"No, you can't. I send her money when she gets in a bind, as much as I can, and today I took my savings down to nothing again."

"I'm sorry. You shouldn't have to do that, but it's amazing that you do."

"How could I just let her drown when I can help?" A small, hard, shameful part of her wished Erin would say something that would give her permission to do just that.

"Other people would. A lot of people do."

"I don't need a pep talk." The words had a hard snap to them.

"Okay. What do you need? I can tell you what you already know, that the whole thing is wildly unfair and that it's too much to ask of you to bail out your mom when it should be the other way around. Is that better?"

"I think that's worse. I should let you go. Nothing's going to make me feel better right now, and you have a meeting."

"Can I see you tonight? I'll meet you at Dialogue. Maybe I can do better in person."

Seeing Erin was always a balm, but in her current ornery state, something bothered her. "Why haven't you invited me to your place?"

The quiet stretched out long enough that Iris pulled the phone from her ear to make sure they hadn't gotten disconnected. Finally, Erin said, "Would you like to come over tonight?"

"I'm not trying to strong-arm you into an invitation."

"I know it's gotten weird, and I want to fix that. It'd be great if you would try not to have any assumptions or expectations about my situation, though."

Iris frowned. "I'm not sure what to expect at this point, so, sure, I guess."

"Okay. I'll pick you up after your shift, and we'll walk over together."

"You sound a little strange."

"I'm fine. I'm just trying to figure out what to do with the twenty-five-foot python I let slither around the place. I'll see you tonight, and in the meantime, try to remember how incredible you are for what you did today."

They hung up, and Iris didn't know what to do with herself. What she should do was get back to the library and take advantage of the hours she had left until she had to get to work, but what she did was turn in the opposite direction and walk down Boylston until she reached the Public Gardens. There, she made her way across the pond to the weeping beech where she'd encountered Erin. She'd been in a state then, one that Erin had helped her forget for a little while, but that wasn't happening this time. She was still twisted up about her mom and now unsettled by what might await her at Erin's place.

She sat on the bench they'd used before and tried to lose herself in the tree like Erin seemed able to do, its curtain of deep-green leaves, the peeks of the skeleton of branches supporting them. Everything was so easy for this tree, needing just sunlight, soil, and water to live. Whereas, with her today, complications threatened to swallow her whole. She was afraid at how easy it would be to slip and end up like Naomi. Yes, she had better options with her degrees, but there was endless debt to service, both hers and her mom's. She'd be dragging them both along shackled to useless problems—like this car—that only money could solve. History professors weren't particularly well paid, and that assumed she could get something other than an adjunct position, which would leave her trying to claw her way to a living wage.

At times like these, she wondered if she should have gotten a more practical degree, like business or accounting, even though the thought made her feel like dying. Pursuing your passion was a privilege she had browbeat the universe into letting her have—at least for now—but things changed, and she might have to change with them. She needed money, not only for Naomi but also for herself. She'd only just paid off her credit card debt from the last time she'd bailed her mom out, which had been another major car expense.

Why wouldn't Naomi try to get a better job? As much as she didn't want to, Iris suspected her of keeping herself down, which made Iris resent turning her own life inside out to assist her. And even if Erin was right that a lot of people wouldn't do what she did for her mom, there were times when she resented the hell out of it. The thought made her stomach cramp in shame. Things would be better in a few weeks after she'd gotten a couple of paychecks and a lot of tips and could know for sure that she could pay her portion of the rent and utilities. Hopefully things would be better tonight when she saw Erin and learned what was up with her apartment.

She wished Erin were sitting next to her, not saying anything, just contemplating the tree, quiet in the face of this curated slice of nature. They could hold hands, palms warm together, fingers intertwined. Time would tick by more easily, and she'd have an anchor when Naomi would call—with a car or another problem. It had been remarkably easy to tell Erin a bit more about her family, and the way she reacted hadn't tripped any red flags. She hadn't offered to come in and save the day, and she hadn't minimized Iris's problems.

She knew that when she got off work and met Erin outside the staff entrance, she would walk right into a ready hug, tight and long, smell the last remnants of her perfume. Erin would ask how her shift was, if she was okay, if she was ready to meet this python. The way Erin knew what to say and how to hold her was dangerous, but Iris wanted acutely to be able to rely on Erin and for Erin to rely on her. She wanted to fast forward and know how they would turn out before she invested any more of herself. She smoothed her hair back and sighed. Nothing would happen unless she let herself run on faith for once.

The afternoon turned around her until she'd sat on the bench for a full two hours. She had to get to work, not to mention pee. She stood gingerly to restore her circulation. Her phone rang. Naomi.

"Did it work out?"

"I'm now the proud owner of a Chevy Impala with blood-red interior and only sixty thousand miles on it. It took every last dollar, so thank you. I wish I could make it up to you."

Her frustration from earlier returned. "If you want to do something for me, interview for some jobs in Allentown now that you have a car that'll get you there and back."

"I know I've been a burden to you—"

Iris interrupted her. "Just say yes, that you'll do it. I don't want your thanks. I want you to have a better life."

"And to not have to bail me out."

"That's not what I said." But it was true.

"You didn't have to. Thank you for it, but I would have figured it out somehow."

"Mom, don't. Neither of us wants any of this, but it's what we're stuck with until something changes. I'm working on changing things on my end, but that doesn't help us now. All I'm asking is that you do this for yourself."

"Okay."

"Okay. I love you, but I have to get to work. Enjoy the Impala."

Iris hung up and set off toward Dialogue on the same path she'd taken with Erin on that stormy afternoon. She was crackling with emotion: anger, frustration, sadness, and a feeling of being betrayed by whatever was ultimately in charge of this mess. It was so unfair—even though fairness was a ridiculous concept, useful only for those privileged enough to feel entitled to a reasonable, rational, and measured world. Just look at her grant: ripped away from her on what felt like a whim—or at least inscrutable bureaucracy—and reinstated at the stroke of a magical pen. Naomi's thanks reminded Iris that she owed this anonymous donor a thank-you note. She assumed she could send one care of the foundation. It just kept slipping lower on her to-do list despite her usual attempt at good manners. And now she had to smile her way through the evening to maximize the tips she suddenly needed desperately.

At least Erin would be on the other side of it.

* * *

Finally, Iris stepped into the long-awaited hug. It grounded her like a deep, cleansing breath. They walked back the way she'd come in this afternoon, toward the Public Gardens, talking about her shift and Erin's meeting, sidestepping the upheaval of the day and the mystery waiting at their destination. They covered some blocks in the easy quiet of Iris's emotional and physical exhaustion. She didn't care what Erin's place was like as long as there was a bed.

They walked between the Commons and the Gardens, then crossed into Beacon Hill. A couple of blocks in, they turned right and started uphill.

Erin said, "It's at the top. Sorry."

"At least you get a workout in."

"It makes you think twice about whether you really need to go to the grocery store or not."

"Why do you live in this neighborhood?"

"I like to be able to walk everywhere, and I actually like the density. It feels efficient while still being satisfyingly old."

"How long have you lived here?"

Erin ushered Iris over a curb and across a cobblestoned street. "Two years. Catherine and I lived in a tiny place in Malden before that where everything was tied to the commuter rail schedule."

"I didn't know you two had lived together."

"We did everything together from the time we graduated college until a little bit ago. It's kind of a long story. I actually planned on telling you tonight, so let's get inside and comfortable. It's just on the next block."

The building Erin walked up to was a redbrick, square structure with several large windows looking out onto the street. She let them through the shiny black door and into a landing with a white door on the right and a staircase in front of them. Erin started climbing the stairs, and Iris followed. There was another white door at the top. Erin slipped her key in the lock. "This is me."

She opened the door and motioned for Iris to go inside first. Erin followed, switching on lights and dropping her keys in a bowl on a slim table that hosted a small spray of mail. "Do you want a tour or would you rather explore?"

First, Iris noted, the place was immaculate. Second, it was large—how large, exactly, she wasn't sure until she'd walked past the good-sized living room, dining room, and full-on chef's kitchen. A couple of more rooms were on this floor, one that looked like an office, and a staircase headed upstairs to god knew what but at least one bedroom since she didn't see one down here. She blinked around, taking it all in until her gaze landed on Erin, who was leaned back against the wall in the hallway, her hands in the pockets of her worn jeans and her feet bare.

She said, "Do you want to see upstairs?"

Iris said, "I think you need to explain a couple of things."

"I know I do. Do you want some hot tea or water or anything?"

"I want an explanation. I can't even imagine how much this place cost."

"Come on." Erin led them back to the living room, which looked like it was out of a magazine spread, and waited for Iris to sit on the couch before settling herself in front of her on a large, leather ottoman. "Can I touch you while I talk?"

"Anything as long as you tell me everything and start right now."

Erin's hands landed on the sides of Iris's knees, her fingers hooking around to the backs of her legs. "Catherine and I started a software company right out of college. In ways, it was a stupid thing to do. I had student loans coming due, and Catherine had six-figure offers from more than one company. She's a tech wizard. Programming. We split responsibilities down the middle, technology for Catherine, everything domain- and business-related for me. We bootstrapped it with part-time jobs and made do without everything we could dump and still survive. I can tell you all about what we built together for law firms, but it doesn't really matter to what I'm sure you actually want to know."

"Probably not. But I thought you were a consultant." Iris's hands were cold, and she felt trapped in Erin's gaze.

"I am now. I'll get there, I promise. It took a year, but we got our first institutional customer, which meant we could quit our other jobs and focus all our energy on the company. We grew slowly after that, hiring only one additional person that second year. More contracts fell into place, and when we hit some magical threshold of customers and profitability, I raised a five-million-dollar investment so we could grow the way we needed to. It was only then that Catherine and I were able to pay ourselves a decent salary."

Iris's eyebrows quirked of their own accord, which Erin clearly noticed.

"Not enough to afford this place but enough to have money left over after my loans—oh, and finally save a little bit."

Iris couldn't wait to get to that place. It sounded magical, but it was certainly not the end to this story.

"After the investment, Catherine and I still retained eighty percent of the company together, and we planned to run it indefinitely. The investment wasn't just a jump start on our individual finances, it was a shot of adrenaline to the business. We grew like crazy, both our team and our customer list. The backlog of things we wanted to do was two years long, and we finally started making headway on it. Then, after another year and a half, we were approached by Nuvio, which is a huge player in the industry."

For the first time, Erin looked away from Iris. Not only that, but she took her hands from Iris's legs. "If anyone could have competed with us on this product, in our essential niche, it was Nuvio. We'd forced them into a place where they had to make a build-versus-buy decision—build a competing product from scratch or buy us outright."

"And they bought you."

Erin nodded. "We never thought we'd sell, but they had resources we couldn't dream of. We agreed to an acquisition that stipulated that Catherine and I would come to Nuvio with the rest of our team and work there for at least two years. About six months ago, when I was able, I left Catherine at Nuvio and went on my own in consulting, which is a long story itself." She looked at Iris with a sharp intensity. "I am a consultant. I have clients and a reputation. I wasn't lying about that."

"What were you lying about?" Iris felt like one big held breath.

Erin's face spasmed into a look of disgust. "Nothing, not exactly. It's just not something I come out and tell people who are new to my life." She looked to the ceiling and took an audible breath through her nose, her chest and shoulders rising with it. She met Iris's gaze and said, "Nuvio bought us for a lot of money."

Iris's throat was tight when she said, "What's a lot?"

"Sixty-five million dollars. I'll save you doing the math in your head—that left us each with twenty-six million, some of which we both used to give very large bonuses to our team. After paying off my loans, helping my family out with a few things, buying this building, and charitable giving, I have over twenty million dollars."

Iris wasn't sure what she felt, but she felt it a lot. She sat back to put more distance between them. It was partly a feeling of immense betrayal that was eroded almost immediately by the understanding that they'd each kept their financial situations quiet for similar but opposite reasons. But, still. Twenty million dollars? That was a huge amount to hide. That was huge in general. Iris felt like she had no idea who Erin was anymore, which she knew was unfair, but she'd already established that fair wasn't applicable to much in her life—especially today.

As if she couldn't sense Iris's turmoil, Erin went on. "It can easily change things I don't want it to, so now I protect myself and pretend it doesn't exist until I trust anyone new. It isn't fair that people expect me to disclose my financial situation right away when I would never ask that of them."

There was that word again. Fair. Iris was furious. All the care Erin had taken to keep them on a level playing field, walking along the river, in the North End, around the arboretum, now felt like a slap in the face. The amount of inequity left her speechless. She stood, getting all into Erin's space before she could slide to the side and breathe.

"Iris?" Erin got up and gently took Iris's forearm in her hand.

Iris shook it off with more vehemence than she'd intended. Erin's face went small and tight. "I need to go home."

"Can we talk about it?"

"No, not after my day today." Maybe not ever.

"It doesn't have to change anything."

Iris laughed like the wind was knocked out of her. "It takes a staggering amount of luxury to say that with a straight face."

"I'm exactly the same person as I was an hour ago."

"You lied to me."

"Did you really expect that I would sit down across from you at The Thinking Cup and disclose my finances? You didn't tell me anything remotely like this until today. How can you blame me for wanting you to see just me and not my money?"

Iris moved away from Erin, across the room and toward the hall. "How can *you* think I wouldn't be blindsided by this?"

"Iris, please." Erin shimmied past the ottoman.

"I need to go home." Her phone was in her bag by the front door, and she moved toward it so she could call a ride, wanting to get away faster than the T could take her.

"Okay, but let me get an Uber for you."

"I don't need your charity!" The words were so loud that shame filled the void they left inside her.

Erin raised her hands and backed off.

Iris gazed at the refinished wood floors. "I'm sorry. That was...I just need to get out of here so I can feel whatever I want without you looking at me or needing to be *fair*." She shouldered her bag and clutched the handle of the door.

"Will you call me when you get in?"

"Not tonight, okay? This is just...not tonight." She thumbed the deadbolt and was out the door and down the stairs in a rush. Then, instead of hailing a ride, she walked down the hill they'd come up and hurried to the T after all. The ride out to her apartment was long, and she needed the buzz of amplified motion around her to drown out the noise inside her head.

The figure was staggering. She couldn't conceive of that much money. Just a small fraction of it would fix everything for her mom and pay off her loans so she wouldn't start out so far behind. Erin wouldn't even notice—that's how much of a footnote their suffering was to her. Erin's lies were sharp, flayed her open in shock. How long would she have kept up the ruse if Iris hadn't tried to find out why she hadn't been to Erin's apartment yet? Not an apartment, even. A whole building. In Beacon Hill.

The train was mostly empty, and she sat in a window seat facing forward, her bag on her lap and arms around it. In the darkness of the tunnel, she could see her face reflected in the window. She looked the same, but everything felt different. She'd confided in Erin, had greedily opened up to her comfort and praise, and now this? She knew she should give Erin at least a small benefit of the doubt, should empathize with her motivations, but there wasn't room for that in her head, which was wholly occupied by the grotesque sum in Erin's bank account.

Everything was just so hard. Maybe Erin had gone through some lean times getting her company started, but it had been temporary and for a larger purpose. She could have quit any time it got more difficult than she wanted. Iris's situation was completely different, not only because it was involuntary. Erin had no idea what it took to unstick yourself from the generational trap of the lower, working class. The discipline needed was beyond measure. But Iris was doing it even when Naomi's deadweight dragged her down.

Thinking about her mom that way made her feel sicker. The worst part was that she knew Erin was being truthful in her desire to protect herself. She understood that the money changed everything in ways Erin maybe hadn't bargained for. But these were problems that one had to be so far beyond privileged to have in the first place, and Iris couldn't drum up any sympathy tonight. Still, there was a small part of her that wished she hadn't been so unforgiving with Erin at the end, hadn't accused her of coming in as some great, white savior when all she'd done was offer basic kindness when she was letting Iris go.

CHAPTER ELEVEN

Erin had never really minded when Iris woke her up too early. It had only happened a handful of times, and it messed with her sleep, but she'd grown accustomed to a hand sliding up her arm to her shoulder, soft breath on her cheek, and the firm press of lips against her jaw.

"Time to get up," Iris would whisper, which Erin would answer with a grunt before prying open one eye to see Iris leaning over her, smiling. Who could resist that?

Now, though, she slept even later than usual, in a bed emptier than the one she'd lain in for the last year and a half. She missed slipping into bed hours after Iris, seeking the warmth of her sleeping body, the smell of her hair done up in its habitual braid, the gentle rise and fall of her chest when Erin encircled her with an arm. She'd felt so at home sleeping next to Iris. Not to mention in their sex, which had combined a deep vulnerability with electric eroticism. Sometimes the naked want on Iris's face, her pulse visible in her neck, made Erin combust.

This morning, eleven o'clock had gone by before she'd pried herself from between her sheets. She regarded herself in the bathroom mirror, forgetting the toothpaste and toothbrush in her hands in favor of studying her ragged reflection. Her hair was everywhere, and baggy, dark skin bruised the area below her eyes. She'd been staying up later to avoid having to confront her empty bed, but those early morning hours hadn't been any comfort. Though she'd missed Iris over the last week, she'd also spent that deathly quiet time seething with anger.

Her money was an easy, useless target for her fury. Was the only way to remove it as an obstacle to romantic connection to date only women who were wealthier than she was? How many of those were in the Boston area, how would she even meet them, and how would they possibly compare to Iris? What had seemed an exciting, staggering windfall when the deal had gone through now grew rotten in her investment accounts even as it multiplied. It had come to own her in a way she couldn't even feel bad about without tripping over her supposed privilege.

Yet again, she wondered if she really should give it all away like MacKenzie Scott or Melanie Perkins. It would do some good, and it would force her to get fully back in the workforce in one way or another. She couldn't count the number of times she'd considered this, but she always had a bevy of excuses why not to go ahead and do it. The right charity, the right vehicle for gifting, the right timing. There was always something. Which, Erin supposed, meant she didn't really want to do it. Which seemed monumentally selfish.

When she wasn't hating her money, she hated Catherine at least a little bit for not having the same kinds of problems with her distribution as Erin did. Catherine, who found purpose in her work, had made a comfortable home and had given away notable sums without driving herself crazy over any of it. Catherine, who had a partner she'd found before it all happened, a partner who also managed to deal with Catherine's wealth without any issues. Catherine, who dispensed advice to Erin like the solutions to everything were obvious.

Then, in her darkest, most desperate hours, Erin directed the dregs of her anger at Iris. Her double standards. Her self-righteousness. Her slap in the face when Erin had offered to call a ride for her. That hair trigger that was too delicate to avoid. In her mind, having money of any kind went directly to inequality, so where did that leave Erin? She knew Iris had suffered and had had to make hard choices—still did—but why couldn't she let Erin in instead of using their inequity as a weapon to put Erin in her place?

As they agreed, none of this was fair. Nothing was fair, not even the fact that she wasn't allowed to think of fairness in her fundamentally unfair position. She could never do enough to make up for how she'd been rewarded for four years of hard work, and that made everything impossible. Being with Iris, giving an extra-good tip, keeping her situation to herself, donating money, not donating money. She was hemmed in by the impossibility of doing the right thing, and that infuriated her.

She brushed her teeth, tamed her hair, determined that her face was a lost cause, and, like every other morning, contemplated her phone. She'd been giving Iris space, white knuckling it until, hopefully, she heard from her again. Despite her nighttime anger, in the light of the early afternoon she wanted to figure out how to make things work between them.

She checked the clock. She had only ten minutes until Shannon was due for a mentoring appointment, which seemed like the worst time to try Iris, but that also made it irresistible. She thought of a dozen different things she could start with and rejected them all as being too intimate, too cold, too potentially manipulative. I miss you, she wanted to write. I don't want to lose you over this. We can figure this out if you want to (please want to). I hope your mom's doing okay. Instead, she typed, *How are you?* She slipped her phone into a pocket so she wouldn't watch it for a reply she wasn't sure would come.

Shannon rang her doorbell, and Erin trundled down the stairs to get her. "Come on in. Coffee? Water? Anything?"

Shannon brandished an impressively large water flask. "I'm all set. I'm trying to be better about drinking."

"If you make your way through that, you'll be doing better than I ever do."

"It's aspirational, like you taught me."

They crossed the living room into her office and took their habitual spots, Shannon pulling her laptop from her bag and settling it across her legs. It was festooned with stickers, one of which said, simply, "Women Rock."

She said, "Do you have any proposals for me to work on? What about those website changes you were talking about the other week?"

Erin settled an ankle over the opposite knee and leaned back into the comfortably curved chair she sat in. "Where do you stand on honesty?"

Shannon blinked. "Do you mean do I think of myself as an honest person?"

"No, that's too easy. Of course you think you're honest—or at least aspire to honesty. I wouldn't be working with you otherwise. I mean where do the limits of honesty sit in you and what is it that puts up barriers to being honest?"

To Shannon's credit, she really thought about it, having gotten used to quiet between them when Erin was asking her to consider a concept. "There's a difference between truthfulness and honesty, isn't there?"

"Yes. How would you define them?"

"Honesty is that everything you actually say is true. Truthfulness means that you're saying everything there is to say about something. Or is it the reverse?"

"I think you got it right. Now how do they live in you? What kinds of things keep you from honesty or truthfulness? And I'm not talking about something like not telling someone that you don't like their outfit or their hair or their laugh. I'd never advocate being a social pariah out of truthfulness. I'm talking about stuff that matters."

Shannon gazed at her hands, fingers intertwined on top of her closed laptop. "I don't tell people about some family stuff because I don't want to deal with their reactions. Sometimes I'm not entirely truthful about what I hope to do after college because I don't want to disappoint people if I don't make it happen."

"Right. There are lots of justifiable reasons to fall short of honesty or truthfulness. I'd hazard to say that most of them boil down to self-protection and fear."

"Now I can't stop thinking of ways that I'm not truthful or even honest."

"Don't feel bad about it. We're all in the same boat. At the same time, keeping things secret or distorting the truth can cause us more harm than what we're trying to avoid by being dishonest in the first place."

Shannon went back to considering her fingers, and Erin knew she had to get to whatever point she was going to make pretty soon. Still, this was exactly the time when people Shannon's age were deciding who they were, and this was a big part of it. While she stewed, Erin looked around the cool gray walls of the room, wondering if she should paint them a color with a little more life. That was something she could do herself and would make her feel unequivocally accomplished—albeit on a small scale. Her phone buzzed where it still reposed in her back pocket, and it took all her strength not to look at it.

Instead, she said, "What I really want to talk about is truthfulness and honesty in business. One of the signs of a sick business culture is a lack of tolerance for the truth. In extreme cases, this leads to whistleblowers, but in milder forms, the truthteller is branded as a problem employee and ignored. People who sugarcoat or conceal or mask situations can get promoted over people who are honest. Sometimes the honest people are gaslighted into submission. So, what do you do when you're coming in as a consultant or a new hire and identify this kind of culture?"

"Well, you have to get them to trust you before you can do anything meaningful, right?"

"Right."

"Would you do, like, a Trojan horse kind of thing where you get them to like you first and then reveal the truth to them?"

"No. That would violate your own integrity. You always tell the truth, but you can change how you tell it."

Erin went on for a little while about ways to present facts to make them persuasive in different situations and with different audiences before role playing with Shannon where she was the consultant and Erin was the client who didn't want to hear what she had to say. It was one of the better mentoring sessions they'd had, and Erin felt loose and affable by the end.

While Shannon was sliding her laptop into her huge backpack, she said, "Are you taking on any other mentees? A couple of my friends would love something like this. Without the administrative work, even though that's not heavy at all. They might even be able to pay for it if that would make you consider it."

"I mostly conceived of this as a job with benefits, so I don't really know. I'd have to think about how something like that would work."

"That's okay. I get it. I'd just like other women to be as lucky as I've been working with you. I know I don't always get to the reading on time, but you make things concrete and push me to really think about them. My classmates would get a lot of value out of it."

Erin laughed. "Well, you've obviously learned the hard sell, so my work here is done. I'll think about it, I promise."

She showed Shannon out and surveyed the stack of mail she hadn't gotten around to opening. Then, like she hadn't been thinking about it for the last half hour, she checked her phone. There was a text from Iris.

I need more time.

She dropped her head back, anger surging again behind her forehead. Given that reaction, she guessed she needed more time, too. She wished she could take back telling Iris about her money but immediately called herself a liar. This was the truth, and if they couldn't both get on board with it, they couldn't be together. Under her anger pooled a sadness at that possibility, but she wasn't about to give up without a fight.

* * *

When Erin saw the McCallister Construction truck, she knew she was at the right place. The Uber pulled over behind it, and she grabbed the bag of sandwiches next to her and headed up the walk toward the house, veering off at the last minute to detour around to the back, where the addition was going up. Even though the bag only held two sandwiches, it was heavy. Sam LaGrassa's made an art form out of piling meat between kaiser rolls. The roast beef was Rory's favorite, and she'd decided to surprise him with it for lunch today.

Erin used to have friends, but the ones from college had wilted on the vine while she was bootstrapping Tribar, and the ones from Tribar had faded when she'd exited Nuvio. She knew that was on her and her hang-ups, but she was where she was now, and since she couldn't hide it with overwork, she had to deal with it. And today, pestering her brother was the way she was doing it.

Through the wood framing, she could see Rory going over plans spread out on a sheet of plywood over two sawhorses, talking to another man in dirty jeans, who was nodding and pointing at the paper. Rory made some hand motions she couldn't decipher, and she was reminded of the occasional visits she'd made with her mother to her father's job sites. This addition was a good-sized one, and Erin knew from Rory that they'd been doing more of these bigger jobs in the last couple of years. Rory was good for business, and Stephanie worked part-time as their bookkeeper around raising her kids. Erin was on the outside, which she'd felt acutely since the money had landed in her bank account. Not that she wanted to be swinging a hammer or coding expenses to a chart of accounts.

When the man walked away from Rory, Erin said, "Hey," but it was swallowed up by the buzz of a saw. She walked closer to the wide opening that would someday hold a set of sliding doors.

She tried again, holding up the bag of sandwiches while she called, "Rory."

He looked at her and smiled. "Is that Sam's?"

"You know it."

"I knew I liked you for a reason." He came to her and motioned to a couple of overturned five-gallon buckets next to a pile of lumber. "Take a load off."

She handed him the bag while she made herself comfortable. He passed a sandwich to her and took the other. They both unwrapped and then swapped without a word, leaving him with the roast beef and her with the pastrami. He dumped the rest of the bag onto the grass, scattering packets of mustard and mayo along with some chips. Salt and vinegar, which Erin couldn't abide but Rory found finger-licking good.

"So, why are you here with this bribe—not that I'm complaining." He slathered condiments on his sandwich, drowning the meat.

Erin squirted some Dijon on half her sandwich, knowing that she'd take the other half home. "It's not a bribe."

He raised an eyebrow and took a big bite, thumbing mustard from the corner of his lips. "Ulterior motives, then," he said around the food in his mouth, which bulged out one of his cheeks.

"Can't I just want to say hi?"

"Not really." He chewed a few times and swallowed. She wondered how he was even able to taste his food. It was in his mouth so briefly. "I know you don't like coming up here."

Only because the rest of her family was so weird about everything. "Fine. I had some time on my hands and didn't want to eat lunch alone." It was close enough to the truth.

"Must be nice." He tore off another bite. "Thanks, by the way." He raised his sandwich as if Erin might not know what he was talking about.

Must be nice. She felt a flash of shame for not feeling that it was nice to be at loose ends like this. It was probably something Iris hated about money—besides the whole inequity of it all. Money meant you could waste your life with impunity. Still, arguing would just pull her deeper into the morass.

Instead, she said, "How much would I have to shell out for dinner to get you to come into town for once?"

"Wow." His laugh was muffled by a full mouth. "You make me sound like a lady of the night. You know, I don't whore myself out for just anyone who offers me a meal."

"I know you don't like making the drive."

He actually put his sandwich down and took his time chewing and swallowing. "You don't have to buy me shit for me to hang out with you."

There it was again: shame. She sighed and squinted at the sun high and bright in the sky. Her freckles were multiplying by the second. "I'm not. I mean that's not what this is. Being alone too much makes me kind of crazy."

"What happened to that new girlfriend? The...what was it? Beautiful and smart one?"

Usually, it was pretty easy to avoid her own life when hanging out with Rory, but he was on her today. She tried to hold tight to Catherine saying things weren't her fault when she said, "She has a problem with my money. And she clearly thinks I should've told her sooner."

"What kind of problem could she have? It's way better than the alternative, right?"

"She doesn't have much, so the whole thing is...a whole thing. Anyway, she says I lied about it, and that's kind of hard to come back from."

He made a dismissive noise and picked up his sandwich again. "Well, at least she's not like Hayley and wants it all for herself. She'd be way nicer to you in that case. Still, does she think you should have your bank balance tattooed on your forehead?"

The fact that he was as much on her side as Catherine about this made her feel a tiniest bit better, but it didn't solve anything.

"So, is she out of the picture or what?"

"She's taking some time."

Another bite. "That's such a chick thing to say. Are you going to process next?"

She hit him on the arm. "I never should have told you anything about lesbians."

"And to think my friends only know what they've seen in porn."

"God, men are disgusting."

He smiled, then opened his mouth to flash her some partially chewed food.

"Gross. Case in point."

"I'm just saying, she's got to be really something to be worth this kind of trouble."

"I'm not sure I should be taking advice from someone who hasn't had a serious relationship since high school—and that was only because you were afraid no one else would date your scrawny ass." He wasn't scrawny anymore. Sandwiches and physical labor had turned him into a strapping specimen.

"Nothing wrong with waiting for the right one."

"The right one doesn't mean you never disagree."

"But with the right one, you'll actually want to figure things out and not just chuck it. At least that's how I see it."

"You're a poet."

He winked. "Your words, not mine."

Was Iris the right one? She'd certainly been heading in that direction, what with the speed Erin had fallen for her and how painful this radio silence was. Erin wasn't ready for things to end now, especially on this note. She wasn't ready for it to end, ever, to be honest. She knew it was too soon to think things like that, but she was done bucking the truth. She'd laid it all out on the table now, honesty the only thing between them, if not absolute truthfulness. All they needed to do was build from here—as long as Iris never found out about that donation, which was something else entirely.

* * *

Partly because Erin couldn't go to Dialogue, she did something crazy and looked up recipes for spaghetti carbonara, wrote down what she remembered of the steps Iris had gone through to cook it for her, and procured not only ingredients but whatever kitchen implements she needed that didn't reside in her embarrassingly empty drawers and cabinets. Then she invited Catherine over for dinner, knowing she could order a pizza from down the hill if things ended up in disaster. She felt a desire to push herself, to be uncomfortable in a way other than what she felt waiting for Iris to deliver her verdict.

Before Catherine arrived, she put on some music and did as much prep work as possible: crushing the garlic (new tool), shredding the cheese (new tool), cubing the pancetta (sharp, unused knife), and cracking and whisking the eggs (only a few shell pieces to be retrieved). She felt awkward with it all, grating her finger along with the pecorino romano, struggling to clean garlic remnants from the crusher, being incredibly timid with the knife and probably looking like a fool. Within the awkwardness was a determination she hadn't felt in a while, and she knew that needing to order in a pie would feel like a failure out of proportion with reality.

While waiting for Catherine, she put together a salad (new veggie wash and greens spinner) and set out two different dressings for them to choose from. It suddenly felt like she was getting ready for a date, or maybe even an interview, and she wondered what she was doing. What did she have to prove to Catherine? What was she trying to prove to herself? That she'd be okay alone again? She hadn't thought that was up for debate, given how long she'd been alone between Hayley and Iris, but right now it had real urgency, given the massive question mark hovering above her love life.

Maybe this very minor amount of cooking was simply an attempt to distract her unruly mind. If so, she had chosen the exact wrong tack if she was trying to avoid thoughts of Iris. All she could think about as she fumbled around was sitting on that worn-out couch, watching Iris be masterful in the kitchen. Iris's place was warm in its shared disarray, her bedroom a cocoon of intimacy. None of which she should be reminiscing about right now. Maybe Catherine would provoke a resurgence of anger that would displace these honey-toned memories.

Erin was halfway through a hazy IPA and watching the lettuce wilt when the doorbell rang and she hurried down the stairs to let Catherine in. Her friend started talking before they even headed back up. This time, it was about some idiot in marketing, which, if Erin had a nickel every time Catherine had said something like that, she'd be even richer and have more to stress about. Catherine had always had the luxury of not having to think about sales and marketing. Granted, her problems were an advanced level of gnarliness, and solving them had been a feat of both intelligence and tenacity. Erin wouldn't have had a product to sell without her, but Catherine wouldn't have been able to sell her product (not to mention have the idea for it) if it hadn't been for Erin. They'd made good partners because they hadn't taken each other for granted. The fact that now Catherine had very little positive to say about anyone who had replaced Erin in her role was warming.

As Catherine sank down on the couch with a sigh, Erin asked, "Are you hungry?"

"Starving. What are we ordering in?"

"I'm cooking, actually."

Catherine laughed. "Then we'll definitely need to order in."

"I'm serious. I'm all set up in the kitchen."

She considered Erin for a while. "What's wrong?"

"Just come into the kitchen so I can finish making things. It won't take long. A lot of it is pasta, which you know is one of the things I can handle."

"Fine. You can cook, then you can tell me what's wrong."

Catherine accepted a beer and sat at the breakfast bar to finish talking about the inept marketing guy. Erin filled a big pot from the spigot over the cooktop and set it on a burner to boil. In a skillet on the next burner over, she drizzled too much oil and stood in indecision whether to pour it out into the sink or live with it. Catherine didn't seem to notice, just rested her chin in her hand with her head tilted to the side, so Erin shrugged and turned on the heat under the pan.

Proving that Catherine was paying closer attention than she looked, she said, "You probably don't want the fire up that high."

"You don't even know what I'm cooking."

"You probably never want the fire up that high unless you're boiling water."

Erin leaned over and turned down the knob, watching the blue flames shrink. "I'm perfectly capable."

"Everyone needs help when they start out. Are you going to tell me why you're doing this?"

"Don't you think it's past time for me to grow up and stop eating out so much?"

"Come on, Erin. You're talking to me." Meaning Catherine's bullshit detector was pinging.

Erin scraped the cubed pancetta into the pan, but it didn't hiss like she'd heard it do at Iris's. She stood with the cutting board (new) suspended over the skillet, not knowing what to do.

Catherine said, "You didn't wait long enough for it to warm up. It's self-correcting. Oh, and the garlic?"

A thump of panic reverberated through her chest since her knife was poised to scrape it in on the pancetta. "What about it?"

"Don't put it in until the meat's almost done otherwise it'll burn."

"Do you want to come in here and make it?"

"Not remotely. I'm just trying to help."

"I can figure this out."

Catherine came around the bar into the kitchen. "Hey." She leaned against the fridge. "I'm serious now. What's going on?"

"I can't talk about it with all this." Erin motioned at the cooktop. "Why don't you eat your salad and tell me something good about work or Nathan or the house. Anything."

Catherine's hesitation was palpable, but she held up her hands and backed out of the kitchen as if being held at gunpoint. She didn't start in on her salad, which was on the counter, but wrapped her hands around her beer and talked about the alarming noise the air-conditioning was making at the house and Nathan's cute but useless attempts to diagnose the issue. "The blind leading the blind at the moment. If only one of us was a mechanical engineer. Anyway, we're going to have to call someone to come around and fix whatever's broken."

She went on about finding a place she could trust and what else they'd have to do if they needed to replace the whole system. She went on in the same vein while Erin stirred the sticking pancetta in the oily pan and dumped a whole box of spaghetti in the water that finally reached a rolling boil, nearly sending it over the pot's lip.

This was a terrible idea. Why had she ever wanted to feel so inept? Still, could she consider herself a full-fledged adult if she didn't know how to do this stuff? Clearly she couldn't count on having another person around to fill this gap in her skill set.

The pancetta was getting hard and dark by the time she added the garlic as Catherine had instructed. Too late, apparently. She lost her nerve and turned off the heat in less than thirty seconds, probably before the garlic was ready. At least she got the pasta right, fishing out strands and biting them in half to gauge their doneness until one felt right in her mouth. She drained it (new strainer) and dumped it into a warmed bowl (new stainless steel set) with the egg and pancetta. After tossing it until there weren't any dry spots on the noodles, she used a couple of forks to dish it out into two shallow bowls. A sprinkle of cheese on both of them, a dash of pepper, and she took the food out to the table she never used.

When they were both settled with their dressed salads across the corner from each other, Catherine took a bite of the carbonara and nodded. "Pretty good, really. Great for your first time out."

"The pancetta's overcooked."

"Never deflect a compliment about your cooking."

"At least I know you wouldn't lie about it."

Catherine put her fork down. "Believe me, not everyone is as enamored with my honesty as you are."

"Nathan?"

"Sure. Him and legions of others. I should probably learn to temper it, but it's kind of like you learning to cook. Are you ready to talk about it now?"

Erin spun her fork, picking up a tidy ball of yellowish noodles, but instead of lifting it to her mouth and finding out how far her rendition of this dish was from Iris's, she let her fork drop. "I told Iris about the money."

Catherine hummed and waited, taking a bite of her salad.

"Her family doesn't have much. She sends money she probably doesn't really have back to her mom for big expenses."

"Oh, shit."

"It's been a week, and she still won't talk to me. Anything I said about it made it worse at the time, so I don't know how anything will be different if she stops freezing me out."

Catherine pointed at Erin with her fork, and Erin braced herself for what was coming. "You've done nothing wrong, and don't let her convince you otherwise."

"I know."

"Do you? Because you've been chastising yourself for this since you left Nuvio."

"She thinks I lied, which I know isn't true, but it feels true. Even though I didn't know her exact situation, I knew right from the beginning that she'd have an issue with it, and I let things progress anyway."

"Are her problems with it the same as yours?"

Erin questioned why she'd set things up to have this conversation over a quickly cooling meal that she'd made herself, but a bigger question was why she hadn't been spending money on therapy so that she might have some answers. "It's not fair that I have so much and she has so little, and she feels that really acutely."

"No, it's not fair, but you're not personally responsible for it."

She shoved spaghetti in her mouth. Her anger from earlier was staging a resurgence, and she didn't want to show it to Catherine, especially since a sliver of it was aimed at her. She went at her bowl with some serious intent, watching Catherine out of the corner of her eye as she relented and started eating again. They sat in a quiet broken only by the crunch of lettuce and some laughing from the street that wafted in through an open living room window.

When half her pasta was gone, Erin said, "It's just that I really like her. I mean, I'm pissed and sad right now, but before I saw her face when I told her about the money, I liked her in a seriously deep, uncomplicated way. Now that's gone."

"God, when did you get so fatalistic? Because you weren't that way before Nuvio."

"Catherine, she bitch-slapped me for offering to call an Uber for her, saying she wasn't a charity case. I'd be a fool to think she's going to come around when now I'm everything she hates—inequality and privilege."

Catherine sat back and dropped her fork in her bowl. "She—What? Over an Uber? She's as bad as you."

"Right. So how is it possibly going to work out?"

"Maybe it won't, but you have to own your part of it. If you can't figure out a way to be okay with what you have, you're never going to be okay with someone else."

"Yes, Yoda."

"I'm serious."

Erin looked at Catherine, really scrutinized her face, the set of her mouth, the cast of her eyes, trying to see behind her skin to the brain underneath and the truth that lived there in a way she'd never seen in another person. When Catherine said she was serious, her seriousness was absolute, but Erin didn't want to hear it, not now.

"Let's just finish eating."

"I don't want to be the bad guy here."

"You're not. It's just a lot, and it seems like I have to figure it all out to get anything."

"You can do it. I mean, if you can make this meal on your first go, you can figure your way out of this."

They dropped the subject in favor of less volatile things. Catherine ate all her dinner, which was a truth Erin was happy to see, but she left after a second beer. Erin was alone again, her place chafing her, her kitchen an absolute disaster. She passed the time washing the pot and skillet, then the bowls they ate out of as well as the large one she'd used to mix the pasta in the first place. She avoided her phone, but Iris's last message haunted her as well as Catherine's matter-of-fact declaration that it was possible—if not probable—that Erin and Iris wouldn't find a way to work things out.

If she thought it would do any good, she would hop on a train and ride out to Iris's apartment to force a conversation. To do it on Iris's turf this time, the scene of their more intimate moments, the warm, comfortable room where they'd bared so much to each other. The truth was that her anger was nothing compared to her continued regard for Iris and her sadness that anything at all stood between them.

It couldn't be over. It just couldn't.

CHAPTER TWELVE

Somehow, the back half of August was already upon Iris. Even though she was practiced at the lead-in to a new school year, nothing felt right this time. Her duties as a teaching assistant—and the stipend that went along with it—would start up in two weeks. This would usually trigger a reduction in the hours she spent at her other job, but with the disaster that was her current bank balance, she was holding on to every shift she could get at Dialogue. Having a buffer of money was nonnegotiable, because anything could (and would) happen—either to her or Naomi. If she sniffed the air carefully, she could smell something like an impending root canal for Naomi on the breeze. She just hoped she could keep the damage to her studies to a minimum.

It was for the best that she not be distracted by a relationship, she'd decided. But that didn't stop her from thinking about Erin at the most inopportune times: while taking orders for a four-top, while in the library searching for more primary texts, while lying in bed at night, unable to sleep. The last was the worst because in her weakness, she ached to have Erin next to her, warm and solid and the person she'd been happy to let dominate her thoughts for months. Things hadn't necessarily always been easy between them, but she hadn't felt that kind of rightness ever before.

But it had been built on a massive lie. The amount of Erin's money had thrown up Iris's walls, but they had been reinforced by the subterfuge involved. Yes, she had withheld information as well, but she felt like she was on the high moral ground here, even though her more rational side knew that was up for debate. She'd just gotten so mad about too many things, and it was hard to walk back from that.

She hated that she didn't know what to do with the space Erin was giving her. Was she open to continuing their relationship? It seemed impossible with this one difference eclipsing all their commonalities. How could Erin really be the same person before and after this disclosure? What did she really think of Iris and Naomi and their financial difficulties? It had felt so easy to tell her about the car and wiring money, but she never would have said anything if she knew Erin sat in a position of judgment.

Besides, what else was she hiding?

In the darkness, when she was unable to fall asleep, she really couldn't believe in a judgmental Erin, not with all her musings about privilege and her seeming desire to improve herself at every opportunity. Iris couldn't believe she could fall so hard for someone fundamentally duplicitous or condemnatory. And she wondered why Erin wasn't trying to win her back instead of keeping her distance as Iris had requested.

Then she'd wake in the morning and start the cycle over. Getting angry again. Not believing a word Erin had said during all their meandering conversations. Being so certain it was over that she didn't even have to come out and say the words to Erin. She wanted to scream at her out-of-control feelings and her inability to boil things down to a single pro/con list that would tell her exactly what to do.

When she'd received the text checking in on her, she'd felt all of this in one flushed, stomach-dropping moment. There'd been an immediate happiness at the communication, a warmth at it being a genuine question instead of something more demanding. Then her hurt and defensiveness had squashed it.

Still, that initial reaction meant she couldn't end it just then. Soon, she promised herself, but it had been several days, and she still hadn't done it.

This afternoon, in the library, Candice appeared as if out of nowhere, backpack over a shoulder and some books tucked under her arm. "How'd I know I'd find you here?"

Iris nodded at the books Candice was carrying. "Great minds, huh?"

She sat down next to Iris and leaned in, lowering her voice to a whisper while she looked around at other students dotting nearby tables. "I haven't seen Erin lately—or heard you guys trying to be quiet while knocking boots." Candice's room was next to Iris's, and this was exactly why she'd tried to keep things stealthy when Erin was over. "Why don't you ever go to her place? I assume she's got one to herself with her being a fancy consultant and everything."

This was about the last conversation she wanted to have—and the last person she wanted to have it with. She would do anything to avoid inevitable "I told you so" vibes about Iris not having googled Erin right at the beginning. When she'd finally done it, it'd been too late, though everything she found supported what Erin had disclosed to her that horrible night.

Iris said, truthfully but still evasively, "We're…not right now."

"You're kidding. Why? I liked her—even after she creamed us at Scrabble."

She felt a pang at remembering that night, board games with Erin and her roommates over greasy Chinese food Erin had picked up on her way over. For once, it had seemed that all parts of her life had come together in a single, sparkling whole, but now that was shattered. "It's complicated."

"Ah, see, this is why I choose to remain uninvolved. Or only lightly involved. Emotionally uninvolved."

"Yeah, I get it. I know how you roll." Mostly, Candice rolled through light relationships centered more around sex than anything else. She'd disappear from the apartment several nights a week for a month, maybe two, until things flamed out—or she got sick of whomever she was doing the nasty with. Trish, on the other hand, apparently went from one longer-term thing to the next with only the width of a sheet of paper in between the two relationships. Iris had been the old maid of the bunch…at least until Erin had shown up. But now Erin wasn't there anymore. Or Iris wouldn't let her be there, which amounted to the same thing.

"So, are you guys over over? Or is this one of those fights you have just to have great makeup sex after?"

"I think we might just be too different. And I don't know if I can trust her."

"Well, different is one thing, but trust is another. Do you think she's stepping out on you?"

"No, she would never do that." The words came out so quickly they couldn't be anything but the truth as she saw it. "I just…I thought I knew her, but it turns out I've been wrong the whole time." But was that true? Had she been wrong about everything? Her inability to end things cleanly told a different story.

"Ah, so you caught her out in a lie. It must be a big one, 'cause, you know, everyone lies about something."

"I don't."

"No? Have you told her everything that went down when you grandfather sold the house out from under you and went to live in the jungle after your grandma died? That whole saga?"

The saga where they'd been homeless for a month, bouncing around couches when they could find them or in the shelter when they couldn't? The incredible betrayal of her own family during the intense grief of her grandma's passing? The way Naomi refused any help that her grandfather's church might have offered—not that Iris was up on the details of that since Naomi had kept as much as she could from Iris at the time. No. She hadn't told that to Erin, and now she was glad.

"That's not a lie. That's just not something you tell someone when things are still new."

"You guys seemed to skip right past new into serious."

"Not everything is everyone's business."

Candice held up her hands. "I'm just saying. I'm on your side, though. Fuck Erin, right?" The student at the next table over glared at them at the increased volume of Candice's words.

Something twisted inside Iris, and she couldn't entirely echo Candice's sentiment. She wanted to. She wanted to shout the words, be definitive about the inevitable end to them, but she couldn't quite get there. "I don't know," she admitted.

"If you tell me to hate her, I'll hate her. If you tell me to hope things work out, I'll hope things work out. But, you know, if you two get back together, please, for all that's holy, have the makeup sex at her place."

Iris shoved her, playing at being playful when she felt anything but. They talked about the rest of their day and coordinated about the evening before Candice got up, gave Iris a hug around the shoulders, and disappeared to another part of the library.

She tried to start reading again but closed the book without getting anywhere even though there was no time for this kind of distraction. She had a shift coming up at Dialogue. Still, she knew she wouldn't be able to focus until she got outside and breathed some fresh air. Laptop in tow, she took the stairs down and pushed her way through the glass doors of the library to the muggy day. She slipped her phone from her pocket, checked the time, and tried her mom. Talking to Candice but not telling her everything made her itch to disclose, and Naomi was the one she wanted to do it to.

"Is it slow?" she asked.

"Not slow, dead."

"Are they playing cards in the kitchen?"

"Let me look." There was a pause. "Not yet, but give it another ten minutes."

"I can picture it."

"Is everything okay?"

"Yeah, why?" Iris started walking the perimeter of a square of red bricks that made up most of the plaza in front of the library. It was crosshatched with lines of white stone just the right width to pace along.

"Your voice. It's got that 'something's wrong' vibe."

Naomi thought she could discern Iris's every mood by the sound of her voice. It was infuriating—she was mostly right, though Iris had managed to talk to her mom several times since that horrible night with Erin without suspicion. She weighed the pros and cons now and said, "I think Erin and I are over."

"Oh, I'm sorry. What happened?"

"She lied to me. Well, by omission, but it was a big one." She turned a corner and continued her pace in a different direction.

"You don't have to tell me," Naomi said after a long pause.

Iris considered keeping it to herself, but all it was doing inside her was fermenting into something malevolent. "She apparently built a company from scratch and sold it to another company for an unfathomable amount of money."

Another pause. "What's unfathomable?"

With her voice lowered, she said, "Her cut was north of twenty million dollars."

Her mom's laugh was a burst of breath.

"Right, exactly. I don't know what's worse, the lie or the truth."

"Good for her, though, for being so successful."

Iris had been so focused on her anger and sadness that she hadn't managed to get to the point that Naomi went to immediately. Erin's had been quite an accomplishment, but thinking about that now was too confusing.

"We can't be together after that, though. I mean, can you imagine? It's impossible."

"Does it have to be?"

"Of course it does, especially if she feels sorry for me and wants to swoop in and save me from poverty."

"Is that what she does?"

Iris wanted to yell about the damn Uber, but she felt like it might not make as strong a case as she hoped. She turned another corner and kept walking. "Isn't it inevitable?"

"How should I know? I don't rub elbows with folks who have anything extra."

"Anyway, I'm not sure when she would have told me if I hadn't put her in a position where she pretty much had to."

"I can see how that would be a problem."

"Right?" Her relief at being validated was shot through with a vein of disappointment. "It's not official yet, but I can't see a way this would work in the long run."

"I'm sorry to hear that. You seemed to really like her, and you haven't met someone like that in a while."

No, she hadn't, but she could wish all she wanted, and it wouldn't move the universe's needle. They went on to talk about other things until Naomi had to get back to work and Iris had to return to her studies. The fact that Naomi hadn't been entirely on her side about the impossibility of things with Erin gave Iris a slim hope that Erin would find the just-right way to convince her to give things another try. Life—her life at least—didn't often leave room for hope, though. So she pushed it aside.

Regardless, Erin at least deserved an answer. It wasn't fair to leave her hanging, thinking that Iris was contemplating a way through this if she was already convinced one didn't exist.

* * *

Those conversations with Candice and Naomi had Erin even more top of mind than she'd already been over the last couple of weeks. While serving her tables at Dialogue, Iris kept looking around as if she might spot Erin in another section, nose in a magazine or book, taking slow bites of her dinner. At the same time, she didn't think Erin would come here without them talking, and she felt a little bad at taking this place away from her. When things had been going well between them, electricity had been in the air when Erin had come in to eat, and they would trade glances and smiles across the dining room. She always sat in someone else's section like she didn't want to play favorites, which Iris liked very much. Besides, it would be strange to get a tip from her. Late in the evening, Erin would go away, coming back when Iris was done with her shift, even if they only had ten minutes to talk while Erin walked her to the T.

It wasn't like Iris *wanted* things between them to be over. It was more like the universe was twisting her arm, and she had no choice but to comply. History was not on her side here. Inequalities like this were constantly going awry: white saviors or gold diggers being the most common tropes. What good was studying history if one didn't learn from it?

She was in the back with Greg, waiting for orders when he said, "Have you heard from Erin? She hasn't been here in a while."

"No. Why should I?"

"I thought you guys were, you know, close." He leaned on the word. "I've seen her hanging around after close, waiting for you to come out."

Why hadn't they been more circumspect? Greg didn't need to be involved in her love life in any way, shape, or form. "I'm not her keeper. Maybe she found another restaurant to frequent, something even more expensive than this one."

Greg took a conspicuous step back from her.

She grimaced. "Sorry. I don't know why she hasn't been in," she lied. "Is it me or have the orders been slow tonight?"

"Carl's out. Stomach flu."

"Ah, that's the worst."

"I'd rather do almost anything than throw up. Here's mine." He took two earthenware dishes from the counter separating them from the kitchen and turned toward the dining room.

Was she not going to be able to escape Erin even if she actually ended things? At least Erin hadn't dragged it out even longer. Getting over her would be a lost cause otherwise. She took this opportunity of the kitchen's sluggishness to slide over to where the staff put their things and check her phone. Speak of the devil, there was a text from Erin. It was long, and she didn't really have time to read it, but she did anyway.

I know you're angry, and you have every right to your feelings even if they don't conform with my desire to hear from you. There are some things I want you to know that I haven't had an opportunity to tell you. Most notably: I had been in a relationship with someone when the sale went through. Over time, the money changed everything. She expected things, assumed things, wanted things, and it was like I was just a means to an end. Almost immediately, we weren't in the same place. She wanted the money more than me.

Iris watched her phone as if the power of her gaze would make another text appear. When one wasn't forthcoming, she slipped her phone back in her bag and went to serve her next order and get back to business. Through rips in her focus as she serviced her tables and managed the customers' response to the delays in the kitchen, parts of that text kept surfacing. Erin as a means to an end was a terrible thought, as was someone fixated on the money.

But there hadn't been lies in that scenario. No one had been blindsided.

The next lull, she went back to her bag and her phone, not knowing if she wanted to have another text or if she hoped that was all Erin had to say on the matter. There was another message, as long as the previous.

We loved each other, and she betrayed me for my money. It broke me, not just my heart but my ability to trust people with the fact of my wealth. Clearly, I'm not the best judge of character, and I've spent the last year and a half protecting myself. I wanted to trust you from the beginning, but I couldn't allow that. I was afraid at our start that if I told you, I couldn't be sure if you liked me for me or for my bank account. If you insist on seeing my keeping this close to my chest as a lie, I can't argue with you. But I'd hope you see that motive counts for something, and maybe now you understand mine.

Iris put her phone away with some reluctance. Since she'd walked out on Erin, she'd thought she needed an apology—though whether that would make her stay was another matter. But Erin wasn't contrite. She stood by her decisions, and where that should have made Iris angry again, it gave her pause. She knew a cautionary tale when she saw one and had intimate knowledge of people's natures being as changeable as the weather. While Erin's issues were beyond even the one-percent's problems, she had struggled with them. Was still struggling with them. Iris could appreciate that.

The rest of the shift was bonkers until the very end when her section eased toward peacefulness out of attrition. She had one obvious date at a two-top and another table with two couples she imagined had babysitters at home and were stretching out their evening of freedom. While she waited for these tables to ask for their checks, she composed a response to Erin in her mind, not sure if she'd actually send it or not. She'd say that she understood, that she doubted she would be changed by Erin's money, that she was still hurt by the underhanded approach, that she still felt the same way about the whole thing, that she was sorry she'd taken Dialogue away from her.

She told herself she didn't have to respond right away. She didn't have to respond ever, though that felt more and more like cowardice. What if Erin tried to convince her that the money wasn't a problem, that they could be equal despite it? Even though Erin claimed to be through with fanciful notions where her money and other people were concerned, Iris didn't want to take part in any kind of experiment that was likely to end in disaster.

At the end of her shift, she looked at her phone before she was even out the door. As she expected, there was another text.

I understand that part of your issue with me is due to the dramatic difference in our financial circumstances, and there's nothing I can do about that. In fact, there's nothing I can do that might convince you to give us another try. I can't help where I am, just like you can't help where you are, but isn't there room for a lot of you-and-I between our different worlds? We were you-and-I in a deeply satisfying, exciting, and profound way in such a short time. Isn't there a way for us not to get back there but to go forward in a way equally as good, now that the truth is between us?

There it was: the question. What she'd been dreading since the first text. Her answer had seemed much clearer this afternoon than it felt right now. She couldn't deny that their connection had grown strong very quickly. From the beginning, it had seemed like Erin had always been there. All of her good qualities were still on display even as she wasn't atoning for her lie of omission. Iris had trusted her, and even though that trust was broken, she couldn't keep herself from trusting these texts as Erin's best truth. It was increasingly difficult to consider walking away from all that.

On her way to the T, she thought about what to do now. Those kinds of texts shouldn't go unanswered, but the only answer that still seemed like a safe bet was "no." She blamed her rapid stride for not taking out her phone and typing just that, softening it enough to spare Erin the worst of it, but something else was keeping her from being so definitive. The truth was that she wanted what Erin was proposing, but she couldn't let herself have it. The want was an insidious temptress, whispering about possibility and exceptions. The want, though, spelled disaster more often than not.

Still, she couldn't answer Erin.

* * *

Two days later, after her shift at Dialogue, she shouldered her bag, pushed her way out of the restaurant, and almost ran right into Erin.

"Sorry." Erin gripped her arms to steady her. Almost as quickly as her hands were there, they were gone again, shoved neatly in her pockets. "Sorry," she said again.

"What are you doing here?"

"Did you get my texts? I thought maybe you might…" She had a pinched look on her face, and Iris hated herself for wanting to soothe it away.

"You can't just show up like this."

"I know. I do, I swear. I guess this is what I do when someone ghosts me. I just…did you get my texts?"

Greg exited the restaurant and gave Iris an impressively raised eyebrow at her present company but headed away without a word. Iris followed his lead but turned left at the sidewalk to his right. Erin stuck with her like she was at heel.

Iris said, "I got them."

"So you understand why I did what I did?"

"Yes, but not what you're doing now." She was hoofing it but was unable to shake Erin, not that she was sure she wanted to, which was infuriating. "I told you I needed time."

"And I needed you to talk to me. Or let me talk to you. I can't stand imagining the absolute worst of what you might be thinking. Turns out I don't have endless patience when a big part of my future is on the line."

"We're barely anything yet."

"That doesn't mean that I don't want us to be more. Right now, if possible. Listen, can you slow down?" Iris couldn't, not yet. "Fine, okay. Listen. Catherine and I started our company on an idea, a hunch, the barest of market research and planning. I believed in it that much, and I believe in us in exactly the same way. Listen, okay? Iris." She stopped walking.

Iris let momentum carry her several steps away before she turned around, her arms crossed over her chest. "What?" The word was too loud for the hour and Erin's entreaties.

"I knew right away that I wanted to invest myself in you like I did in my company. Maybe it was idealistic and naïve, but I felt like something special would grow between us, given half a chance. I think we both gave it every chance, and now you're already inside me." She put her hand over her heart. "I would have bet everything that you felt the same. If we let my money ruin that, it would be many times worse than what it did to me and Hayley."

The worst part was that right until Erin had come clean, Iris would have agreed. Truthfully, she couldn't get herself to entirely disagree now. Erin standing there, open to Iris's gaze, shrouded in the aura of truth, was a compelling sight. The pro/con list in Iris's mind shifted precariously.

She dropped her arms to her sides. "I know you're not worried about me and your money, but I still worry about you."

"That was pretty clear with the whole charity thing."

"That was a knee-jerk reaction."

"A pretty vehement one."

"Because I know you well enough to see how you might want to become a savior to me and maybe even my family. Maybe you'll start by chipping in on an emergency or maybe you'll think I'm working too hard and want to help so I can reduce hours or whole jobs. You won't be able to stop yourself because it'll feel good. It'll feel fair. But it'll reduce me to a charity in your mind. We'll never be equal because of it."

Erin gestured at the road next to them. "Calling you an Uber isn't charity. It's a vehicle for affection and concern for your safety."

"I'm not saying it's going to be this way right from the beginning, but you'll start paying for activities or meals I can't afford because you want them. You'll want to go on a trip and will pay my way so you won't be alone. Balance in relationships is so important, and there are so many ways this will screw with that."

"Iris, you're not hearing me. I don't need expensive things. I just need you." This was said with her hand still over her heart.

In her truest self, Iris admitted that need was an expansive, terrifying word and that it pretty accurately reflected how she felt about Erin under her fear and reason. But if she didn't have reason, where would she be? Waiting tables at the Main Street Diner next to Naomi, praying that nothing, including herself, would break down because she could never scrape together enough savings to be prepared for an emergency. Reason had gotten her to where she was and would get her into a profession she loved and one that provided dental.

With her hand lingering over her heart, Erin was such an arresting sight. After over two weeks away, Iris saw her anew. She was so earnest, shoulders back and neck straight, her hair stirring in the evening's breeze, darker in the night's velvet, her fingers spread over the navy blue of her T-shirt. So much of Iris wanted to go to her, pull her in close, say she felt the same way, endeavor to try this grand experiment.

The rest of her stood rooted to the spot. Being disciplined and realistic had never been so difficult before, and that made her pro/con list fiendishly challenging, each side weighted by different levels of effort for various degrees of benefit. The truth was that she wanted what Erin was offering, wanted so much to be able to convince herself that she should believe in them like Erin had believed in her company.

"Iris?" Erin whispered.

"I don't know what to do."

Erin took a small step closer, her body quiet like she was trying not to startle elusive wildlife. "Can't we just try? Go into it with open eyes, come up with some rules that make each of us feel safe, and know that if it doesn't work, it'll hurt, but the world won't end. Can't we do that?"

The world might not end, but Iris already knew that it would feel like it. Was Erin worth the risk? Was she allowed to give herself this thing she wanted so desperately?

Erin slid closer. "Iris. Just decide about tonight. We can deal with tomorrow in the morning."

"You can't lie to me anymore."

"I'll try not to keep things from you again."

Iris laughed. "That means nothing."

"I'm being as truthful as I can. No one can promise not to lie. I've got a whole history I'll try to be as open about as possible. I'll be honest in our discussions and in answer to your questions. I'll keep you in mind when I make decisions. I won't promise something I don't know if I can keep."

Iris took her time digesting that.

"I pride myself on being a good person and doing what I say I'm going to do, and I hope that's enough for you." Now Erin was right in front of her, her gaze direct and searching.

Despite everything, she believed Erin. And that made the decision for her. She groaned in surrender and pulled Erin to her, her arms trembling where they snaked around her ribcage. Erin returned the tight squeeze, saying, "Okay," in Iris's ear on repeat, like she was trying to convince them both. They stood that way for a long time on the deserted sidewalk before Iris finally loosened her grip and spoke.

"You said something about deciding about tonight?"

"Tomorrow's another day."

"Will you come home with me?"

"Lead the way." Erin gestured with an outstretched arm.

They started walking to the T, hand in hand, quiet now, the tension between them softened and diffuse. When they'd gone another block, though, Iris stopped. "Wait. You don't have roommates."

"Nope. I also have an unwrapped toothbrush I bought for you weeks ago."

They turned around without another word and started walking again. "A toothbrush, huh?"

"Like you recognized on our first date—I'm an optimist."

"You're lucky I'm the forgiving sort."

"No, you're not."

Iris laughed, relief crackling through her chest. "You're right. I'm not."

They covered a couple of blocks in companionable quiet before Erin said, "I didn't mean to ambush you just now."

"Yes, you did."

"I didn't want it to seem like I was trying to strong-arm you. I mean, I was, but only so you'd talk to me, not anything else. At least I didn't just show up to eat and ask to be seated in your section."

"I might have accidently dropped a bowl of carrot soup in your lap."

"I realize I'm going to have to earn your trust again and that it won't happen overnight."

Iris tightened her fingers where they were entwined with Erin's. "I know that 'tomorrow's tomorrow' isn't the best foundation for a relationship, and I'll try to stop imagining the worst and having one foot out the door."

"That's still way better than both feet out the door."

"Maybe we need some ground rules. Like, you need prior approval for purchases related to me that are more than twenty dollars."

"I've been having a great time with you for way less than that. But does that mean I can never take you for dinner? That seems like a typical date-night scenario. Right now, all I can kind of cook is carbonara, but it was a far cry from yours."

This got Iris to stop. "I haven't known you very long, but that seems kind of momentous."

"It felt momentous, aside from my practically incinerating the pancetta."

"Are you going to cook something for me?"

"Probably not." Erin laughed. "That's way too much pressure. Hence my desire to take you out to dinner every once in a while."

Iris pulled them back in motion again. "As long as it's not egregious."

"Once a month? Biweekly? I'm sure weekly is too much to ask."

"We'll take it as it comes. Tomorrow's tomorrow, after all."

They'd come up on the Public Gardens. Erin steered them inside and to the weeping beech. They stood contemplating it for a while. Its leaves, dark in the fuzzed light from the streetlamps, fluttered in the sweet, late-summer breeze.

Erin said, "Now, whenever I'm here, I think of you."

Iris pulled her close and kissed her. Right. Erin's lips had grown familiar so quickly. She let the kiss linger until her mouth eased open and welcomed Erin's tongue. Right, again. Their kiss deepened quickly and steadily until Iris knew they shouldn't be doing this in the emptied-out public park, but she still couldn't quite get herself to stop. Erin obliterated her self-restraint in every way.

Erin was the one to pull away. "One traffic light and one hill, and we'll be there."

Their talking was over, and their pace became more determined. They dashed diagonally through an intersection and hoofed it up the hill to Erin's place until they were both breathing heavily. The air between them was taut with tension while Erin pulled her keys out of a pocket and slid one home. This time, the steps to the second floor were familiar, though the feelings they evoked were entirely different.

At the top, Iris grabbed Erin and kissed her again, untucking her shirt and running her fingers from her stomach around to the warmth of her back. When that wasn't enough, she pulled up on the hem of the shirt, getting it to under Erin's arms but unwilling to stop kissing long enough to rid her of it completely.

Again, Erin was the one to pull back. "One more flight of stairs to the bedroom, then no more interruptions."

Iris felt herself pause at the idea of a whole additional floor in this house-like apartment.

Into her hesitation, Erin said, "It's okay. I know it's not as appealing and cozy as your room, but I promise that my bed is comfortable."

Iris relaxed and smiled. "Your charm will only get you so far."

"As long as it gets you upstairs, I'll be happy."

Two other rooms and a bathroom shared space with Erin's bedroom suite upstairs. One had exercise equipment in it, and the other had a sterile-looking bed, nightstands, and dresser. Erin flipped on the light to her room. It was large and painted a deep green that made the watercolor artwork of nature scenes stand out in bright relief. The bed was made, its silvery comforter lustrous against the matte walls. Three big windows were decorated with heavy draperies and wooden blinds that matched the trim and crown molding.

Erin looked around with Iris as if seeing it for the first time herself. "I had help—with the whole house. A designer. I would have been lost otherwise."

"It's beautiful."

"Come here." She pulled Iris to her. "I like how much of you is in your room. I don't want to stop staying over there just because I don't have roommates."

"I think you've got more than no roommates going for you here."

"Fine, but can we maybe stop talking now?" Instead of waiting for an answer, she kissed Iris, picking up where they'd left off downstairs.

They shed their clothes with sharp desperateness between rough kisses, leaving a trail of garments from the door to the bed, not able to get naked fast enough. Erin ripped the comforter and sheet half off the bed and ushered in Iris, who quickly scooted over to make room for Erin. She rolled over on top of her to feel all of Erin's skin against her own, the press of her bones, the heat of her belly. Erin was both familiar and startlingly new after their hiatus, and she wanted them to mark each other in this way after having been marked by deception and fear earlier.

Erin's hands roamed over and across her back and down her arms, nails dragging across her flesh, which was a pleasure tinged with pain on her sensitive skin. Iris kissed and bit her neck and whispered, "What do you want?"

"This. To be close to you."

"Close like this?" She slipped one leg between Erin's.

Erin's head pushed back into the pillow, her chin sliding past Iris's ear with a quiet whoosh. "Yeah, like that. I want to touch you. I want to taste you. I kind of want everything." She blew out breath in a laugh.

"Me, too."

She pushed Iris off and onto her back and, without another word, took one of her small breasts in her mouth, sucking hard on the skin and nipple, engulfing it in warmth and wetness. Meanwhile, her hand cupped the other breast, pinching its nipple in rhythm. Iris tilted her head down to watch Erin, red hair falling across an eye, a flush in her lightly freckled cheeks. Close like this. Only now did Iris let herself feel how much she'd missed Erin over the last few weeks, how much she'd wished what had happened hadn't.

Erin spent a delirious amount of time lavishing attention on Iris's breasts, having learned that they were a gateway to the nirvana of Iris's orgasm. By the time she moved down Iris's body, her nails dragging down her sides like their first time, Iris's nerve endings were almost unbearably sensitive from her scalp down to her ankles, and all she could think about was what Erin was going to do next. The soft heat of Erin's cheeks brushed against her stomach as she nuzzled the skin around Iris's belly button. Iris's breath was shallow with anticipation, and she clutched at bunches of Erin's fine, electric hair, moving her head this way and that. The ceiling was the white of ceilings everywhere, and the only thing there was in this room, in this apartment, in this whole building was her and Erin.

"Come on," she urged, and Erin answered by settling herself between Iris's legs and covering Iris's center with her hot mouth. Pleasure rolled through her in a wave, and she closed her eyes to keep it inside. She opened her legs wide and held Erin against her. Erin's tongue probed her entrance and circled back up to her clit, the motion both lazy and purposeful. She kept it up for a while until she pushed two fingers inside Iris, which loosened a groan she remembered she didn't have to stifle.

Iris could relax into Erin, whose ease and persistence made her feel expertly taken care of, made her unashamed of how long it might take her to come, made her not even wonder if she would come in the first place. She abandoned herself into the slow build of hot pleasure that radiated through her body, feeling Erin inside her, against her, so close and intimate. She knew acutely that it was Erin doing this, but she felt untethered, released from everything but what she was feeling. She arched her back, and it built and built and built, until she couldn't contain it anymore, and orgasm washed over her, her torso cramping with the power of it, and she cried out, satisfyingly loud and long. Erin teased out aftershocks until Iris collapsed, boneless and wonderfully out of control.

Erin crawled up her, her knees on either side of her hips, her chest pressed to Iris's, face in her neck, moving it just enough to breathe rapidly into Iris's ear. "That was amazing."

All Iris could do was nod. It felt so good to have Erin pressed against her, grounding her on the comfortable mattress, the ceiling holding them inside, keeping them together. Erin was quiet while Iris's blood rearranged itself throughout her body, making things like thought possible again.

Close like this. Maybe this was makeup sex, but Iris felt changed by it. By the way Erin was clinging to her, she suspected this change was mutual. Instead of picking up where they'd left off before the cliff of Erin's truth, it was as if they'd jumped far into the deep end of the waters below with only each other to keep afloat. As much as Iris may have wanted to maintain a certain remove of distrust, she felt differently now. What should have frightened her only made her run her hands up and down Erin's back, scratching in echo of what Erin had done to her until Erin let herself go and settled herself even more fully on Iris's chest.

But as much as Iris loved the weight of Erin, she said, "Sit up."

Without delay—and without asking why, which thrilled her— Erin complied, settling back on her heels, her pale chest flushed red, her breasts tempting in their fullness. Iris reached up and thumbed their nipples until they pushed hard against her fingers. Erin's gaze remained adamantly on her, her fingers pressing lightly against Iris's ribs for balance.

Iris moved one of her hands between Erin's legs, Erin lifting herself up a couple of inches to give Iris room. Iris smiled at the wetness she felt, the slippery evidence of Erin's arousal. She slid one finger inside, then a second one, making slow, even strokes, Erin's hips moving in time. Erin felt so beautiful, and this was another way of coming home.

Erin made a soft whimper, but instead of increasing her pace, Iris said, "Touch yourself." Despite everything they'd said about equality, Iris wanted this kind of power over her.

A raised eyebrow answered that, but Erin moved one hand between her legs, and her fingers started to circle her clit. She bit her lip, and her eyes fluttered closed, her head tilting back, showing her neck. Iris wanted to bite it, partly for her own pleasure and maybe a little to punish Erin for lying, but she was committed to this course of action. Erin's motions sped up, and Iris matched her, thrusting faster and more deeply. Her breath quickened along with Erin's in the delicious lead up to her climax, which caused Erin to still and groan, then again and again while both their hands worked together to draw out the orgasm until Erin collapsed on her back next to Iris, tangled in the sheets.

"Jesus," Erin said.

In response, Iris turned on her side and sank her teeth into Erin's shoulder, not being gentle or quick about it.

"Ow."

Iris relinquished her grip. "That's to remind you not to hurt me again."

"I'd already come to that conclusion, but okay."

"I'm serious. This has been incredible, but it doesn't erase what happened."

"I get that. I'm not likely to forget it, either. Listen. You're important to me. Very important. But you can't freeze me out like that. We need to be able to talk things through. I'm going to screw up sometimes, we both will because we're only human, so we need to be...gracious with each other."

Iris slipped an arm across Erin's chest, which was still red. "As in treat each other with grace?"

"Is that too religious for you, given your grandfather?"

Iris thought about it. While grace had a certain religious overtone, it felt different coming from Erin. Erin's texts had grace, her open declarations right there on the sidewalk had grace. She had gracefully turned Iris's pro/con list into a pro/pro list. Grace in this meaning required Iris to hold on to the softening that had let Erin back in, extend trust to her, treat her with the care Iris now knew she deserved.

"It's perfect. The only thing that would be more perfect is if you stayed in bed and went to sleep with me. It's almost late enough, isn't it?"

"Turn over." Iris did, and Erin fit herself behind her, chest to Iris's back, one arm under her neck and the other draped over Iris's waist. "At the very least I'll hold you until you're asleep."

That was all Iris could ask.

CHAPTER THIRTEEN

Beside the fact that Iris was always working, Erin's life was so far beyond good that good was a laughable concept. As soon as they had gone beyond their hurt and anger, they'd found another gear of togetherness. Now, Iris stayed at Erin's place half of the nights she worked at Dialogue, and Erin made the trek out to Allston at least once a week, spending the wee hours at Iris's desk, occasionally working on a consulting deliverable and sometimes reading the thick volumes and journals that cluttered its surface. Heavy stuff indeed, and it gave them even more to talk about, not that they needed help in that area. Given that it was a part of Iris's family history, Erin better understood her staunch pessimism. So much harm—or at least foolishness—had been done in the name of God. How a man of the cloth could abandon his daughter and young granddaughter to try to save people who should be left alone was beyond Erin's wildest imagination.

Still, though Iris tended to expect the worst, or at least prepared for it, she walked around seemingly as happy as Erin. Though it had been happening on its own before their grand pause, their fracture had accelerated their ability to confide in each other: about family, about studies, about discrimination, about hopes and dreams, though Erin had precious few of those and still paid lip service to her consulting business. It bothered her, but it was easy to bury under her relationship with Iris. The farther they got from Erin's donation to reinstate Iris's grant, the easier it was to push that action aside and consider it part of the deep past that never needed to be spoken about.

They took walks along the river, had coffee at The Thinking Cup, sat together in the Public Gardens, read across from each other on Erin's couch or the dilapidated one in Iris's apartment. Iris consented to being taken to an Italian dinner back in the North End that wasn't too expensive, and Erin never ever offered to call an Uber for her again. She did catch herself wanting to buy Iris things: frivolous clothes, organizational tools, weekly date nights out, a new skillet. Most of them were things she would have gifted her girlfriends with, even before the sale of her company, but now Erin stifled the urge. Maybe later, when the inception of this rift was well behind them and Iris could find some grace in accepting presents like that.

Grace was working out well as a guiding principle for them. They deeply considered each other, elevated common courtesy, communicated regularly, and gave and took compliments without pause or argument. Erin wouldn't say that they were careful with each other, but they did treat each other with care, which felt different. Either way, it was working, and as the days peeled off the calendar, she felt more confident in them as a couple, which was thrilling.

When she was alone, though, which was still most of the time, she worried over her lack of ambition. Iris was one of the most driven people she knew, and she was coming up short in comparison. If she didn't figure it out soon, she might not be what Iris wanted in a partner. As it was, Iris didn't know exactly to what degree Erin was or wasn't working on her consulting engagements. Leaving this fuzzed followed the letter of the law about honesty but played around with the spirit of it. It was temporary, she told herself, just until she figured out her next move.

Meanwhile, as a distraction, she and Shannon put together an afternoon session for some classmates of hers, one where Erin was supposed to talk about interviewing techniques. She cleared off everything from her dining room table, turning the room into a seminar environment with just enough space for everyone who was scheduled to show up. This talk was supposed to be part of follow-up engagements with her consulting contracts, though since she hadn't pushed to get one converted, she'd never used the material in front of a live, studio audience. Nerves sparked under her skin in a not-unpleasant way as she paced around, waiting for her "students" to arrive.

Finally, her doorbell rang, and things began, the attendees arriving in one big clump, carrying huge backpacks and small purses, wearing Chuck Taylors or sandals or big Doc Martens boots. Most of them had hair longer than Erin's, and they all sported jeans or leggings in comparison to Erin's deep-green slacks and cream-colored blouse. The eight- or nine-year gap in age between Erin and them loomed large.

Erin stood at the head of the table, a recently purchased whiteboard propped on the buffet behind her. "I think you all know each other, but for my sake, let's do a quick round of introductions before we start in."

It was easier than she thought it would be. She started with the lay of the land.

"An interview is an interrogation, and you can't leave the table until you've gotten what you want." She followed that with lecture-style content: "Nothing happens without a rapport, so let's break down how to create one." Then came the all-important exercises: "Pair up and try to get information about the other person's favorite meal. Remember rapport. And details!" She closed it out with a question-and-answer session. The two hours she'd planned on went by before she knew it—and before she'd delivered all of her material. The whole thing was electric, and by the time she was done, she was sure she wasn't going to be able to sleep that night, even though bedtime was still almost twelve hours away.

As the young women packed up their laptops and chatted amongst themselves, Shannon came up to Erin. "Thank you so much. That was exactly what we need that isn't covered in our curriculum. We get bits of it from projects and group work, but it's not nearly this comprehensive."

"Good, I'm glad you found it valuable. It was my pleasure."

"Do you have other topics you could cover with us? I know that's kind of presumptuous, because you're not getting paid for this, but everyone would definitely come to more of these. Right, guys?"

There was a general, enthusiastic assent from the group, which warmed the cockles of Erin's heart. The last time she'd felt needed in a professional way was right at the sale of the company, and she only realized now how much she'd missed it. Though she couldn't imagine a reason why she'd say no to more of what had just happened, she played it cool. "Let me look at my schedule and get back to you."

"That would be great. Just text if you're willing, and I'll get the crew organized again."

When "the crew" vacated the apartment, Erin lay on her couch, her head buzzing like the best parts of being tipsy. She wanted to do something, but she just put a hand under her head and crossed her legs at the ankles. The soft beige of her walls was made darker by an overcast sky outside, and she thought about calling Iris, then Catherine, but she didn't make a move toward her phone. Instead, she lived with the last two hours, replaying the good parts and the misses, trying to sear some of her phrasing into her memory for the next time she might be called upon to deliver the material.

She wanted to do just that, like she hadn't wanted anything since Nuvio. Her desire moved beyond hosting eight young women in her dining room and presenting the second part of the interviewing material. She wanted to do something like this a lot more, for a lot more people. That had been a vague part of her vision for her consulting company, but she hadn't thought to position herself as an educator first. Wasn't it kind of pompous to consider herself a teacher? She had no training in pedagogy or actual experience running a classroom. Mentorship, yes, that had been a part of her management style since employee number three at Tribar. Was it possible to make a mentorship and educational business that operated at an angle to what she was marketing herself as right now?

She sat up, brushed hair from her face, and thought again of calling Iris. Her watch told her that Iris was in a sectional, actually teaching a real subject to serious students. Iris would have tons of information and advice for Erin, though she wondered how Iris would take Erin wanting to jump into education without all the groundwork Iris was right in the middle of doing with her PhD. What would she think of Erin's quiet epiphany? Would she be supportive or suspicious of this new educational push? Would she wonder, like Erin did, who her students would be and how she could get herself recognized as an expert in the many things she now wanted to teach? Would she see this and extrapolate back to how little Erin had invested in consulting? Would she see Erin's subterfuge about her company? Would that break where they'd gotten to now?

Lying was such a strong word for how Erin presented her consulting. But the reality was that her rhetoric had been aspirational more than anything and lacked a strong sense of direction other than "help change things." She wanted to make an impact—which she'd assumed would be through consulting to corporate clients. It had presumed substantial hourly rates, in part to make the content seem valuable, but now she saw more clearly that making money was a secondary matter. How could it not be, given how much she already had—and how problematic that amount had been for her?

Leaving her phone on the kitchen counter, she walked into her office and sat at her desk. She opened her laptop, started a new document, and rode a wave of concentration through dinner and into the evening. The amount of information about teaching, especially about teaching adults, that she found out there in articles, blogs, and books shouldn't have been surprising, but it made deciding where to start challenging. She wanted to know it all right now and relished the idea of having her nose in a book for the foreseeable future. Learning new things was almost as good as teaching new things, and she felt the snap and crackle of inspiration. It wasn't like the pop of her idea that had driven TriBar, but it was remarkably close.

There was so much she didn't understand yet—how to get students and of what demographics, what kind of curriculum would work best, how to make the material tangible and facilitate the practicing of ideas, and even how to expand and get recognized experts to teach what they knew best. For the first time since selling out to Nuvio, she felt like she'd found a worthy investment for her attention. If she could pull it off (and pulling it off was still wildly ill-defined), it might make the kind of impact she'd been pining after for the last few years.

She was ordering a dozen different books, having them shipped out as soon as possible, when she heard Iris's special ringtone coming from the kitchen. Though she still had some hesitation about talking to Iris, professional teacher, she answered with a smile on her face. "Hey, I wasn't sure I'd hear from you." Iris's schedule had dictated a quick commute directly from her sectional to Dialogue, and now it was in the middle of her shift.

"It's weirdly slow tonight, so I snuck out for my union-mandated Erin break."

"I knew I liked unions. How was your class?"

"Really good. They're still getting used to each other, though, so sometimes conversation is difficult. It'll flow better in a few more sessions."

"They're probably all intimidated by you."

"Doubtful. How was your mentoring today? I imagine you cut a more intimidating figure than I do."

"It was great. Really got my juices flowing. It actually made me want to talk to you about some things when you have any downtime." Erin sat on one of the counter stools. "Speaking of, are you coming over tonight?"

"If I think I can get there without falling asleep on my feet."

"I'm going to have a firm talk with your workload."

"Don't. I'll be there tonight, I promise."

"It's okay if you need to go home."

"No. I'd rather see you even if it'll only be for a few minutes before I pass out."

The words warmed Erin beyond the glow she'd gotten from her research. "Your key will be under the succulent pot." Erin had been gently trying to get Iris to take a key to her place, and Iris had been just as gently refusing. Hiding one under the big planter by the front door was Erin's way of giving it to Iris without actually giving it. Erin wasn't sure why Iris wouldn't take this next step—maybe she thought it was too soon or was afraid to get too comfortable in Erin's home—but Erin only pushed it this far. She liked hearing a key other than hers slide home in the lock and Iris's light step in the front hall while Erin waited supine on the couch.

In her office, Erin circled back to the thought of including other people in this enterprise. Wasn't the most exciting thing about the idea that it could be much bigger than herself? Starting the company with Catherine had been both deeply personal and about creating an entity that existed beyond the bounds of either of them. They served it first, then each other, then themselves, and that hierarchy had felt perfectly appropriate. This was what had been missing with the consulting company. It existed on the back of her name, she was the face at every meeting, it was her approach behind everything. Her her her.

She had no idea how to achieve the image that was forming inside her head, but she hadn't let that stop her before. Catherine would understand, but Erin wasn't ready to tell her anything. She would be supportive, but she would ask too many questions. Her ability to poke holes in still-nascent thought was legendary and was part of what had made them work together so well, but there were enough holes in the idea already without Catherine's laser-like commentary. Instead, Erin went back to her desk and researched 501(c)(3) nonprofit organizations. She wasn't sure it would play into what was taking shape in her head, but it seemed useful information regardless.

Still engrossed in her research, Erin missed the sound of the key in the door, even missed it opening and closing. She only came around when she heard Iris call her name and the key clink against the stone top of her entryway table. She hustled from the office to where Iris was dropping her things on the dining room table.

"Hey," Erin said and pulled her into an embrace.

Iris sagged against her. "Hey."

"Long day?"

"You mean it's not over yet?"

"Come on." She pulled away and took Iris's hand. "Let's get you to bed."

"You seem happy."

"To see you? Of course."

Iris followed her up the stairs. "No, in a not-related-to-me way."

"I have an idea, but it's too early to talk about it."

"An idea for what?"

"Just an idea. I'll tell you more when I know more."

They arrived at the bedroom, and Erin took the initiative to unbutton Iris's black work shirt and untuck it from her pants. Iris said, "Personal idea or professional?"

Erin considered that for a moment before smiling. "Yes."

Iris shoved her lightly. "I'll get it out of you one way or the other."

"Oh, do you have ulterior motives? Because I'm all for that."

"You're way too awake right now."

Erin unhooked her bra and unbuttoned her pants. While she pulled the zipper down, she said, "Definitely."

"Does that mean you won't come to bed with me? I want to go to sleep with you."

"I'll at least stay until you're asleep." It had become a common refrain.

Their conversation petered out while they brushed their teeth and washed their faces, Iris in one of Erin's T-shirts and a pair of workout shorts that hung low on her hips and brushed her knees. She sat on the edge of the bed and redid her braid in a looser configuration for the night, a sight Erin would never tire of seeing. It was so automatic and quick and intimate, and Iris was half-asleep already when she did it.

Then, finally, they were settled together under the covers, Iris's head pillowed on Erin's shoulder, her arm heavy across Erin's ribs. After a quick, chaste kiss, Erin said, "Wake me when you get up."

"I don't know why you insist on that."

"Because I do."

Iris chuckled, resettled her head, and was asleep in a matter of minutes, which left Erin staring at the ceiling, at least a couple of hours away from being able to follow her into slumber. In the deep quiet of the bedroom, Iris's breath was a low, rhythmic hum, and Erin listened to it for a while, trying to calm down to its soft push and pull. Sometimes it seemed crazy for Iris to come here, given that she fell asleep right away and woke up while Erin was still deeply asleep herself. It was more than sex, though that was certainly part of the allure. It was still, quiet moments like these, everyday conversation, seeing Iris in her clothes doing nightly routines next to her in the bathroom.

Erin had only been partly kidding about having words with Iris's workload. Her exhaustion wasn't healthy. Erin suspected that Iris could exist well enough without working so much at Dialogue, with her grant and stipend from being a teacher's assistant, not that Erin knew what that amounted to. Dialogue was a buffer, was savings to help her mom, was the fear of not having enough. Iris was right about Erin feeling an itch to help out. There was no one more deserving to be comfortable, but it was Iris's decision. Erin had done more than enough already, though Iris, thankfully, would never know who was behind that anonymous donation. Sometimes, Erin wished she could come clean about it and have nothing between them, but it was impossible. Best for it to melt away into history.

Iris impressed Erin deeply, and Erin wanted to deserve her. She wanted to do something worthy of Iris's admiration. Maybe this idea would get her there. She itched to go back downstairs and continue researching and reading, though she should actually watch some mindless TV or listen to music that might calm her enough to sleep. If only there was a way to stay here, warm with Iris, and also be in her office. Alas, she hadn't mastered the art of being in two places at once, even though the skill would have been handy in the early days of TriBar. She'd never wished it so completely as in this situation, though. She'd always been happy enough to abandon girlfriends to sleep, even Hayley, while she burned the midnight oil.

Iris was different, not that Erin didn't already know that. Erin lay there, pinned in place by Iris for a long while, warm and comfortable even as her mind spun. She waited a half hour before disengaging herself from Iris and easing the door closed when she exited.

* * *

Iris woke her after maybe half a night's sleep, which was an insult of the highest degree. Truly, why did she insist on her doing this? Everything was too bright, the slide of Iris's hand down her arm jarring her roughly from a dream. She mumbled something garbled, not even remotely words produced by thought, and buried her face in her pillow.

Iris's fingers sifted through her hair, which felt kind of nice, and she kissed Erin's ear, which could have been worse. Maybe waking wasn't absolute hell after all. Erin opened one eye to check the bedside clock. "You didn't sleep enough."

"You're one to talk."

"Why are you up so early?"

"I have things to do."

Erin finally turned over and really looked at Iris. She was smiling and very awake, though with a hint of the bruising of exhaustion under her eyes. Erin reached up to run her thumb across one cheek. "Stay for breakfast?"

"I already had some cereal."

"You were supposed to wake me when you got up. I would have eaten with you."

"It was too early for you to eat."

"Well, I would have sat across the table from you and stared at you while you ate."

"Erin, you need to go back to sleep."

Erin sat up, the covers falling from her. "I'm just trying to get as much time with you as I can."

"I'm sorry I can't take afternoon walks with you anymore."

"I'm not asking for walks, though they would be awesome. I just want some time in the morning before you leave."

Iris frowned, and Erin regretted pushing her.

"I can't be as flexible as you are. School and work keep me busier than your consulting."

"I'm working on changing that."

"I'm not commenting on your time. I'm talking about myself." But she slid one hand down Erin's arm when she said it. It didn't help.

"In relation to me."

"Hey, I didn't mean anything by it. I'm just complaining. If I didn't have these obligations, I'm sure I would spend my time more like you do."

Somehow that didn't make Erin feel better. "I'm figuring it out."

"Figuring what out?"

"How to make a contribution."

"I'm sure you make a contribution to your clients."

"That's not what I'm talking about. A larger contribution. An impact." Now that she'd done it once with TriBar, anything less, especially in the face of Iris's dedication, was akin to failure. She hadn't always felt like this, but that level of success changed things.

Iris took Erin's hand and squeezed it. "I'm not judging you. It's just that in some ways we're in very different places."

Erin took a breath. "I remember being in your place. It's not fun, but it's also exciting. I wish you didn't have to work so hard, not only because I'd be able to see you more."

"I want that, too. This is temporary."

"Three years doesn't feel temporary to me."

Iris brought Erin's knuckles to her lips and kissed them. "I love that you want to spend more time with me. I want to spend more time with you, too."

"Just not today."

"Just not today."

"Okay. I'll come downstairs with you and demand kisses before you leave."

"What a hardship."

Iris was gone too soon, and Erin was too awake after that conversation to go back to sleep. Iris had tried to cover for it, but it was clear that she would have only so much patience for Erin if she wasn't really working. The idea of Iris being disappointed in her made her chest tight. It was already bad enough that she had too much money, but if she used that money to just slide through life, Iris would lose all respect for her. Erin had to hurry up and create something tangible before the untruths about her consulting business broke through her happy façade and ruined everything.

CHAPTER FOURTEEN

Iris hadn't often been this happy, and she wondered how much she could trust it. The only thing that would make it better is if there were more hours in the day. Everything with Naomi was steady. She'd even applied for two different jobs in Allentown despite her reservations. One didn't even have to materialize. Iris was just happy with the intent. There were no problems with the new car (yet), and slowly but surely, Iris's savings were inching their way upward, having nowhere else to go. In another few months, she could stop worrying about expenses that came out of left field because she'd have a buffer to take care of them—or help Naomi take care of them. Nothing made Iris relax more than a buffer…and Erin.

If she had the chance, she'd lavish the extra hours she wished for on Erin. She'd watch Erin sleep in the morning, reading quietly next to her in bed. She'd cook her a meal or two—and teach her a straightforward recipe in that chef's kitchen of hers that was woefully neglected. She'd have more energy after her shifts at Dialogue and would spend them having luxurious sex with her. The way they were emotionally and mentally connected with each other in bed was far more of an aphrodisiac than oysters and chocolate. They could take an extended, ambling walk along the river or in Forest Hills Cemetery, where Erin had promised to take Iris for the trees and statuary.

Iris hadn't forgotten about Erin's lie about her money, but she'd softened to her privileged dilemma. After all, she wasn't about to open up her bank account for inspection by just anyone, either. Or anyone, period. Erin was proving to be the same person after the revelation as she'd been before. She had an incredible place to live and more time on her hands than a normal person, but she didn't seem inclined to drop money at the smallest whim and still ate premade supermarket salads several times a week even though she easily could have a personal chef. Not that Iris wanted her to. No, Iris wanted that job along with many others that centered around Erin. As for the money, there was so much of it that it refused to move from abstraction to something concrete in Iris's mind.

What Iris loved irrationally was that Erin still spent nights at her apartment, riding the interminable T through BU to the far hinterlands of Allston to then be pinned between Iris and the wall when in bed and forced to use a bathroom shared by three different women and all their hair. When Iris turned over, an hour or two into sleep, she would catch Erin, silhouetted by the desk lamp, bent to one text or another, and she'd feel a narcotized version of love that chased her all the way into morning. She wasn't ready to declare it to Erin yet, but she rode high on its swell of deep affection and more.

But the day didn't have extra hours, and she had a sectional to teach for the Africa in World History course. The classroom was in the College of Arts and Sciences building in the middle of a long hallway with institutional brick tile on the walls and dark, wooden doors. She held one of them open for a couple of students, smiling at them in greeting. Hidden from the view of the classroom at large, she could hear the chatter inside, which rose to the phrase, "She's playing at being Black." When she stepped inside the door, the general murmur choked off in such an immediate and damning way that Iris knew who the "she" was in that sentence.

She walked to the table at the front of the room, slipped off her heavy backpack, and dug through it to buy time and composure. The worst thing would be to show any reaction, not even one that would indicate that she'd even heard those words in the first place. She just hoped her voice would cooperate and not waver in her turmoil and anger. It wasn't the first time she'd heard something like this, just one variation on the theme of her skin not being dark enough, her hair not kinked enough, people thinking she was some other flavor of brown despite the flare of her nose and shape of her lips. But, somehow, it felt even more personal in this professional setting.

After finding her lecture notes, she scanned the room full of Black students, most of them darker than she was, not knowing if she wanted to find the guilty party or not. It didn't matter really, since it clearly had been a group discussion. Several people found other places to look than at her face, and her rage distilled down to a hard nugget that made it difficult to swallow. "Everyone ready?" Before waiting for any answer, she started in on the day's material—material she was more than qualified to deliver, no matter the color of her skin.

She stayed back after the class was over and was still at the head table, her notes spread out, when the next lecturer arrived. Despite the fact that she was supposed to go back to the library, she gathered up her things, found a bench along a rare square of grass in this urban campus, and felt a wave of heat flare through her under the still-strong, early-fall sun. Everything about her birth had been accidental, and she lived with the consequences of having a single mother and skin that didn't match anyone else's. Naomi was significantly darker than she was—dark enough that she got discriminated for the exact opposite reason that Iris had gotten flack for today.

Her choice of thesis was almost painfully personal, despite it not showing on her face. Her grandmother had been such a formative presence before she'd died, and Iris had always had a desire to understand her life first in the Congo and, later, Angola.

She wanted to understand her grandfather's sense of God-mandated ownership of the soil of Africa. She wanted to train her historian's eye on intersections like this because she was so emblematic of the same crossing of cultures and genes. But she couldn't win either way, being just dark enough not to be white and white enough to be considered an interloper to the study of African history in any form.

This was going to follow her through her academic career, so she'd better get used to it and grow a thicker skin than what she already had. The only thing she could do was be unimpeachable in her scholarship, which she'd already known and was why she worked herself hard enough that Erin took issue with the toll all her endeavors took on her.

She pulled out her phone but hesitated before calling Erin. Naomi would understand to some degree and would at least be offended on her behalf, but it was prime lunch hour, and she would be busy. Would Erin understand? Had there been anything in her life she was deemed ill-suited for by some physical characteristic she had no control over? Was there such a thing as discrimination against redheads? The freckle police? Not that Erin would have needed to personally experience something to commiserate with Iris, but she would feel better about it if she had. Instead of empathy for the hurt she had felt at that comment, she wanted the just-right constructive outrage that would only increase her fortitude for the course she was on.

Since calling Erin at any time was generally a good idea, Iris chose her name from her recents list and listened to the ringing of Erin's phone across town. She was about to hang up when Erin answered.

"This is a pleasant surprise. I thought you'd be buried in a book already after your sectional. How did it go?"

Sometimes Iris wished Erin wouldn't remember the intricacies of her schedule so well. "It was fine," she lied. Or at least withheld, since the meat of the class had passed without incident, and she'd covered all the material she'd slated for the hour.

"That's a rousing assessment."

"Clearly it's been a long time since you've been in school. Fine covers at least seventy-five percent of all lectures."

"True. I guess that's why I've preferred my learning to take place outside the classroom."

One of Erin's qualities that Iris loved the most was her seemingly insatiable desire to take in new information and become an expert on this thing or that. They were so well suited in that regard. "What're you up to?"

"Finding out how charities work."

"Is this for that thing you won't tell me about yet?"

"Patience is a virtue."

Iris laughed. "Patience is a bore."

"I know. Isn't it? I skip as many steps as I can…and some that I can't."

"It's good to hear your voice," she said around a smile.

"Ditto." A pause. "Is everything okay?"

"Yeah, why?"

"I don't know. You don't sound like yourself, and it's strange for you to call me in the middle of the day. I'm not complaining. Or prying. I swear. Just a concerned citizen."

"You can pry, but it'll probably make me clam up."

"It's okay if you don't want to talk about it or if I'm wrong and there's nothing going on."

Something about that made Iris slide even closer to love, and it took her breath for a moment. Then, even though she hadn't wanted to a minute ago, she told Erin what she'd overheard in the sectional.

"Are you kidding? That's beyond crass and wildly inaccurate."

"Thanks for saying that."

"I'm so sorry. I'm offended on your behalf. Is it any consolation that you can wipe the historical floor with them?"

It was, actually. "They're not the only ones who have ever thought I wasn't Black enough."

"Since when do you care what other people think?"

"It's just a thing I can't escape. At least not until I'm established in the field." She leaned back on the bench and showed her face to the sky. "African history and Black studies are pretty exclusive in terms of race. Black people don't want other people telling our stories or putting their grubby hands on our history."

"Is a genetic test required?"

Her surprised laugh made a passing man turn in her direction. "Can you imagine? It'd be like when slaves were categorized as things like octoroons. Or the tests to claim native status. At least I can just show pictures of my mom to people to prove that I belong in the club."

"It's really a shit thing for you to have to go through. Maybe you can spin some of your righteous indignation into strengthened resolve. I know I can't understand, but I'm on your side."

"It would be like your being too freckled. Or not freckled enough. Have you just been able to avoid anything like this?"

"In the most anemic comparison ever, Catherine and I got discounted a lot for being women in technology. But that lacks the kind of nuance and history of what you go through."

Iris couldn't remember why she'd hesitated to tell Erin about what had happened. She was so good at saying the right thing. It was uncanny, and Iris wondered if this skill applied to everyone or just her. She liked the idea of being special. Before she could stop herself or even think, she said, "I love you."

"Iris." Erin's voice was low. "You can't say that to me over the phone."

"Why not? It's true." And saying it had left a lightness in her chest.

"Because you're not here for me to hold while I tell you that I love you, too."

"I know it's not a planned night, but will you—"

"Yes. Anything."

"Meet me on campus and ride with me back to my apartment? I can't stay at yours tonight, but I need to see you."

"I'll wait outside the library. And, Iris?"

"What?"

"You're enough. Period."

After they hung up, Iris pressed the phone against her chest like some swoony fourteen-year-old. But, really, was there any feeling better than loving and being loved in return? She lived so much of her life in the future, preparing for the worst, planning for stability and professional success, but love was right here, right now. Everything was happening exactly at this very moment, and today, on this bench, she couldn't be happier about it.

She swam around in the memory of Erin's voice, how it had sounded so intimate after Iris's declaration. She could have this. She deserved it, however little deserving had to do with anything, but luck was at least on her side with Erin. There were so many ways they either couldn't have met or would have stayed merely server-and-well-tipping-customer. At this moment, she could forgive any of Erin's real or imagined transgressions, because she felt who Erin was at her core so acutely. She was incandescent to Iris, a shining beam of positivity that existed outside her privilege.

After spending a while on this happiness trip, she stood, hoisted her backpack on her shoulder, and headed into the library. Finally, after weeks of procrastination, she was in the right mindset to write that long overdue letter to her anonymous donor and savior. Her thankfulness at having Erin in her life slipped its bounds and spilled over on so much else. When she'd initially gotten the grant, she'd written to the Foundation in gratitude, but it seemed like the Foundation had little part to play in this donation and funding. She'd talked to an administrator there who was like the anonymity Gestapo, but she'd eventually convinced them to forward a letter to the donor for her. Now she just had to write it, and she'd never felt more inspired.

* * *

Iris's phone rang, the display showing "Mom." She paused before answering it, hating that she immediately wondered what was wrong. Naomi called her plenty of times for no reason other than to talk to her daughter, but the specter of disaster had clung to their communication since the car. Iris took her phone and buried herself in the stacks so she wouldn't disturb anyone in the work area.

"Hi, Mom."

"This is all your fault."

Her pulse quickened as she cast around for what she had possibly done.

Before she could find anything, Naomi went on. "I got a job at Forage." One of the Allentown restaurants.

"Mom—that's great. I mean, it's great, right?"

"It's great, but it changes everything, and I'm not one for change, as you know."

"Are you quitting the diner?"

"No, of course not."

"How are you going to work at both places at the same time?"

"I'll only be at Forage weekend nights when they need more help. I'll just have to cut back at the diner. Don't you think they'll be okay with that?"

Iris rested her head on the metal shelf of the rack in front of her. "How could they not be okay after all the years you've been there working breakfast, lunch, and dinner? They'd be fools to do anything but say that they'll make it work."

"It's a busy time at the diner, too."

"They can hire someone else. I just wish you'd cut back even more."

"You know I can't do that."

She did know that. It was exactly the same reason she was still working four evenings a week at Dialogue. With both of them, more was rarely enough. "I'm really happy you went through with it. It wasn't that hard, was it?"

"Things aren't as easy for me as they are for you."

"Come on, Mom. Lots of things are hard for me. They're just different from what's hard for you. Things change, and you have to be okay with that."

"Change is rarely for the better."

She had a point, but Iris didn't feel like conceding it. "Passivity is even worse." She shut her mouth, her lips pressing into a firm line. "I didn't mean that."

"You always say whatever comes to mind."

"That's not true. Why are we fighting? Didn't we start this with good news?" Good news that Naomi had turned into a problem. Now Iris had to turn herself around to fix it. "I'm glad you're doing this, and I think it'll be positive all around and not as scary when you settle into the new routine. When do you start?"

They talked about the job for a while, Iris keeping her voice low but still drawing a stink eye from a student passing through the stacks. When they had exhausted the subject, Iris should have found a way to get off the phone and back to her research, but she didn't.

She said, "Erin and I are doing really well."

"So you think you can trust her and that the money's not going to get in the way?"

"She practically acts like it doesn't exist."

"But it does."

"She's careful with me. Things like that are on my terms."

"And you think that'll last?"

What was up with Naomi this afternoon? The negativity was relentless. "Mom, I love her. We love each other."

A rustle of breath. "I'm happy for you."

"But…?"

"Nothing." But then she negated that with, "I just hope she doesn't want to fix everything in your life or is going to get tired of you not being rich like her."

"Good thing I know her better than you do."

"Agreed. I don't want anything more than to be wrong."

Iris turned around and leaned back against the seam between the two racks of books behind her. "I'm not stupid, okay? But Erin's proven herself to me. I trust her. She's such a positive force in my life, a positive force in general. We both want to make a difference, and that means more than the relative size of our bank accounts."

"Iris. I'm happy for you, I am. Can we leave it at that?"

They did, but a sour taste remained in her mouth. She couldn't blame Naomi for anything she was feeling: it was all justified by her lifetime of experiences. It was just that sometimes Iris wanted an uncomplicated happiness. She knew that she and Erin were sequestered in their little world of two, but wasn't that okay right now? Did every moment have to be about the next disaster?

* * *

Having Erin at Dialogue while Iris was working was one big, aching distraction. She was seated in Greg's section and doing an admirable job of staying focused on her book, but Iris couldn't resist sneaking peeks at her while she was supposed to be tending to her tables. The night couldn't go fast enough during this second seating, and Erin was going to stay until the bitter end because she was going to walk Iris back to her place after closing.

It made Iris remember the night months ago when Erin had flagged her down with an apology. Even though she'd been short when Iris had thanked her for the beyond-generous tip, her apology had been unexpected and warmly genuine. Now, Iris thought she understood Erin's reaction, her desire to be generous but still fly under the radar. Her relationship with her wealth seemed uneasy, which Iris didn't really understand. Maybe it was because it was still new, or because she'd had such a bad experience with that ex-girlfriend, or because she didn't feel deserving, or maybe it was all of the above. Iris realized she didn't have to know the exact reasons because what really mattered was that Erin was, above all else, thoughtful about everything.

There was such care in how Erin met Iris where she was and didn't pretend to know anything about Iris's experience. It was such a comfort to know that Erin wouldn't drop a tone-deaf analogy into the conversation or try to make an easy understanding from small snippets of Iris's life. Instead, she asked questions aimed at getting Iris to articulate things from her point of view, which often helped Iris as much as Erin.

Iris buzzed her table when the dining room was half empty. It took Erin a moment to look up from her book and smile. "Hey, you."

"Are you getting dessert tonight?"

"No, I'm stuffed. I've already settled up, so now I'll just sit here until I'm kicked out."

"No one's going to kick you out. You're the golden-child customer. Or would be if you ordered dessert more often."

Erin's smile went wider. "They'll probably make you kick me out."

"If I stand here and talk to you any longer, they probably will."

"I'm not complaining."

"You're the worst."

"If worst means the best, then I agree."

Iris didn't want to encourage this line of conversation so she just gave Erin an eyebrow raise before going back to her duties. With Erin right there, in this environment, it was hard for Iris not to think about Naomi, who apparently had no faith that things would work out between her and Erin. Normally, Iris would concede some of Naomi's points, but she was unwilling to slip into the doomsday stance that had underlaid so much of her life—or at least her financial life. Her studies had always been an easy positive, buoying her through the worst times. She was good at them, they were satisfying, and they brought her outside herself to a larger context and bigger problems. Erin, with her expansive list of interests, and desire to be as well informed as possible about all of them, held some of the same qualities for Iris. She knew that love could make you stupid, but if that was the case here, she couldn't get herself to care.

The rest of the night went quickly, and Erin disappeared when they locked the front door without her noticing. Iris liked the hurried camaraderie of the end of the shift, jokes and gentle teasing while everyone went about their closing duties. It was an atmosphere as familiar to her as the classroom.

Greg passed her, saying, "It was good to have Erin in the dining room instead of just hanging around out back."

"You just like her for her tips."

"Yeah, and you just like her for her tits."

She slapped him hard on the arm. "Rude," she said, though he wasn't entirely wrong. Erin had many fine qualities, but her breasts were the just-right size and shape, and Iris was looking forward to having them in her hands as soon as possible tonight.

Iris was still pulling on her coat when she pushed through the door to the chilly night. Fall had turned cold recently, and she liked this version of Erin, clad in a knee-length black wool coat with a bright-blue scarf tucked under her chin. Her hair was windblown from her wait, and she smiled when she saw Iris.

She gave Iris a firm kiss. "Ready?"

Iris took her arm, curling her already chilly fingers into the crook of Erin's elbow. "Lead the way."

They walked the now familiar route, making their standard detour into the Public Gardens to visit their tree, which was just starting to turn a bronze color with the changed weather. The color was muted but noticeable in the streetlamps' glow.

"They keep their leaves well into winter," Erin said. "They're a rustling tan. I'm not sure why the tree doesn't drop them, but it probably drives the caretakers a little nuts to be raking up leaves in January."

"I like that kind of perverse perseverance. I feel like there's a lesson there."

"Like the opposite of the early bird getting the worm? I could get on board with that."

"You don't need a reason to sleep in when you stay up so late. For this, though, I was thinking something like the rewards of hanging in beyond what everyone accepts as the end."

"True. You never know what might be out there if you hold on a little longer." Erin slid her fingers between Iris's. "Your hand is so cold. We should probably stop contemplating this tree and get home and warm. I turned up the thermostat for you before I left for the restaurant."

That thoughtfulness made Iris take Erin's face in her cold hands and kiss her thoroughly, a move Erin reciprocated with enthusiasm until they were moments away from being arrested for public indecency. They reluctantly pulled apart and walked the rest of the way, the hill finishing what the kiss had started, warming Iris from the inside out.

At the doorway, Erin nodded at the big planter. "Your key or mine?"

"I wish you wouldn't leave that out there where anyone could get at it. You're just asking to get burgled or worse."

"The solution to that is simple—accept the key and keep it safe yourself."

Iris couldn't articulate why she'd been rejecting this next step in their relationship. It had something to do with independence or safety or deprivation probably, but tonight it just seemed silly. Erin wanted her to have the freedom to come and go as she pleased. She trusted Iris with her home, and tonight, Iris could find no reason to hold on to this rejection until her fingers cramped.

She held out her hand. "Okay."

That brought Erin up short. "What?"

Iris opened and closed her fingers in a gimme gesture. "Okay. I'll take the key."

Erin blinked twice in the muted light from the street. "That's the last thing I thought you'd say." As if to keep Iris from reconsidering, she swooped down to the planter, tilted it up, and retrieved the key. She handed it to Iris. "You're welcome literally anytime. You know that, right?"

Iris closed her hand in a fist around the chilly metal. "Thank you."

"I love you."

They didn't seem anywhere near tiring of declaring this to each other, and Iris hoped they wouldn't. It felt so good to hear and to say. She followed Erin up the stairs and waited for her to unlock the door to her apartment, unwrapping her own scarf and scratching the itchiness from her neck. Inside, they both shed their coats and hung them on the rack opposite the narrow stone table in the entryway. There was loose mail on the table's surface as usual, including something that caught Iris's eye. It wasn't her place to look at Erin's correspondence, but she shifted one piece to expose the return address stamp on the letter underneath it. A stamp that bore the logo of The Foundation for Modern Historical Studies.

In her confusion, she asked, "What's this?"

Erin had already wandered away but turned around. "What?"

"This letter." Confusion was morphing into something else. Iris couldn't get herself to pick it up.

"I don't know. Probably a solicitation. I get a ton of those."

"From The Foundation for Modern Historical Studies?" A new emotion had a stranglehold on her throat, making it hard to talk.

"I honestly don't know what that is. I mean I know who they are from you, but I don't know what's in that envelope."

The coldness that the walk had dispelled came over her again. "I don't believe in coincidences, Erin."

"I know you don't. I talked to them months ago after you brought them to my attention."

Iris finally took the letter between her forefinger and thumb like it might combust and extended it to Erin. "Open it."

Erin looked like she was trying to think of a good argument not to but eventually reached out and took it. She ran a finger under the flap and took out a small note and a folded envelope. She read the note and closed her eyes. "Please let me explain."

"That's the letter I wrote to the anonymous donor, right?" It wasn't really a question.

"It wasn't only about you."

Iris scoffed and realized her fingers were trembling in a mixture of disbelief and rage. "You're not supposed to lie to me."

"I'm not lying. It started with you, of course. It started with my trying to right a wrong, but what I ended up doing is going to help people for the next decade. Even more with good management." The letter and its envelope were in her hands at her hips. This open posture was infuriating.

"How much did you give to them?" Iris watched Erin's lips press together and twist. "How much?" The words were loud between them.

"A million, give or take. Directed to the Margaret B. Johnson Grant and with stipulations that they can't ever use it for anything else than its original purpose."

The amount made her breath catch. "I can't believe this."

"I didn't tell you because I didn't want you to take it the wrong way."

"There's only one way to take it."

"It wasn't charity. Isn't."

"The hell it's not, and you barely knew me when you did it. How could it be anything other than charity when all I was to you then was a needy almost stranger?"

"You were clearly deserving, and they'd done something wrong that needed to be fixed. They needed to be held to their word to you."

Iris scoured Erin's face for any recognition of what she'd done but came up empty—which was how she felt now. "I told you you'd try to become a savior. I just had no idea you'd already done it."

"I wasn't trying to save you. I just…"

Iris rolled her eyes and put the key on the table with a click, needing to get it away from herself. "You just what, Erin? What were you trying to do?"

Erin gestured a vague shrug with the papers in her hands. "I thought I could fix something. I thought I could help."

"I don't need your help."

"You were going to have to leave school."

"I can handle my own problems."

"I'm not saying you can't."

Iris crossed her arms, tucking her cold fingers into her armpits. "I go through life on my own merits."

"Your merit won you that grant, and stupid bureaucracy took it away from you. It was wrong on every level. Besides, why can't you take help every once in a while?"

"A million dollars of help?"

"I told you. It wasn't just for you. It's for future recipients, too."

"That's a story you're telling yourself, and you know it." She stretched her neck to look up at the ceiling. "I can't believe you lied to me again, and this is so much worse."

"I'm sorry. I just—"

"Save it, Erin. You knew how I would react and why. You selfishly wanted to avoid it. You made a fool out of me."

"You're not a fool. I didn't want you to see it as charity."

"It's literally charity! You're probably getting a big tax write off for it."

"You deserved it. You earned it."

Iris felt tears forming and was desperate for Erin not to see them. She took her coat from the rack, put it on, and wound her scarf around her neck. "I'm leaving."

"Wait, no. Please, will you—"

"I'm leaving." There was just enough give in her anger to make saying this hard. "I'm leaving you."

"What? Iris, please."

"I have to go."

"No, you don't."

But Iris already had the door open and was halfway across the threshold. A glance behind her showed Erin sagged against the wall, her eyes wide and mouth open. Before she could say something that might, miraculously, make Iris stay, she closed the door behind her and ran down the stairs and outside, not slowing until she was at the bottom of the hill, where she leaned against the nearest building and let herself cry.

CHAPTER FIFTEEN

Erin sat down on the floor where Iris had left her. She dropped the letter and its envelope like they were on fire and covered her face with her hands. All evidence to the contrary, she couldn't believe Iris was gone. Just like that. No discussion. No chance at all to stop her. Just, "I'm leaving," and then the door was closed, and Iris was on the wrong side of it. "I love you," then "I'm leaving you," all in a span of ten minutes. Nothing could hold together long enough for Erin to grasp except the black hole where Iris had just been standing.

Erin had been such a fool. Foolish to think the façade of anonymity would hold and Iris would never find out, that this lie was justified and beyond reproach. All Iris had asked for (demanded, really) was truthfulness, and she hadn't given it to her, not until she literally couldn't get away with withholding it a minute longer. She wanted to kid herself into thinking the withholding was what drove Iris away, but would this have gone any differently if she'd disclosed this donation when she'd told Iris about her wealth? It had been one of the best things she'd done with her money, and it made her a monster in Iris's eyes.

It couldn't be true that Iris was really gone, but the hot pain in Erin's chest certainly made it feel true. Tears filled her eyes and spilled down her cheeks, and breathing was a chore she wished she didn't have to bother with, especially when it pinched her chest with every inhalation. She thought about Iris's face right at the end, twisted and hard, and that broke whatever control she had left, her sobs curling her into herself, the floor unyielding when she tipped over onto her side, her face landing on the opened envelope.

Time passed until her mind was one bruised *no*, and she was hollowed out enough to not be able to cry anymore. She just lay there, in a tight ball, her hip numb against the floor, sniffing in mucus with rhythmic regularity. It had been so fast, going from exchanging that key to Iris being apocalyptically angry, so angry that there was no way past it and into the part of Iris that must still love Erin. That couldn't have evaporated so quickly, could it? Or was the inside of Iris built like one of those rooms you saw in spy movies that self-immolated on a simple trigger? The thought made Erin even more miserable.

She sat up, wiped her face on her sleeve, and slowly got to her feet. Before she could stop herself, she picked up Iris's letter, opened the envelope roughly, and started to read the handwritten page within.

Dear Generous Donor,

I wanted to take this time to thank you for your donation to The Foundation for Modern Historical Studies. It has truly changed my life. These days, too many people have to pay for their studies by incurring crippling debt, debt that follows them from job to job, delaying the possibility of reaching milestones other people might take for granted, like buying a home or investing for retirement. I already have a frightening amount of student loans and would have been unable to pursue my graduate work with any fiscal responsibility were it not for scholarships and grants like the one this foundation has extended to me. Without your generosity, I would have been forced to leave school, perhaps permanently, making it impossible for me to pursue the research I believe is important in understanding our human condition.

I am the daughter of a single mother, and we have worked hard for every penny we've earned. I can assure you that I will do the same in the time this grant affords me. The world needs scholarship in history, and I applaud you for believing the same.

With profound gratitude,

Iris Patterson

Erin let the letter drop to the floor and climbed the stairs to her bedroom, where she stripped and slipped into bed, pulling the comforter up to her ears. She refused to believe things were finished between them. Iris had gotten over her money in general, and she would get over this donation in particular. Too raw to consider any other alternative, Erin just breathed warm exhalations into the blanket, knowing it was impossible to sleep but unwilling to face any more of this day.

By the time she dragged herself out of bed the next day, it was nearly noon. She made her way to the shower—and suffered a crying fit so prolonged that she ran out of hot water and looked like she'd been punched in the face when she cleared steam from the mirror with the side of her hand. That was enough. She couldn't get Iris back if she was crying all the time. Before she could think about it too hard, she grabbed her phone, ignored all the notifications that had piled up since the day before, and texted Iris.

I would do it again.

Maybe not the most strategic thing to say, but it was the truth, which was what Iris said she wanted. Erin wasn't going to step back this time and give Iris infinite space. She was going to fight for them—being persistent but not an asshole, which was a line so fine Erin was already sure she was going to transgress it.

After securing a dinner invitation to Catherine's for that evening, Erin distracted herself with whatever was most likely to keep her attention. Today, instead of books or the articles she had set aside to read, she devoted her time to considering the art of the email. She channeled her former self, back when she'd been selling their product as well as fundraising. The question was how to ask for something in a way that didn't feel like asking to the recipient. It needed to feel like a gift curated just for them. An opportunity.

What Erin wanted most was to write something infinitely compelling, something that would convince Iris to talk to her again, but that was a task miles away from the favors she was intending on calling in or the requests for information she was going to make to people she admired but hadn't ever met. For these, all she had to trade on was what little name she had, which was featured prominently on her website, along with the marketing content for her consulting. What she wanted to find out from those she contacted was this: was she crazy to consider starting a nonprofit to teach college-aged women the skills that they needed to be successful and confident in business environments? Skills not usually taught in the classroom? Though she could fully fund and administer a 501(c)(3) nonprofit, she had no illusions that she could (or should) do this by herself. She would need a lot of help with the rest of it.

Help—everyone needed it in one way or another, but Iris didn't want any. Or wanted it only on her narrow terms. Erin got that, but she'd thought she was working within that construct when she'd funded the grant Iris had already won.

Okay, maybe she hadn't been thinking exactly that when she'd opened her wallet, but she'd never consider just handing Iris a check for God's sake. Iris worked so hard, had so much merit, something which had been easy to see from the beginning. What was wrong with Erin giving the universe a little nudge—okay, a shove—and encouraging it to fix some bad breaks and make Iris's life just a little easier?

Erin wasn't above asking for help for herself, after all. The women she was writing to had information or experience that could pave the way to success in this still-nascent endeavor of hers. Curriculum building, accreditation, guest speakers, community outreach, working with universities, and additional funding, of course. Erin was made of money, but she already knew that nonprofits like this could never have too much.

The more she wrote, the clearer her vision for the enterprise got: offering three or four college credits for a semester-long seminar taught by masters in the field, projects that took students out into the community, mentorship during the course, and access to a growing alumni group after they passed. It was a lot like what Erin had hoped to accomplish with her consulting, only decanted into the classroom and focused on individual women instead of businesses. This wasn't supposed to replace existing college curriculum but was something that filled in the yawning gaps between theory and practice. How do you talk to people? How do you present yourself? What matters in a presentation? How do you listen and meet people where they are? The list went on and reinforced Erin's purpose.

Was this charity, especially given that she'd start out with her own money? Was charity a bad thing? How did she do good with her money without it being charity? Was it possible for Erin to win in Iris's eyes? If she held on to her money, she was a dragon counting its gold. If she gave it away, she was making beggars out of the people she helped. Was it charity for these women she wrote to, to spend their time answering her or signing up to help in larger ways? If it was, Erin didn't feel bad for taking it.

She was twenty-five emails in and numb to enthusiasm when the afternoon drew to a close and she pocketed her keys, slipped on her coat, and headed out into the chilly evening to get to Catherine's house. Boarding a green line train at the Park Street station reminded her acutely of the long ride out to Iris's apartment, and she thought she might start crying again. She took a deep breath, pulled out her phone, and texted her.

I was helping on your terms.

Again, not so much the tail between the legs that Iris might be looking for, but this was what was coming out today.

Erin took the ten-minute walk from the train to Catherine's house to compose herself—or at least decide what she wanted to tell Catherine about Iris. It seemed strange now that the two of them hadn't met. Yet, she reminded herself. They hadn't met yet. Catherine would be happy that Erin was in love. She would be impressed with Iris. She would get it. Not that Iris cared.

Everything had been on her terms, which Erin had understood and honored, but this leaving was something different.

The front door was cracked open, and Erin knocked hard before going in and closing it behind her. "Hello?"

"Kitchen."

Of course, given the aromas thick in the air. Meaty and spicy. Erin followed her nose, hugged Catherine and Nathan, and peeked into the big stock pot on the stove. Chili. And a pan of cornbread was cooling on the island. Her stomach growled, reminding her that she hadn't eaten anything today, which then reminded her so strongly of Iris last night that words came out of her despite herself. "Iris left me."

Then it was a fight to the finish between her composure and her tears; she feared cracking a molar with how hard she was clenching her jaw.

Catherine watched the whole thing, and Nathan went to set the table. "I don't know whether to ask or not."

Not would be safer, but Erin ground the heels of her hands against her eyes and said, "I'll tell you over dinner. I need something to settle my stomach."

"I just need to know if I'm supposed to hate her."

Her sorrow reared up again, and she kept her hands over her eyes. "I love her." Then, before Catherine could ask again, she said, "And no."

After a brief respite in the powder room, Erin regained the control she'd held on to all afternoon. She still looked like crap, but she and Catherine had spent so much time together that they mostly saw through each other's skin to the spirit within rather than every deepening wrinkle.

Nathan set a steaming bowl in front of her. "Chili heals everything."

Erin took issue with that statement but said nothing. She buttered her cornbread, took a bite, and sighed while her stomach growled, her appetite awakened from its daylong slumber. "I did something," she admitted and told them about the donation and her secrecy.

Catherine stared at her, but Nathan said, "You gave her a million dollars?"

"I gave the foundation a million dollars. They gave her her grant back."

"And she's pissed? I mean, pissed enough to break up with you?"

Erin let her spoon drop. "We're not broken up. She's just taking some space."

"Erin," Catherine said. "You knew she would have a problem with this, even back when you did it—which is a topic I'll save for another day."

"Her reaction is based on a pathological amount of pride. She needed help, and I could give it. I would have given less, but a million was what was required to do it right." And to have it not be entirely about Iris.

Catherine focused her laser-like attention on her. "Why did you do it when you barely knew her?"

Erin toyed with her chili for a while, pushing beans over to one side of the bowl and the ground meat to the other with onions, tomato, and corn in the demilitarized zone between them. Finally she looked at Catherine.

"Her resilience and pride are compelling. She's so passionate about what she does. Her independence was irresistible. It was a travesty that they took that grant away from her. She needed it the way you and I don't need anything anymore." Except love, she reminded herself with a pang. "And I thought she'd never find out."

That left the room quiet. Erin watched Nathan and Catherine look at each other in silent conversation and missed Iris with such a twist in her gut that she couldn't eat any more.

Catherine said, "What does she hate more? That you did it or that you lied about it?"

A bitter laugh bubbled up past her bruised heart. "They both featured prominently when she took me to task." *I can't believe you lied to me again.* And *it's literally charity.* "She had no problem taking the money when it was an anonymous donor. She earned that grant, beat out a long line of people for it. Why is it suddenly a handout when the money came from me?"

"It's a lot to do that. To have done that when you did. Don't you think Iris feels uncomfortably indebted to you?"

Honestly, the thought hadn't crossed her mind. "The gift was to the foundation. It's going to be used for decades."

"That's semantics, and you know it."

"She doesn't owe me anything. It was a gift."

"A handout, you mean."

Erin slapped the table, then looked anywhere but at Catherine. "She earned that grant. Mismanagement took it away from her. If the foundation was any good at fundraising, it wouldn't have been a problem." She wiped her fingers on the napkin in her lap. "I couldn't bear to see her give up what she'd worked so hard for. You and I had lean years, but it's nothing like what she's been through most of her life. I could tell you stories, but it's not my place." She finally met Catherine's gaze. "I can't bear for this to be what ends us. I can't bear for us to be ended."

In typical Catherine fashion, she replied, "You may not have a choice." She shrugged.

Erin glared at her. "She's surprised and hurt, but I can't believe it made her stop loving me. I've never a felt a connection like this, and she wouldn't blow smoke about it to me. She's got too much integrity for that." Erin glanced down at her half-full bowl of chili and inched it away from her. "And, what, maybe I don't because I lied?"

"Erin," Catherine said, but it took a while for her to look up. "You have integrity. This is a unique situation. She's probably shocked, and maybe it would have gone marginally better if you'd brought it up when you talked to her about your wealth."

"Because that went so well without this complication. This whole thing is ridiculous. I should have gotten rid of the money years ago."

"All right. Let's not get dramatic."

Erin gripped her thighs under the table, squeezing them until it was uncomfortable. "I'm trying. I have ideas. I have an idea that might make an impact if I can get it off the ground."

"Good. All I'm saying is that you need to prepare yourself for the possibility that you and Iris might not be able to get on the same page."

"No, I don't. Did we prepare ourselves for failure when we started out?"

Catherine's smile was small. "Well, I mean, a little, but for us it just meant we'd have to get real jobs."

"I didn't let myself conceive of failure. It just wasn't an option, and that made a huge difference. I knew I had limited power about our outcome, and I know the same thing is true here, but I'm not going to hand any of my power over to the universe—or even to her."

"Will you just be careful?"

"Probably not." Erin found a grin under her steely, weepy resolve and picked up her spoon again.

In the velvety dark on the way home, Erin unlocked her phone and wrote one more text message to Iris.

I got as much out of it as you did.

* * *

Iris had yet to respond to any of Erin's texts, not even to tell her to knock it off, so Erin continued to send one a day. The latest was *It was a way to help that I understood.* The passing days had only served to harden her determination to persist, even though she suspected that keeping on Iris like this might not be the best approach. It might just be making her dig into her considerable stubbornness. Still, what was left for Erin to do? Iris would definitely not take well to Erin showing up at work again or at school or her home.

To limit her text messages—and keep herself from despair—Erin poured her energy into her nascent new venture, moving from sending cold-call emails to tending to legal matters, setting up the entity and signing and filing all the documents that her lawyer insisted were necessary. It all felt a little cart-before-the-horse as she waited for responses and excitement from women both inside and outside her network. There was so much to coordinate, and the thing wasn't even a thing yet. She wondered again how different the help she was asking for was from what Iris had received through the grant. Help was help was help, right? Only, somehow, it wasn't.

Was there anything Iris could give her that Erin wouldn't accept? Besides this most recent "no," of course. Erin wanted nothing disingenuous or dangerous. She just wanted Iris as is. Unfortunately, Iris only wanted her with one big caveat.

She looked like a wreck, she knew, and mostly felt like one. She avoided people's gazes when she walked to the market or into the Public Gardens to sit in the fall chill and look at their tree. Theirs, she stressed to herself. Its foliage was now fully turned to bronze. The color made it easier to see the crooks of the branches where they turned from growing upward to trending down. Why did these weeping varieties flout the traditional laws of nature? The only thing that grew downward were roots, not things above ground. It was a beautiful perversion, which was probably why Erin liked it so much. Wasn't that what she aspired to? Not physical beauty but more…a beautiful sense of purpose? Unfortunately, however kin she was to this specimen, it had no answers for her.

Her phone rang when she was considering getting up and going somewhere where she could get warm. She snatched it up, but it was from an unknown number. Wary of spam, she considered not answering, but curiosity killed the cat.

"Hello?" The word was gruff with don't-fuck-with-me vibes.

"Erin McCallister?" It was a woman.

"This is she."

"Hi, it's Delia Swanson. I got your email."

Erin took the phone from the side of her head and held it out in front of her, looking at it in disbelief. Delia Swanson was the COO at Barnaby Technologies and one of Erin's personal heroes for the way she navigated expectations both realistic and not. Erin held the pose long enough that she heard a tinny, "Hello?" from arm's distance away.

She brought the phone back to her ear. "Ms. Swanson, hi. Sorry. I'm just surprised."

"In these days of texts, I still like for some conversations to happen in real time."

"Agreed. You've caught me outside, though, so I apologize for the traffic noise. What can I do for you, Ms. Swanson?" The question was a stupid one, but before she could take it back, a laugh came across the line into her ear.

"Call me Delia, and I'm pretty sure the question is what I can do for you. I'm intrigued by your proposal, though it still seems half-baked."

Delia sounded so much like Catherine right then that Erin relaxed. "It's absolutely half-baked. I'm looking for help to refine and realize my vision. At this point, I'd take whatever you're willing to give."

"You can use my name, however much that helps, and I'll commit to being a guest speaker once every semester, assuming you really do plan on aligning with the school year, which I think is a good idea."

"What do you want to speak about?"

"Something topical. I'll decide later if you get this off the ground. I can make some introductions, but understand that none of these women have time to spare."

Erin sat up straight. "Absolutely. I know I wasn't keen to do anything outside my company back in the day. Introductions would be great. Names mean everything right now. I have a lot of ideas about content, but I don't want this to be only about what I think, and I certainly don't want it to be all about me as a teacher. I mean, I'm passable, but there are so many more qualified people out there. I want to be surprised by ideas and approaches."

"You want to be the ringleader."

"That's my sweet spot, yeah." A woman with a squalling child in a stroller took her time passing Erin. "Sorry about that," she said when the coast was clear.

"I have two of my own, so I understand."

Erin wondered how Delia could balance kids with the kind of career she'd had, rife with startups and responsibilities. "Maybe you could speak about that."

Delia laughed, which thrilled Erin. "Making it through something hardly means one is an expert. I do have ideas about topics you might want to include in the curriculum if you've got a way to take them down."

Erin put her phone on speaker and opened up a notepad app, typing with her thumbs as quickly as she could so she wouldn't have to make Delia repeat herself. What she offered was a gold mine, so many things Erin hadn't considered that she felt like an idiot. Yes, she should definitely be the ringleader and not on the hook for content or delivery.

"Thank you for this, Delia. You've been incredibly generous when you don't owe me anything."

"We need to lift each other up. If you can make this work, it'll have an impact. I have to run, but keep in touch. I'll send a few introduction emails to women in my network when I get a chance."

"Thank you so much. This has been amazing."

Delia laughed. "I don't envy the amount of work ahead of you."

But work was all she had now, and every day it grew clearer in her mind. Providing supplemental education and mentorship for female undergraduate and graduate students on a variety of subjects geared toward filling in the gaps of business school. Elevating these women as polished, well-rounded candidates who would make continued impacts in the workforce. The specific curriculum and format, the criteria for applicants, and who she'd have to pay and who would volunteer were all up for debate. Most of it was up for debate, actually, but she was looking to put together a solid advisory board (that maybe Delia would join?) which would help with the countless decisions that needed to be made before anything could really begin. If she got pie in the sky, she would love to start offering parts of the curriculum to younger students, targeting underfunded high schools. Talk about an opportunity to fill in gaps, but she needed the rest of her business model in place first.

Doing this reminded her of working alongside Catherine before they'd been bought. Juggling and talking and thinking through all the angles, hoping to avoid making a wrong decision, knowing there was so much at stake, having a sinking suspicion about everything she didn't know but forging ahead regardless. It had required a kind of faith Erin hadn't known she'd had until she'd called on it. Now was the same, but the faith felt more blind than ever, both in this new venture and in her and Iris weathering this storm.

Thinking about Iris, and with this excitement and positive boost simmering inside her, she wrote the day's text to Iris.

I ask for help all the time.

No one could live entirely on her own merits. Everyone learned from other people or leaned on them, built on top of other achievements or accepted an introduction or friendly word of warning. Everyone was beholden to each other, and Erin wouldn't want it any other way. Did Iris not see the books and journals she read as sources to her research as help? She would probably argue that it was a different kind of help from the kind Erin had given to her, and maybe that was true, at least in magnitude and directedness, but her scholarship required both, no matter what she thought about it.

Of course, arguing with Iris when she wasn't there to argue back was fruitless. It made Erin sick, with a heavy tinge of anger. Iris was so stubborn, so unimpeachable, so burdened by that massive chip on her shoulder. Erin loved these traits as much as she hated that they were keeping them apart. What was Iris going to do, give her grant back to the foundation? Would she go that far? Erin couldn't imagine it. Wouldn't. Because if Iris kept it, there was a chance she could be convinced to keep Erin, too.

* * *

Erin wished she could be at the kids' table in the kitchen instead of squeezed into the dining room in her parents' house. She wished she could take back the bouquet of flowers and bottle of wine she'd presented to her mom at the front door when she'd arrived, which had just been awkward for everyone. She wished she belonged to a different family or had done something completely different with her life or at the very least had worn a T-shirt instead of the button-up she'd pulled on in stupid indecision an hour earlier before catching an Uber up here.

She wished Iris were here with her. Even Rory had a date, a pleasantly curvaceous brunette who seemed to fit in exactly as much as Erin stood out.

For some ungodly reason, her mother had requested that they do a full family dinner. This was something she insisted on every year or two, a midyear Thanksgiving-type event where she would cook a ham or a roast and Stephanie would bring a couple of side dishes, and they would all gorge themselves on white rolls and some kind of fruit pie at the end. It was a time for them to catch up, her mother always said, but the only one out of the loop was Erin herself. Her brother worked with her father, and her parents were very active grandparents to her niece and nephew, seeing them and Stephanie weekly. Even the couple of cousins who were invited saw everyone regularly, their kids having play dates with Stephanie's.

If Iris was here, the evening would be entirely different. It would be a lot for Iris to be introduced to everyone all at once, but having everyone around would dilute the impact she would surely make. Not that the impression she'd give would be negative, but it would be different, and Erin knew how that went with her family. Instead, Erin kept herself busy eating ham and casseroles while following the conversation as it bounced around the table.

An ornate tiling job, preschool for her nephew, a new rule from the IRS and needing to file before their extension ran out, Rory's girlfriend's job as a dental hygienist and the cavity that had brought the two of them together, how insurance was screwing everyone over. She hadn't always been on the outside. Before she'd gone to Tufts, the only strange thing about her was how much she'd liked reading, which was not generally a McCallister pastime. But then she'd broken the mold with college and again with TriBar and again with her wealth until now she felt more like a far-distant, long-lost cousin than a daughter and sister.

She was doing a good job at flying under the radar until, probably to get her goat, Rory asked, "So, Erin. How's consulting?" At least he didn't use finger quotes around it.

Everyone looked at her. She immediately wanted to evade, but she imagined Iris next to her and her reverence for the truth. "I'm actually starting to focus on something else."

Her mother said, "Is it law school? You spent all that money on a prelaw degree, and you've never used it."

"I have used it. Just not as a lawyer. No, it's not law school. I'm never going to law school, okay? I'm starting something new. It's a nonprofit, a good use for my time and money."

"You mean a charity?" This was Darrin, Stephanie's husband, who actually tried to engage Erin in conversation every once in a while.

"It's a training program for young women going into business. I'll offer scholarships to women in need, but other people who can would pay for it." She glanced around the table at a bunch of blank faces. "It'll start with my own money, but as we mature, we'll get to fundraising. At some point, I hope to be able to pay myself a small salary."

Stephanie said, "Not that you need one."

Erin sat back, letting those words evaporate into the air with the savory smells of dinner. "I'm trying to plug a gap in college curriculums, give these women a head start toward really being successful. Teach them things that I learned starting my own company. Kind of like how Dad's taught you," she said to Rory.

"And by that, you mean something other than knowing which end of a hammer you use on a nail." He winked. She reminded herself that he was on her side even if it sometimes didn't feel like it.

"Yeah, like how to talk to customers. How to manage subcontractors. How to set expectations. How to communicate when things don't go according to plan. Stuff you had to figure out as you went along," she said to her father. "You wouldn't have been as successful if you didn't have those skills."

Her father gave a sideways nod. "It's the hardest part of the job."

Though he had just conceded her point, everyone was quiet after that. Erin looked around the table, bristling with frustration. "I don't understand how it makes sense to everyone that Dad started his own business, but it's something strange and suspect when I did it. When I'm doing it again. What I did at TriBar wasn't hard to understand, but you treated it like I was doing something totally out in left field. I don't need you to be proud of me, but maybe you can not act like I was switched at birth or something."

She put her napkin on the table and scooted back her chair so vehemently that it knocked into the wall behind her. "I'm going to get some air."

She scooted past Darrin, gave Stephanie a wide berth, and strode out the front door and halfway down the walk before she stopped and growled. She should've handled that better. She should've kept her mouth shut. She should have been more patient. She should educate. That's what she wanted to do with this new venture, right? She gripped her head and looked up at the sky, which was starting to grow pink with sunset.

She didn't turn around at Rory's voice. "That went well."

"Fuck you."

"When I asked how things were going, I thought you'd say, 'Fine,' maybe tell a funny story about a client, and we'd all move on."

She turned around to face him. "Yeah, well, I didn't feel like coddling everyone anymore. I'm either a part of this family or I'm not. I think it's pretty clear that I'm not. Tell me the truth. Is it the money?"

"They're just people, Erin. That's one of the first things I learned working with Dad. They're just people with the same stupid hang-ups everyone has. They're probably just embarrassed that they don't really understand what you do. You work hard but in this way that's kind of invisible. It's all in your mind, right? Or is this still kind of virtual thing that some lawyers use. They don't get it, they don't really get you, and they don't handle it well."

His patient tone deflated her.

"Why didn't you bring your girlfriend?"

She laughed. "Like they'd get her any better. Besides, she's not talking to me right now." She held up a hand. "I'm working on it. Everyone makes choices. Abdicating is as much of a choice as anything else, and they don't even try."

"What happened with the girlfriend? The money again?"

She sighed. "I was too generous in a way she didn't like."

"Okay..."

"Forget it." She scrubbed her face with her hands. "Dammit. I probably need to go in and apologize or something. I just...it should be easier."

"Shoulda, woulda, coulda," he quoted their father.

"Part of me thinks they would love Iris. She's got such a keen work ethic that you can't help but admire her. But the rest of me knows they would look at what she's doing in graduate school and what she wants to do with her life and decide they can't understand that either. Or at the very least don't appreciate it. But I don't think I'm asking for anything special."

"You're not. You just have to give them more of a chance than you do."

"It's been years."

"We McCallisters are a dense bunch."

That was the first thing to ring true all evening, especially when she applied it to herself now. If she wanted things to change, she had to own the situation first, which she'd avoided doing. She needed to extend her will to improve to these relationships as much as she applied it in her professional life—and with Iris.

While Rory lit up a cigarette, she pulled her phone from her pocket and texted Iris. *I fell in love with your sense of family, and I aspire to match you, with you.*

CHAPTER SIXTEEN

Ignoring Erin's texts did not make them stop coming as Iris (mostly) hoped. They were hard little grenades of...truth? Pleading? Argument? Iris read them all despite her best intentions and railed against them in her mind—though not on her phone to an Erin clearly fishing for a response.

Giving gives me purpose. That had nothing to do with anything. None of the texts answered the question of how in the world Iris could be with someone who had done something like she had—and when she'd done it. Erin hadn't even loved her yet, had known so little about her beyond this one specific need that the "gesture," as Erin might call it, was absurd. It could be nothing but the most brazen charity.

Then the lie. And she'd tried to cover it up right until the end. There were many worst parts of the whole thing, but Erin pretending she didn't know why she might have gotten correspondence from the foundation, lying right to Iris's face, might be the one truly unforgivable one. Not that Iris was ignorant of why she'd done it. Anyone who knew Iris at all could predict she would blow her top at the truth. Which, of course, she had.

Every time she thought about it, she grew furious, and every time she went to the library or paid for anything at all, she felt strangled by the money: Erin's money. Even if she could be completely rid of Erin (which she somehow wasn't yet), she would remain beholden for the next three years. The thought was untenable.

And the absolute truth was that she didn't know what to do.

She was the one who fixed things for herself and Naomi. She was the one who dug up solutions to their problems, money for their expenses, a forced optimism for their despair. She was the one who had things under control and was moving inexorably toward something better. The grant that had been her salvation had been taken away, only to be returned in the most impossible manner. Would she have to give it back? Is that what her honor dictated?

How could she have the money if she wouldn't also have Erin?

The possible ramifications were keeping her up at night, which only made her think of Erin sitting across the room, silhouetted against the light from her desk lamp. Iris craved having her close, turning over half asleep, ordering her to come to bed, not staying awake long enough to see if she obeyed. Then she thought of Erin in the mornings, soft in her slumber, slow to wake, a sleepy smile the first thing Iris saw before she growled and buried her face in her pillow. Iris had loved seeing her like that, especially when it had been in Iris's bed, when Erin had been slotted so neatly into her life.

Suddenly everything became suspect, which turned her stomach. Had it been an act when Erin said she liked staying over at Iris's even after Iris knew about the money? Who would willingly hang out in this apartment with its shared bathroom and creaky couch when she had a huge place in Beacon Hill? Could she even trust that Erin loved her? Or that she had loved Erin?

She was approaching the doors of the library when her phone rang. She stiffened. Erin hadn't called yet, but that didn't mean she wouldn't. She fished it out of her pocket and sagged in relief when she saw it was Naomi. After a detour to a nearby stone bench, she answered.

"Hey, Mom. Is everything okay?"

"Everything's fine. You worry too much. It's just the lull before lunch, and I thought I might catch you."

"You caught me."

"What's wrong?"

Iris made a face. "Nothing. I'm just swamped."

"Maybe it's time to cut back on the restaurant job."

"My bank account doesn't agree."

"Because you gave your money to me."

Iris rolled her eyes. She didn't have it in her to comfort Naomi about that. "We're in this together," she said, not even convincing herself.

"Something's wrong. What is it?"

"Nothing." It was said far too vehemently to be true. Iris put a hand over her eyes before running it up her forehead and across her hair. "Everything's fine."

"Is it your Erin?"

As if there were hundreds of Erins out there they might talk about. "I can't discuss it."

"Hold on, let me go outside for some privacy."

"Mom, no. I'm serious. I'm not talking about it."

"I'm almost there, just going out the back now." There was the thunk of the push bar on the metal door and the faint whistle of a breeze over the phone. Iris could picture the tableau exactly: a dumpster over here, chain-link fencing over there, a red painted outline for the fire alley. "It's not bad out considering how cool it was this morning."

"I don't need a weather report, Mom."

"What's going on with Erin?"

The only way out of this would be to hang up, and that would only prompt more questions. "We're over, pretty much."

"There's a lot of real estate around that sentence. I'm going to need to know more."

At that prompt, Iris couldn't stop herself: catching Erin in a lie, her making the donation that funded the grant, when the donation had been made, Iris leaving, Erin's continued text messages, and Iris's current conundrum about the money. It felt good to get it off her chest but terrible now that it was out in the open. "It's all tainted now."

"That's a lot, and I love you, but you're being ridiculous."

"Did you hear what I said? The size of that donation and the enormity of the lie that went along with it?"

Naomi said, "I heard you. What's the saying—pride goeth before a fall?"

"This is not pride. This is reality, our reality."

"I don't know where you got this hang-up about taking help. It's not from me. I'm all about taking what I can get when I need it."

"This isn't just help, Mom. This is more money than I could ever pay back. It's an obligation I didn't ask for and don't want."

"Would you have felt obligated to the donors who made that grant possible in the first place?"

Iris pulled the phone away from her face and looked at it like her mom was suddenly speaking in Lingala, one of the three languages her grandma had known.

"It's not remotely the same. This donor knows me. This donor did it specifically for me. This donor gave more than what was needed for the grant to have sway in how the donation was used. This donor hid it from me and lied about it to my face."

Her voice had gotten loud by the end. Just one of the many dramatic conversations that happened on campus every day.

"I'm not an idiot. I understand what you said. My point is that you need the money. You would have to drop out of school without it. Even though you earned it, the grant was a gift, and the only thing to do with a gift is to take it and say thank you."

But saying thank you was what had unraveled everything.

"That's not true. You wouldn't take money from just anyone. When you take something from someone, you're beholden to them."

"Erin didn't hold it over you, though. She did the opposite by not telling you at all."

Someone stopped right in front of her, patting pockets and digging around in his backpack, so Iris lowered her voice when she said, "Why are you on her side about this?"

"I'm not. I'm just saying that she's got plenty of money, and she did it in a way specifically so you wouldn't feel like you owed her anything."

"Yes, she was a very ethical liar." Her snark was off the charts, and she hated herself for a moment.

"You're being a brat. I thought things between you two were getting serious. Are you going to let this ruin that?"

"Mom, she *lied*. About something pretty enormous. Besides, I don't remember you being all that positive about her in the beginning."

"Yeah, well, I'm allowed to change my mind. You're going around in circles, and didn't you forgive her last lie? Why can't you forgive this one? She just wanted to help."

"That's not how you help someone!" Several people looked at her with that outburst. "It's just insane. I can't ever repay that debt."

"It seems like she doesn't want it repaid."

"But it's going to sit between us no matter what she wants. Why did she do that? Why did she ruin us when I could've figured it out. I always figure it out." Some sadness sneaked past her fury at the thought.

"Maybe she didn't want you to have to."

Those words made her go still. All she could see was the money because she'd stopped seeing the alternatives the minute the grant was reinstated. That bleak pro/con list had instantly become a thing of the past, and she had moved through her days lighter and with much smaller problems. The money lived quietly in the background, but it was what enabled her everyday existence.

Had Erin known this was what would happen, this relief so deep it became woven into her cells? Could Erin know something so far out of her current experience, or had her thinking stopped at solving the immediate problem?

Naomi went on. "I'm not telling you what to do, but I am telling you not to be rash. You can't do everything on your own. That's not how things work. Relationships are about helping each other, or so I've been told. Not that I got that at all before Mick."

"You and I help each other."

"No, you mostly help me at this point, which I'd like to change."

"It's fine, Mom," she said, returning to where they had started and looking for a way out. "But we both need to get to work now."

After serving up a little more admonishment, Naomi let them get off the call. Instead of going into the library as she had planned, Iris remained on the bench, forearms on her thighs, turning her phone over and over between her hands.

All that stuff was easy for her mom to say. She was obligated only to Iris, and that was by blood and long-standing tradition.

Getting the grant back had felt like a gift from a god she was pretty sure didn't exist. It had opened up her lungs and made her unclench her hands. It had calmed her fevered consideration of any and all alternatives, of the best out of a bunch of bad options. It had let her be herself. Now that she wasn't herself again, she could understand what an incredible gift that had been.

Iris didn't know if it was possible for her to see Erin again without remembering her being caught out and lying clumsily, being careful—Iris now saw—to stay within the letter of the truth while obliterating the spirit of it.

Iris could accept help. Maybe she wasn't as good at it as Naomi, but she'd had plenty of help through the years: free lunches, after-school programs, small scholarships for her undergraduate years, and multiple grants for graduate school. She knew she couldn't do it alone, from helpful neighbors when she'd been a kid, to people who'd given her jobs, to Dr. Rawlings and her other teachers.

She just hadn't wanted to be seen as someone who needed so much help. Hadn't wanted Erin to see her that way. As someone who needed saving.

* * *

The hits from Erin kept coming.

Money is not an end in itself but a means to something better.

And *Catherine and I took whatever help and mentorship we could get.*

Iris wished she could get herself to tell Erin to buzz off. Erin would, she knew. If she was clear and definitive enough, she would get the message and leave Iris like Iris had left her that night.

Instead of doing that, Iris let herself steep in memories of Erin on the T with her, kissing her with delicious purpose, pointing out a tree in the arboretum, waiting for her outside Dialogue. As much as the memories hurt her and as angry as they made her, she couldn't stop herself from hunting them up and caressing them over and over. It felt like she'd have to leave the entire city to be able to move on past Erin.

The truth was, she couldn't give back the grant if she wanted to—or at least not all of it. The bulk of it had already gone to the university to pay for her tuition for this semester and some more of it had been deposited in her bank account to supplement what she earned as a teacher's assistant (and a server at Dialogue). Maybe she could refuse it for next semester, but doing so felt impossibly hypothetical. The truth was, with every step she took she was benefiting from Erin's problematic generosity.

When she got those texts, she wanted to respond, to reopen the argument they'd had in Erin's foyer. But where would that get them?

Still, it sometimes felt like fighting would be better than this forced silence on Iris's part. She couldn't talk about what Erin had done, what Iris was now bound by, without sliding into anger. The problem was that on the other side of expressing that anger was a vast unknown, and the odds were slim that it included her and Erin still together. Their whole relationship seemed impossible now, not just the bad things but all the good ones as well.

Reaching the vestibule of her building, Iris unlocked their small mailbox and snatched out the few letters and one grocery store flier within. While she trudged up the stairs to her apartment, she flipped through the envelopes: bill, something for a roommate, a political mailing, and…something from The Foundation for Modern Historical Studies. She swore under her breath, leaned against the wall, and opened it. Inside, there was a small note and another envelope. The note said, "The donor received your letter and wanted to reply."

Iris weighed the inner envelope in her hand, her heart pounding—with fury and an excitement she hated. This was way more than the sum of all the texts Erin had sent since Iris had broken it off. She didn't have to read it, she told herself, but the words rang hollow. She ran up the rest of the stairs, dumped the unopened mail on the pile already tilting precariously on the table, and leaned back against the closed door once she knew she was alone.

It felt wise to know what she wanted to be inside this envelope before she looked at it, but wouldn't that just leave her open to disappointment? Really, what was left for Erin—for either of them—to say?

If she wasn't going to burn it, she might as well get on with reading it. She slid a finger under the envelope's flap, pulled out two pages with closely spaced type, and started reading.

Dear Grant Recipient,

First: you're welcome, and it was my great pleasure. Despite my means, I don't make donations lightly. I want them to be impactful, for the good they do to be measurable, indisputable, and compounding. I want them not just to be about the person but the activity—both of the charity and the direct recipients. History is such a worthy pursuit, just as important as those pursuits that are supposed to propel us into the future. Because isn't the thing about history that we carry it with us as we step through a present that changes so quickly into another present and ultimately the past? We live in the accumulation of what has come before, and if we remain blind to it, we aren't just doomed to repeat it but will almost certainly make a bigger mess than we already have.

Personal history is a lot like that, too. Our natures are warped by whatever nurturing we did or didn't receive in whatever fortunate or unfortunate direction. Becoming a bona fide adult entails examining what we've been taught, taking what seems right, and abandoning the rest in a heap behind us. We have to forge our own moral compass and have that guide us through the unending decisions we're asked to make in the name of having a life. And we don't do it in a vacuum. We are swayed by family, the media, books, our friends, all of which are laden with history.

We need to be able to look at what has happened in our lives, in our communities, in this country, and in the world as a whole. We need to be able to derive lessons, elucidate warnings, shine light on the deserving, and carry it all inside our hearts and minds to guide us with every step we take. In this way, we can hope to make a new history.

The nature of time dictates that we all have pasts, but it's something different to "make" history. The people who have done this have had the ability to move the needle far beyond their individual circles and effect change. Whether this change is good or bad depends on the person and the circumstances, not to mention perspective, and it is often able to be judged only in far retrospect. The people who've been able to do this have very frequently been privileged and leveraged their position to maximize their impact. Most often, they've done this to the detriment of those who are less privileged.

We the privileged have an obligation to understand history and to do better this time. We need to cede our soapbox to others who might have more important things to say, and we must enable more people to have the opportunities to gain experience and education that gives them something meaningful to contribute. We have to put our money where our mouths are to make any strides at all toward leveling the playing field and giving other people the chance to follow their passions without judgment or penalty.

That's why I made this donation. It was one way of righting a cosmic wrong. I donated because you had already done everything in your power to earn the right to study what you wanted. I donated to fix something that had nothing to do with you but that affected you heinously. I donated because though I didn't have the words yet, I loved you, have loved you from the moment you argued with me before stepping out of the protection of my umbrella.

Love is a lot of things, but to me a big part of it is wanting the very best for my beloved. I want you to have everything you desire, which is an unrealistic goal, but that doesn't stop me from wanting it. It is not accounting, where the exercise is to balance two columns of numbers to keep things as even and equitable as possible. It is an open-ended yes from me to you. It is a torrential downpour, and all you need is a bucket.

My donation was an investment in you because you are you, and I love that. I love your honor and your sadness, your focus and your willingness to sit and look at a tree with me. I love your determination and your unblinking acceptance of reality, no matter how much it might hurt. I love that you've turned a messy family history into the beginnings of a career in which you'll be joining and contributing to a larger, vibrant conversation. I love that you hate my money. I love that you hate my lies. I love how I feel when I'm around you: inspired and restless and wanting in a terrifying way. But also seen, supported, and cherished.

I wanted to help, and I knew you wouldn't let me if you knew, so I lied. I regret that, but I don't regret what I did, even if you can't forgive me. I should have found a way to be open with you, to convince you that you should take help when it's given and that it wasn't extended with strings attached. You are not beholden to me unless you still love me, in which case we are beholden to each other in the very best way. But if you are considering somehow returning this gift, please don't. That would be a slap in the face I might not recover from.

If we don't move, we're lost. I mean that "we" in a general sense but also as you and me. For my part, the only move I have to offer is my very deepest apology—and a declaration in detail of my love. (See above, but that only scratches the surface.) Not having you in my life right now makes me feel empty, like I'm going through the motions even as I try to distract myself with something that might ultimately make you proud of me. I crave your admiration. I crave your body, your smell, the feel of you next to me, the sound of your breath in my ear. I love you, and I know that only goes so far, but I hope that it's far enough this time.

Can you find it in yourself to shift and soften? To accept my help and my love? To understand my lie and know that I won't do it again? To come back to me and let me earn your trust every day? To be my partner, hold me accountable, and be with me in the pursuit of all our passions? Can you? Will you?

I await your reply,
Anonymous

Iris tried to remember how to breathe. She felt empty, too. She felt everything, all at once. She'd spent the last ten days waiting for her feelings to converge in a conclusive way, but now she realized she would have to apply her own will to come to a decision.

As a historian, she spent most of her time digging up the facts of circumstances long gone or far away or both. She examined the current situation.

Fact 1: Erin believed everything she'd written in that letter. It was her truth.

Fact 2: Erin had met Iris where she lived in her talk about history and its importance.

Fact 3: Erin was not apologetic, not really, not at all.

Fact 4: The donation had come from good intentions, however misguided.

Fact 5: Erin was still wildly privileged.

Fact 6: Erin wanted to be a better person.

Fact 7: Erin loved Iris.

Erin loved Iris. Iris had known that, but having it spelled out made a difference. What had she written? Her love was a torrential downpour, and all she needed was a bucket? When it came to relationships, Iris had always operated more along the lines of the accounting version Erin mentioned. Because if things weren't even, they would always be in the other person's favor. But Erin was also saying that not everything was about money, which was an easy thing to say when you had it.

She slid to the floor, her back still against the door. As much as she wanted not to be, she was deeply affected by Erin's note. Underneath all her anger, she craved Erin, too. What Erin thought of her had taken an outsized space in her mind. Her support was sweet and unwavering, and being held in her arms provided an immeasurable comfort.

She loved Erin, but was that enough? Could she learn how to let go of her own internal accounting enough to handle Erin's generosity? Could she learn to see it as investment instead of charity? It was entirely up to her, which was another fact that made her squirm, that made her want to be better, that made her want to drop her defenses and see what vulnerability might bring. But she was afraid.

She heard a key in the lock, but before she could move, the door shoved against her.

"What the hell?" Candice.

Iris scrambled to her feet, the note still clamped in her hand, and opened the door. "Sorry. I was..." She shook her head. "Floored, literally, I guess."

"Good or bad?" Candice asked as she came into the apartment. She glanced at the letter Iris was holding. "That looks official."

"It's..." She shook her head.

"Wow. Something's got you speechless? I need to know all the details. But, first, a beer. Want one?" Candice breezed past Iris to the kitchen and opened the refrigerator, bottles clinking in its door.

Iris couldn't answer.

"I'll take that as a yes." She came back with two bottles and sat on the couch, patting next to her in invitation. "Spill. Can you at least give me a hint? Is it a primary source? That paper you're coauthoring with Dr. Rawlings? Your shifts at Dialogue? Don't tell me it's about your grant again."

Iris blinked at each question and finally went to sit next to Candice.

"Or is it Erin? I haven't seen her for a while, and you haven't been spending nights over there."

Who knew Candice had been so up on her schedule all this time? "I don't know what to do." No pro/con list existed for this kind of dilemma. "I can't even..." She hadn't told Candice about any of it, and though the letter felt deeply personal, she thrust it at her and said, "This is from her. I think it says it all."

Iris wasn't much of a drinker, but she downed half her beer in the time it took Candice to read the pages, her face going through various contortions in response to the words as she went along. It would have been funny if Iris wasn't essentially shell-shocked.

When Candice finished, she said, "Wow. This kind of makes me want to date her, and I'm straight."

"But you see, right? I mean, you get what she did."

"She funded your grant. A while ago. And kept it from you."

Iris blurted, "A million dollars!"

"What? How rich is this woman? I mean, was that a lot to her or not so much?"

"Enough."

"She really loves you. I mean *really* loves you. How do you feel about her?"

Iris put her beer down and covered her face with her hands. "Too many things."

"'Beholden to each other in the very best way'? I mean, come on."

"I can't be in debt to her and together with her at the same time."

"What does your mom say about this? Does she know?"

Iris dropped her hands and rolled her eyes. "She says when you get a gift, take it and say thank you. But this is just beyond… everything."

"How much could she have given that you'd accept? Is it really about the money?"

She scoffed. "Of course it's about the money!"

"I mean, I'd get it if you didn't trust her, but I think I'd find a way to get over that."

"You like that she has money."

"I like that she's on your side. Way on your side. Do you not believe that's possible? That someone of means doesn't just see you as a charity case? Maybe you need to give some people more credit."

"It's always been that way before, not that I've gotten close enough to many rich people to be dismissed like that. But it's how the world works."

Candice folded the letter along its original creases and extended it toward Iris. "Maybe because you've never given it room to work any other way."

Iris took the letter, stopped momentarily by the thought that Erin had held these pages, left her fingerprints along with the words. It felt almost like a touch to be holding it.

"Do you love her like she loves you?"

Change was hard. Risky. She knew she could navigate her life the way she'd been doing for years. Anything else was a yawning unknown, and Iris wasn't big on faith.

"I mean, isn't that the only question here?"

Iris knew the truth but was too scared to say it. Still, if she expected truth from Erin, she had to expect it from herself, too.

CHAPTER SEVENTEEN

After fifteen unanswered texts, Erin received a reply, time-stamped 5:15 p.m.

Come to Dialogue tonight.

She leaned back from her laptop, her back crackling from her intense hunch. Okay, she could do that, but…it felt like it might be an ambush. Did Iris want a public (though not neutral) setting for their official breakup? It would seem more appropriate for them to meet at the Public Gardens in front of their tree, the setting full of anonymous witnesses and poignancy.

Iris's reply made Erin wonder if she had gotten her letter already. Seeing as it had to go through the foundation to get to her, they would have had to be Johnny-on-the-spot for it to arrive so soon, not that Erin hadn't been counting the hours since she'd dropped it in the mailbox. It didn't escape her that if the foundation had dragged its feet a little more in forwarding Iris's thank-you note, she and Iris might not be in this situation in the first place. She pressed hard on one eyebrow. A swift spasm of thought told her that she ultimately wouldn't have been able to live with the untruth of it all.

If Iris had gotten her letter, had she read it? Or had she found the tit for tat of it offensive? Erin had worried about that but had decided that Iris would be more likely to read a letter sent care of the foundation rather than one sent directly from Erin. It had pretty much been a Hail Mary, anyway. If Iris wanted to stay angry and end everything they had together, Erin doubted anything she could say would dent her resolve.

Just when was she supposed to show up at Dialogue? She didn't have an exact usual time, but she generally came in closer to closing than to opening. The restaurant unlocked its doors at 5:30. She checked her watch. Right about now. She wanted to see Iris as soon as possible, but she also wanted to do this right. Eight o'clock seemed a safe enough bet, though that left her with more than two hours to torture herself before setting out for the mile walk.

Were they meeting at Dialogue so Iris could hand her a paper bag with the few things she'd left in Iris's apartment over the months? Toothbrush, pajamas, a couple of pairs of underwear, the lotion she couldn't live without. Not a very big footprint for as emotionally invested as she'd been. As she still was. If that's all Iris wanted from this meeting, it would crush her. She would have to try mightily not to cry—not because she wouldn't want Iris to see that truly honest reaction, but because she didn't want to make things difficult for anyone. And by anyone, she meant Iris. Taking it on the chin quietly would be the last thing she could give to her.

After trying and failing to get back into her research or read one of the books about the challenges of nonprofits stacked high on her desk, Erin confronted her closet. Yet another conundrum. She never went to Dialogue without cleaning up at least a little bit so she wouldn't ruin the ambiance with a scruffy presence. The prospect of seeing Iris made her want to dress up even more. Of course, if she dressed up just to be officially dumped, she would feel worse.

First, her favorite slacks: the ones she'd worn when signing papers for the sale of her company. They were black with a thin satin stripe down the leg—not formal or too fussy but just really nice. Then her shirt. This choice took forever. There were too many options. When had she become such a clotheshorse?

She considered a half a dozen before choosing a crisp cotton button-front one in a soft gray with a black accent on the edge of the cloth. When the buttons were fastened, the stripe bisected her body from neck to belt, echoing the stripe in the slacks. Makeup she kept to a minimum, but she fussed with her hair until it staged a coup, lying wherever it wanted on her head no matter what she did.

The ticking of the large clock in her living room kept her company while she waited for the right time to leave. Which might turn out to be the wrong time. Who knew? She was practically hyperventilating with nervousness and left her place early, intending to make a stop in the Gardens to soothe her nerves with a bit of urban nature. The memories around the beech tree were layered. Some from when she'd first discovered the specimen and did her research to understand what it was—if not why. And some from the last time with Iris, when she'd talked about "hanging in beyond what everyone accepts as the end."

That was what she was doing or trying to, wasn't it? Hoping but not knowing if this "perverse perseverance" was going to pay dividends.

She tried not to rush, but she still made it to the restaurant earlier than planned. She looked around for Iris but didn't see her. She must be picking up an order in the back, Erin decided. When she was taking her coat off, her scarf got tangled on itself as she tried to free it from her neck, and she ended up struggling with it awkwardly until she was able to hand it and her coat to Justin, the host who had always been so helpful. He smiled like this was an ordinary evening.

He said, "Bear with us a minute. We're getting your table ready."

She reached out and touched the podium, running her finger along its wood grain. "I'm actually not sure if I'm here to eat, as strange as that sounds. Is Iris around?"

"We have a table reserved for you, so at least have a seat."

Erin shrugged and glanced worriedly around the dining room. She felt naked without something to read. She realized she'd left her phone in the pocket of her coat but stopped herself before she grabbed the host to get it back. Browsing on your phone in a restaurant was uncouth. Surely she could make it through a meal without that kind of distraction. Iris was nowhere to be seen, and she wasn't sure what that meant.

The table the host led her to was in a private corner of the dining room. This made no sense. Why all this if Iris was just going to break up with her? Because she was sure that was coming. Trying to get her outfit and hair just right felt ludicrous now, but if this was what Iris needed, she couldn't get herself to leave.

As usual, she was not given a menu. Chewing on a corner of her thumbnail to boil off some of her dread, she looked around the room. Everyone else in the restaurant seemed to be having such a nice evening. Like the evenings she'd had when she'd eaten here while Iris was working. It had been so hard to be so near her but not able to interact in a meaningful way. Hard and kind of arousing.

Before she could get lost in reminiscence, Iris emerged from the back, not in her server uniform but in a navy-blue dress with a fitted bodice and sleeves and a full skirt. Her hair was in her typical braid, but it looked freshly done and tight. She headed right for Erin, who stood when she got two tables away. It was an involuntary motion, powered by the pounding of her heart.

"Hi," she said stupidly.

Iris pulled her chair out and sat while Erin chastised herself for not being on the ball enough to do that for her. She sat back down and smoothed out the tablecloth in front of her. It took a moment for her to be able to look directly at Iris. She raised her eyebrow in question.

Iris said, "We need to talk, and I get to be the one in control for once."

"When have you not been in control?"

"I'm paying for this dinner, and you're ordering dessert. And wine."

"That's not necessary."

"It's absolutely necessary."

"I'm not sure—"

"Are you going to have a serious discussion with me? Can you?" Iris was so stern, forbidding.

Erin nodded. "Absolutely." Before she could say anything else, Greg arrived at their table, his hands clasped behind his back, his mouth admirably straight.

"Are you ready to order or do you need some more time? Erin, would you like to hear the specials?"

She rubbed suddenly sweaty hands down her thighs under the table. "Maybe a few minutes wouldn't be amiss."

Iris said, "Listen to the specials."

Erin cleared her throat. "I'd like to hear the specials, please."

The chef's carbonara was on the list. Erin ordered that, not knowing if she was making a statement and, if so, what it was. Iris added an appetizer to share and two glasses of wine on top of two desserts she ordered up front with zero discussion.

To Greg, she said, "No rush."

He nodded and disappeared.

"I want to go along with whatever you've got planned, Iris, but I'm not sure I can eat right now." This didn't *seem* like a breakup, but her stomach hadn't gotten that news, maybe because Iris hadn't softened yet. Judging from the determined expression on her face, she wasn't concerned about Erin's appetite.

"I know you've tried hard to make things equitable for us, but the truth is that they aren't equitable. Not by a long shot."

"I always met you where you were."

"Have you ever thought that might be part of the problem? I can't be the one to hold you back."

"From what? Dinners like this? They're just a way to get me out of my house, which has been empty without you."

Iris took a deep breath. "You're not listening."

Erin held up her hands. "Sorry. I'm trying to, I swear."

"Your meeting me where I am means that you give and I take. This relationship can't be all one-sided. I know you said you didn't buy into the accounting model of relationships, but I can't live with the scales so far out of balance. You give me an open-ended yes, but what do I give you?"

"But I've hardly given you anything at all." Partly because Erin knew Iris wouldn't stand for it.

"You have options available to you that aren't available to me."

"What options?"

"Time, for one. You meet me here sometimes just to walk me to the train. You're always ready for a walk whenever I'm free. Your money gives you options, too. Ordering in food for us instead of me cooking, for example."

If Erin hadn't just found something potentially useful to do with her money, she would have signed it away right now just to get it out from between them. How could she respond without pissing Iris off again?

Iris saved Erin the bother by continuing, "Funding that grant was exactly like putting money in my hand. You can try to tap-dance around it, talk about the future students that will benefit, but no one would benefit later if I didn't benefit first."

"You're right," Erin admitted.

"You can call it an investment, but the truth is that to a great extent you've paid for my life for the next three years. I'm not sure I can live with that, not with the way things are between us now."

Her stomach churned. "I can't take it back. And I'm not sure I would."

"I know that. That's why things have to change if we're going to have any chance together. The fact is that there's always accounting, there has to be accounting. Relationships have to be equitable—or at least mine do."

Iris thought they had a chance? Erin let herself look at her fully, examine her face in the restaurant's low lighting. She looked weirdly calm, given the subject matter. "I hear what you're saying, but…change how?"

"I don't know, not exactly. That's where this becomes a discussion."

"I can't help that I'm in a position to give more than you are right now. That's just now, though. That's not necessarily forever. And whatever you think I'm giving up to be with you isn't a sacrifice at all. You're right that I have more time than you, but if I wasn't able to be flexible, I'd never see you."

Iris's composed façade slipped a little bit. "Fine, but it's not that, exactly." She shifted and straightened her silverware before looking up. "I need to have something to contribute to this relationship. Otherwise I feel like the charity case people of means generally see me as. This has to be different."

Erin was pretty sure they'd trod this ground already, but she tried to listen differently this time and move beyond the money. The money was the ultimate problem, though, wasn't it? Or was Iris saying it wasn't? How was Erin supposed to show her love if she didn't give her things, make time to help, arrange things to be easier for Iris? Accounting was cold and calculated, and there'd be a never-ending game of balancing the ledger, making sure each got exactly what they gave. How could love live in such constraints?

"I want to meet you where you are instead of your meeting me where I am. Does that make sense?"

"You do."

"No, I don't! That's the point. You're so intent on giving that you don't give me room to give back."

"This is why accounting doesn't work. You have different drains on your attention than I do, and the model has to account for that. You have so much on your plate. I'm just trying to make things easier for you."

"Who said I wanted easy?"

"I just—"

"I need you to expect things from me. I can't go around feeling like a chasm of need around you. I've been in that position too much in my life."

"I don't think of you that way."

"But you treat me that way."

Erin stopped herself from arguing. Barely. Iris had told her to listen, so she took a moment to review everything Iris had said. Erin had been so careful not to add herself as another burden on Iris's life, but it sounded like Iris was saying that was a bad thing, that maybe she was treating Iris as poor in more ways than strictly money. Iris wanted an equity Erin wasn't allowing to happen because she didn't like the tit-for-tat nature of keeping track. But Iris seemed to want at least some of that. "You want to do things for me? Like what?"

"I don't know! But you need to let me find out."

Erin gripped her thighs. She'd never tried this hard to understand someone and be this present in a conversation. Iris wanted to meet Erin where she was. She wanted to contribute in an active way. She wanted to give Erin something the way that Erin gave her herself. If this was what Iris wanted, and she was starting to understand why that might be, how could Erin take a step back and Iris take one forward? She thought hard in their silence before saying, "You want to walk me home—even though I'm pretty much always there. Metaphorically. You want to give to us—to me—intangibly."

"Yes! And sometimes tangibly." It still wasn't a happy yes. Her eyebrows were bunched together, willing something more out of Erin.

What else could there be? She had to get this right. She replayed their interactions from the very beginning, her gaze on Iris's forehead, looking and not looking at the same time. Relationships were about give-and-take, yes, but there was more to it. Erin had given, and Iris wanted to give. Iris needed to give. Iris wanted to be needed to give. "And…you want me to expect that of you. That giving."

"Yes!" Iris sat back and glanced around the dining room as if looking for tables to service. "But I don't know if you're wired that way. I don't know if you've been the way you've been with me because of the financial inequality between us or if that's just the way you are. Maybe you're not actually interested in an equitable relationship."

Her conjecture left Erin winded. Into this pause, Greg delivered their appetizer and disappeared without a word. Neither of them made a move toward the food even though the glazed cauliflower looked delicious as always. She was uncomfortable and scared that she'd discover her truth was the wrong answer to Iris's question. Still, if they were to have any chance at all, they both had to be honest. Iris clearly was, which meant Erin had to follow suit.

She said, "I've never thought about it. I guess I've always been more comfortable giving, making a gesture, you know? Not always things but what I considered thoughtfulness. It's how I show love. It's not because I think you need it more or anything, but I did put some extra effort in making things easy for you because you work so hard and push against so many obstacles."

"But do you see how that makes me feel? When you do it all the time? When you're the one who's always doing it? When you don't expect the same from me?"

"Now I do."

"Do you think it's something you can change?"

There was only one right answer to this, but it wasn't that easy. "Giving makes me feel good, like how I tip. I think it brings a net positive to the world—and has always been a net positive in my relationships. But I get that you're saying you want to have that feeling, too, and I'm not letting you."

"No, you're not."

Erin grimaced. "I don't want to account for every emotional dollar, but I want an equitable relationship with you. Does that count for something?"

"That counts for a lot."

"I don't like to make promises I might not be able to keep, but I would try just about anything to make something between us possible."

Iris leaned forward, the table's edge creasing her dress. "I can give you so many things that barely cost anything. I want you to make demands on my time and attention. Let me make the gesture sometimes, like bringing the flowers—not that there have been flowers so far, but you know what I mean."

"I didn't think you'd want flowers because, you know..." Erin had never known if a dozen roses fit into the budget Iris had been so adamant about. Twenty dollars didn't go very far these days.

"Who doesn't like flowers?"

"Only psychopaths and people who think they're too expensive because if you're going to give flowers, they need to be fair trade, which costs more."

Iris's frown returned. "I'm being serious."

"I get that. And I get it," Erin said, trying to salvage things. "You want us both to be equally demanding of each other."

"Yes, exactly."

But Erin wasn't sure how that would work. What could she ask for—demand? Occasional home-cooked meals were one thing, but though they were nice, they didn't seem sufficient for the cause. She knew Iris had more to offer, but with her back against the wall like this, her brain wasn't cooperating.

Then she thought about her nonprofit and all the things she'd wanted to tell and ask Iris during the last couple of weeks. "Okay. I have about a million questions to ask you about your grant application process, and I need to pick your brain about teaching before getting my new nonprofit off the ground. If it helps, you can consider me a chasm of need around this."

Iris's hand pressed flat on the table next to her knife and spoon, and Erin couldn't look away from it. She willed it to move closer, to be open to Erin's fingers and the heat of her palm.

Iris said, "Good. A new nonprofit?"

That little nudge of encouragement rocked Erin further out of neutral, and she went on. "I'll tell you about it in a minute, but I'm not done. I need you to come up with the next date for us unless you just want to repeat the arboretum since it was particularly memorable." All that kissing in the beech grove.

"I'll see what I can do."

"At some point, sooner rather than later, I'm going to have to attend some fundraising events. I'll need you with me, but it might require a new fancy dress or two."

Iris glanced down at her empty appetizer plate. "That's a hard one."

"I could go alone, but—"

"I don't want you to go alone." She raised her gaze to Erin. "I'll let you buy me fancy dresses so I can go with you to events that make my skin crawl just thinking of them."

Erin stretched out over the table to reach Iris's hand. "I want you to think of ways to surprise and delight me so I can keep surprising and delighting you."

Iris swiped at the corner of an eye, and she sniffed wetly. "That's all I'm asking for."

"You keep me honest, and I'll keep you honest. That I can definitely promise."

Iris turned her hand so it was palm up and squeezed Erin's. "Me, too."

The relief that flooded Erin turned her joints to liquid, and she was thankful to be sitting down. She couldn't stop looking at Iris, her tear-shined eyes, soft mouth, and proud chin.

"I love you and need you to come back to my place and take the key I've been offering to you. I know that's giving, but I want you to take up space in my life."

"I love you, too, and I was hoping you'd say that."

They released each other's hand and sat back. Erin felt like she'd just run a mile and needed a minute to catch her breath. She caught Greg watching them, probably to time when to bring the main course, but she was still fathoms away from being able to eat.

"What do we do now?" she asked. "Because I left my appetite at my apartment, and I'm not sure when it's going to catch up."

"Speak for yourself. I'm starving. Who in their right mind eats this late?" Iris started dishing cauliflower onto her plate.

"Please don't tell me we need to negotiate dinner times, too, before we can take the next step together."

She put down the serving spoon. "No, I think a good old-fashioned compromise will do for that."

Erin smiled. "I can see it now—you're going to boss me around, and I'm going to love it."

Iris brought a bite to her lips. "Oh, absolutely. Now tell me about this new nonprofit and how I can help."

"That's all I've wanted to do for weeks. I need your expertise desperately. So much that you might get tired of giving."

"Doubtful."

The last bits of tension in Erin's chest unfurled, and her appetite began to awaken.

EPILOGUE

Iris's alarm was a cheerful rudeness from the nightstand right next to her head. Erin's groan added to its pleasant chime. Iris shut it off and stretched, turning over to envelop Erin in a gentle squeeze. Into her ear, Iris whispered, "Ten minutes." She repeated it until there was a noise of assent. She got out of bed and walked to their bathroom, the bedroom adrift with boxes that people had come and packed for them the day before. It was something Erin had insisted on. She'd said that if they were going to move halfway across the country to Chicago for Iris's new job, an actual tenure-track position at DePaul, they were going to make it as easy on themselves as possible. Why it had to be done exactly around the time of Iris's official graduation was a mystery neither of them could quite explain.

"I guess the date just got stuck in my head" was Erin's take on the whole situation.

Granted, Erin had been juggling several full plates while expanding her nonprofit, Ahead for Business, to three new cities, including Chicago—though Erin had made it clear that she'd have followed Iris to the Windy City even if it hadn't been on the organization's expansion road map. No long distance for them, not if Erin had any say in the matter, which she most definitely did.

Iris softly closed the bathroom door and caught a glimpse of her smiling face in the mirror across the room. When she'd moved in almost two years before, she had willed herself not to get used to everything being nice and spacious in case things didn't work out, but since she couldn't conceive of splitting up with Erin, resistance to a lifestyle afforded by Erin's money had been futile. Not that they were profligate by any stretch of the imagination. The house was Erin's biggest outlay, especially when she didn't renew the first-floor lease and turned it into offices for Ahead, including their first classroom.

Iris had given up her server job when she'd no longer had to pay rent, and the two of them ate out at Dialogue a couple of times a month. It was their favorite date-night place. In fact, they'd gone there just the night before, for a graduation-eve celebration with Catherine, Nathan, Naomi, and Mick, the latter two of whom were asleep across the hall in the guest bedroom. It was the season of celebrations since Catherine and Nathan had gotten married on Patriot's Day in the first throes of spring with the forsythia in golden bloom. The event had been both poignant and huge, given the sizes of both their extended families. Iris had let Erin buy her a new dress for the occasion.

Even now, they still didn't have their give-and-take dialed in. Even though sometimes overwhelmed with work for Ahead, Erin fell into old habits and tried to take care of too much to make things easier on Iris or went overboard on a present. Apparently Iris inspired generosity, which was a cross she was just going to have to bear.

Still, they were keeping their finances separate, at Iris's insistence. When Naomi's new used car turned out to be if not a full lemon then at least half of one, needing increasingly expensive repairs the year after she bought it, Iris and Erin had had what felt like a never-ending discussion about the level of help Iris was willing to take on Naomi's behalf.

Erin said, "I bought my brother a truck. Isn't this practically the same thing?"

"She's my mom, not yours."

"I know she's not officially my family, but she might as well be."

"She's not your responsibility."

"Iris, you need to stop being so all or nothing about things. Besides, haven't we already established that I feel beholden to you in the best way, and isn't that transitive?"

Like the time at which they would eat dinner, they compromised, Erin paying for a better, late-model used car and Iris trying not to panic about it. After a while, once it was clear the world wasn't going to end at this level of generosity, Iris relaxed a little more into the incredible safety net that Erin provided for both her and Naomi. This was the first time they'd had anything of the sort since her grandfather had up and moved to the Amazon, where he apparently still was, out of their lives for all intents and purposes.

She brushed her teeth and washed her face, taking her time in order to let Erin sleep as long as possible. She still thrilled at seeing their toothbrushes sitting next to each other. After the rift that had nearly undone them, they'd doubled down on their relationship, each giving and taking and raising expectations until it became clear that the only way they could make things better would be to live together. It had been so peaceful writing her dissertation at the desk they'd bought for the guest bedroom, far away from Erin's frequent phone conversations in her first-floor office.

Iris loved watching Erin work, the way she paced back and forth while talking, the graceful gestures she made even though the other party couldn't see them. She could concentrate so hard that she was deaf to Iris's voice from where she stood in the doorway. Sometimes it took coming all the way in and putting her hand on her shoulder to drag her from whatever she'd been working on. Her passion for Ahead was thrilling and just made Iris love her even more.

After finishing up in the bathroom, Iris walked around to Erin's side of the bed and squatted down. Erin's love had changed so much. It had helped Iris see generosity as something other than nefarious, a comment on her circumstances. She trusted a little easier, and the chip on her shoulder had shrunk. Now, she brushed hair away from Erin's forehead and watched a lazy smile curl her lips.

"Time to get up," Iris said quietly.

The smile evaporated.

"I let you sleep as long as I could, but graduation waits for no woman."

One eye opened at that. "Cruel and unusual."

Iris stood, knowing that was Erin speak for "I'm getting up."

"Hey, wait. Where'd you go?" Erin reached for Iris's hand and sat up. "Mmm, you smell minty fresh. Maybe I should—" She shook her head. "Sit down, please. Just for a minute."

Iris sat. "Everything okay?"

"Everything's fantastic. I'm beyond my wildest dreams happy. I'm so proud of you for finishing your work here and going to start new work in Chicago. That's so badass I don't even know how to quantify it."

"I was sure I'd have to be an adjunct for years," Iris admitted.

"I know, but I was sure you'd get your dream job."

"I'm still not used to optimism."

"Well, you'd better get used to it. Because you're going to need a lot more of it, starting right about now." Erin leaned forward and opened the drawer of her nightstand. She pulled out something that looked suspiciously like a box that might hold a ring. Iris's breath stilled. Erin placed it in her hand, curling her fingers around it.

"It's not much because you'd rip me a new one if it was. But the intent is the same. Iris, you push me and soothe me. You are uncompromising in the very best ways. You make me rethink everything and test all my assumptions. I love making you smile, making you dinner, which we can both admit is a work in progress, taking what you give, expecting exactly as much from you as you expect from me. I love you, Iris, and if you're willing, I want more than anything to marry you."

Iris's blood pulsed in her temples. Erin let go of her hand, and she opened the jewelry box. Inside was a thin white-gold band with a leaf where one might expect a stone to be. The leaf looked remarkably like the leaves on their favorite tree.

"Did you have this made?"

"Yes. Does that make it too much?"

"No, it's wonderful." She took it from its velvet cradle and put it on her ring finger. Not surprisingly, it fit like it was made for her. "Erin." Her voice was low and thick with emotion. "No one's perfect, but you're perfect for me."

"Should I take that as a—"

"Yes. Absolutely." She pulled Erin to her and held her tight with shaking arms. Finally, she loosened her grip and said, "Kiss me."

"You're so bossy."

"And you love it."

"I do, I really do." Erin closed the distance between them and sealed the proposal with a kiss.